THE DUKE'S DRAGOON

The Duke's Guard Series,
Book Four

C.H. Admirand

Dragonblade Publishing, Inc. is an imprint of Kathryn Le Veque Novels, Inc.
P.O. Box 23
Moreno Valley, CA 92556
ceo@dragonbladepublishing.com

Produced in the United States of America

First Edition March 2023
Trade Paperback Edition

ARE YOU SIGNED UP FOR DRAGONBLADE'S BLOG?

You'll get the latest news and information on exclusive giveaways, exclusive excerpts, coming releases, sales, free books, cover reveals and more.

Check out our complete list of authors, too!

No spam, no junk. That's a promise!

Sign Up Here

www.dragonbladepublishing.com

Dearest Reader;

Thank you for your support of a small press. At Dragonblade Publishing, we strive to bring you the highest quality Historical Romance from some of the best authors in the business. Without your support, there is no 'us', so we sincerely hope you adore these stories and find some new favorite authors along the way.

Happy Reading!

CEO, Dragonblade Publishing

Additional Dragonblade books by Author C.H. Admirand

The Duke's Guard Series
The Duke's Sword
The Duke's Protector
The Duke's Shield
The Duke's Dragoon

The Lords of Vice Series
Mending the Duke's Pride
Avoiding the Earl's Lust
Tempering the Viscount's Envy
Redirecting the Baron's Greed
His Vow to Keep (Novella)

The Lyon's Den Series
Rescued by the Lyon
Captivated by the Lyon

Dedication

For DJ, the keeper of my heart, and love of my life. I miss you.

For Arran McNicol, who gets me back on track when my brain is moving at a different speed than my fingers on the keyboard.

For my loyal readers, thank you for reading my books and letting me know how much you love my stories.

Author's Note

Dear Reader:

Hardheaded Heroes and Feisty Heroines…what's not to love?

This book is for all of you who continue to read the books that live in my mind and my heart, with characters that continue to whisper to me long after I've written their story and shared it with the world. Thank you, from the bottom on my heart.

Settle into your comfy reading spot with a cup of tea (or tasty adult beverage) while I tell you a story…

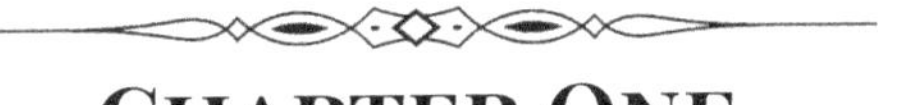

CHAPTER ONE

"YOU'RE LEAVING?" MOLLIE Malloy's heart literally stopped, then slowly began to beat again. "Has His Grace reassigned you?"

Finn O'Malley, one of the sixteen men who guarded the Duke of Wyndmere and his family with their lives, shifted his gaze away from her. "Ye could say that, lass."

She frowned as a flash of *déjà vu* warned her what was to come. She'd been in this very spot before, having this same conversation. "I thought you would be staying at Wyndmere Hall this time."

"Nay. 'Twas only for a week or so, like the last time I returned, when me brother was healing from the lead ball he took protecting the twins. I've been away from Penwith Tower too long as it is. I'm sure ye heard I was in the Borderlands, *visiting* the baron and the duke's sister at the duke's request. 'Tis more than time for me to return to me duties there."

"Cornwall seems so far away." She would eat dirt before she told the stubborn Irishman he was breaking her heart—*again!* She'd been a scullery maid the first time he left her. Since then, she'd risen to the shared position of lady's maid to the duchess and—once Their Graces' twins were born—relieving the nanny in the nursery. The one constant in her life was her love for Finn O'Malley…and bracing herself each time he walked away.

The first time was after she'd nursed him back to health when he was injured in the attack against Wyndmere Hall. The duke's enemies had plotted against him, but thanks to the combined efforts of the duke and his private guard, the attempt failed. She shuddered remembering the violent battle between Hollingford's men and the duke's. He'd walked away after delivering urgent news to His Grace. Was this to be their lot, sharing searing moments of pleasure locked in one another's arms and dealing with long separations while their hearts, and bodies, ached to be together?

Mollie curled her hands into fists at her sides to keep from giving in to the powerful urge to place a hand to her heart to keep it from shattering. She refused to break down and weep like a newborn babe. Malloys came from strong stock, according to her da. She would trade her life, if it would spare Finn's—not that she was ready to tell him that. Wasn't it enough that she tossed her pride away and was his for the asking every time he returned to Wyndmere Hall? After last night, he had to know.

A black thought plagued her... Did he think she gave herself freely to any man?

Dear Lord, she wished she'd been strong enough to resist his crooked smile, dancing green eyes—and those lips! Her heart raced as she remembered how they'd kissed a path from the base of her throat to her...

She still couldn't fathom the power of his desire for her—or hers for him! She swallowed against the lump of emotion lodged in her throat. The passion burning between them could not be denied. His callused hands, the weight of him—

"Are ye all right, lass?"

Mollie blinked, surprised to find herself in his embrace. The worry etched across his brow warmed her heart. Though she knew he would not change his mind and stay, he did care for her. But he'd made a vow to the Duke of Wyndmere and his older brother. To dismiss that vow in favor of another would tarnish the honor of the men in the duke's guard—his brothers, cousins…and his own. He'd die first!

"I'm fine," she assured him. The men in the duke's guard served in a continuous rotation between the duke's estates and the homes of his brother and cousins. It could be months before she saw him again. "Just tired."

The lie weighed heavy on her conscience. What good would it do to tell him the truth? The first time he left had been the hardest to bear. The second time he left, she'd been consumed with worry that her nausea was the result of the night they'd spent together.

Had they been taunting fate one too many times, spending the night rekindling the desire that burned so brightly between them? Why hadn't he asked if she'd been faithful to him? Why hadn't she told him she was devastated—heartbroken—every time he left her?

She drew in a cleansing breath and slowing exhaled. She'd made the choice *not* to add to the responsibilities already resting on the man's broad, but capable, shoulders when she suspected she carried his babe months ago. It turned out she'd fretted herself into an upset stomach and dizzy spells. Would fate be kind to the lovers again if he left without sharing what was in his heart?

She sighed deeply. Either way, Finn was leaving…again.

"If ye're certain, lass. I could fetch Merry or Constance for ye."

The very last thing she needed was the housekeeper or the cook as witnesses when she fell apart at his feet, begging him not to go. By all that was holy, she was a Malloy, and Malloy women held strong till their last breath!

She gathered her resolve and her courage to say goodbye, burying the worry that it might be for the last time. "May God watch over you on your journey, Finn O'Malley." *And the rest of your days,* she silently added.

FINN TUCKED A lock of auburn hair behind her ear, memorizing the curve of her cheek, the love shining in her soft blue eyes. "Will ye miss me?"

A deep ache settled in his gut as he realized he wanted to stay—to hell with duty! The petite firebrand staring up at him with tear-filled, bright blue eyes was the other half of his soul. He knew it in the very depths of his being…just as he knew he had no choice. His word was his bond.

He had to leave.

"Aye, Finn. Every day until you return."

His throat tightened with emotion as satisfaction filled him. Drawing in the scent of her—rain-soaked roses—he dug deep for the wherewithal to release her from his embrace. He tucked the memory of last night, spent locked in each other's arms, beside a similar memory of her waiting to welcome him back with open arms. He'd be back, and she would be waiting. It gave him the strength to leave now.

She was already his, and had been since their first night together. Her unconditional love moved him, branding him as hers. By the saints, he would return! When he did, they would be wed good and proper—not just pledges made in the heat of passion before he'd claimed her heart, body, and soul.

He pressed his lips to her forehead. "Write to me."

She snorted with laughter. "You won't write back."

"Ah, but I'll want to."

"You will be too busy with your duties at Penwith Tower. Constantly on edge, reinforcing patrols, keeping the workmen rebuilding the tower safe. The constant threat from smugglers and wreckers—while the local excise men line their pockets while they look the other way—allows tax-free goods to be sold to the locals."

His eyes widened. "Ye have been listening."

"Aye, Finn. It's wrong for the locals to be in league with those who break the law."

"'Tis more than that. Both sides are against the duke because he dared to rebuild his family's ancestral tower. Like it or not, his coin—and his men—are breathing new life into the village of St. Ives."

"The possibility of both sides attacking those in the middle—you and the duke's men—frightens me."

He met her gaze and held it. He looked past the proud woman struggling to hide what was in her heart, to the woman he'd wrapped in his arms with nothing between them but the night. It took every ounce of his steely control to ignore the clawing need to kiss her until she was weak with passion. Instead, he bent and placed a kiss to the tip of her nose. With a brief hug, he stepped back.

The need to profess his undying love tore through him, but he'd done more than he'd ever intended that night he accepted the gift of her virtue. He would not have her pining for him while he was gone, too. She needed to be able to live her life *without him*—at least for the next few months.

So many things he wanted to tell her, but for the sake of his sanity, and her heart, he rasped, "Be safe, lass."

She lifted on her toes, wound her arms around his neck, and kissed the breath out of him. His body tensed as desire for her threatened to cut him off at the knees. One more moment and he would toss her over his shoulder—again.

"Promise me, Mollie."

"I promise."

He could not resist brushing the tip of his finger along the curve of her cheek one last time. Something in her eyes had him hesitating. Mayhap he could ask the duke if he could remain at Wyndmere Hall permanently—his brother Patrick had after he'd married.

But that would never work. He and Patrick would butt heads constantly, as they had done the whole of their lives. Mayhap after Penwith Tower was rebuilt, and the local excise men put a stop to the smugglers and wreckers plying their trade along the coast of Cornwall, he could claim her heart. At the moment, the situation was too tenuous, too dangerous.

"Mollie?" She lifted her gaze to meet his, and a lone tear streaked across her cheek. He wiped it away and tenderly pressed his lips where it had been. "If ye need me—"

Bloody hell, why couldn't he just say what was on the tip of his tongue? *Send word immediately if you think you're carrying my babe.*

Frustration twined with anger, tearing him apart. His brother had told him how the lass suffered the last time they'd parted, and the added worry that she might be carrying his babe. She hadn't been, but that did not mean she wasn't with child now. A strong believer in fate, he knew you could only tempt it so many times…

He couldn't utter the words to ask. He would never leave if she was. Clearing his throat, he reminded her, "If ye need me, have Patrick send word." The lass remained stubbornly silent, until he wanted to shake some sense into her. "I'll have yer word, Mollie Catherine Malloy!"

She huffed and mumbled.

Good—he'd rather she was angry than sad. "What was that?"

"If I need you—and I won't—I will seek out your brother."

"Not me cousins."

Her soft laughter was music to his ears. "Aye, Finn, your brother, Patrick."

He yanked her to him and gave in to the need tearing at his soul. Molding his mouth to hers, he drew every ounce of sweetness from her lips. "That'll have to last ye till I return, lass."

She pushed back from his embrace, blue eyes narrowed, wisps of auburn silk trailing from where she'd gathered her hair into a knot on top of her head. Mollie studied his face as if she'd never see him again. "What makes you think I haven't found another to warm my bed while you are away?"

He chuckled. "Ah, lass, I know ye like I know me own heart. You'd never have tried to seduce me and have yer wicked way with me if ye didn't love me."

"Why haven't you asked if I've been faithful to you?"

He pulled her back into his embrace and tucked her head beneath his chin. "Ye've a heart as big as Ireland, lass, and eyes that speak louder than yer words. When ye gave yer virtue to me, 'twas a gift to be treasured for the one ye'll love till ye die—*me!*"

"Then why are you leaving me—again?"

"I've given me word to His Grace. Between us—me brothers and cousins—we swore an unbreakable vow. I'll return to ye. Trust me and wait for me, Mollie-lass."

Gently, he set her away from him. The mixture of hope and despair in her gaze tugged at his heartstrings, but he had a duty to fulfill. She had to understand!

"I will."

He saw the moment doubt crept into her gaze. But let her doubt him. He'd show her he could keep his vow to the duke— and the one he'd made in his heart to her. He'd prove her wrong when he returned to sweep her off her feet and plop her down in front of the vicar.

A swift nod punctuated his decision. He turned to go, but not before he heard her softly whispered words.

"I love you."

Those three words carved a hole in his gut. Bloody hell, if he turned back one more time, he'd never leave! It was his duty to go. His honor and his vow would be in question if he stayed.

The first step was the hardest. He put one foot in front of the other, ignoring his bleeding heart as he walked away from the woman he loved.

Duty called.

CHAPTER TWO

FINN O'MALLEY HEARD an ominous creak above him—a split-second warning. The men laying the last course of stone didn't need to be told—they scrambled to the ladder. Half the men jumped to safety when they were a few feet off the ground, rather than wait their turn to descend.

He rushed past his men toward the swaying scaffolding, grabbed the section of framework that threatened to collapse, and dug deep to brace it with every ounce of strength he possessed. They'd spent months rebuilding Penwith Tower's curtain wall...and this was the last section. If it collapsed, his plans to leave tomorrow to surprise the fair lass he'd left behind at Wyndmere Hall would change. It had to hold!

His cousin rushed forward, adding his muscle. For a heartbeat the rumbling and creaking above their heads stopped and Flaherty grinned at him. "Never doubt an Irishman when he's saving the world."

Finn chuckled. "Ye're right, even if ye're a bloody *eedjit!*"

Timbers cracked above their heads. *"Shite!"* There was no saving the scaffolding, now. Finn's heart thundered in his chest as he shouted, "She's coming down!" He grabbed his cousin's arm and shoved him toward safety. "Move yer *feckin' arse!*"

Dust billowed as dagger-like splinters of wood rained down on them. A deep rumble beneath their feet had them lifting their arms to cover their heads as they ran like hell!

Flaherty, lighter by a stone, made it to the entryway. Finn pushed for more speed, dashing beneath the arch of stone. His cousin's warning shout could barely be heard above the crash of rubble that sounded too close to his heels for comfort.

The first stone hit point-blank on his right shoulder. Another bounced off his back. Flaherty motioned for him to hurry. Finn knew he had to reach freedom—the other side of the ancient archway.

He heard the scaffolding and part of the wall collapse behind him as the ground shifted beneath his feet, pitching him forward. He twisted at the last second, so he wouldn't land on his face, and landed hard on his shoulder.

His stomach roiled as his arm was forced out of the socket, but he'd be damned to Hell and back before he gave in to the weakness he'd suffered from the decade-old injury. Ignoring the pain, he lifted his head and locked gazes with his cousin—it would be up to Flaherty to assume command. Flaherty's grim expression alerted Finn that his silent message had been received. Flaherty would take the reins as head of the duke's guard at Penwith Tower should Finn be incapacitated.

On his hands and knees, he took another hit. Sharp pain lanced through him. He ignored the useless arm dangling at his side and struggled to his feet. Arms pulled him to safety as more stones from the wall shook free behind him.

Instead of the sympathy he expected from Flaherty, his cousin chuckled. "Well now, what was it ye've always boasted about brawn over brain?"

Finn shoved free from the two men steadying him. "Nearly caught *you* that time, too."

The amusement in his cousin's eyes faded, and a look of concern took its place. "Sure and I thought ye were done for."

Finn snorted with laughter and nearly lost his breath as the pain jolted through the entire right side of his body. Determined not to appear weak in front of their men, he scoffed, "Faith, 'tis only a scratch." He narrowed his eyes. "A Flaherty will *never* beat an O'Malley in a test of strength."

"Ah, ye may be right, but we Flahertys are swift of foot and canny in a bare-knuckle fight."

Finn narrowed his eyes at his cousin. The memory of the last time they'd sparred—and Flaherty's hard clip to his jaw—surfaced, irritating the *shite* out of him. "Care to put that to the test?"

Flaherty's laughter was a healing balm to Finn's wounded pride at not being able to keep pace with his faster cousin. "Well now, shall we go a few rounds before or after I set yer arm back where it belongs?"

Finn grimaced. The remedy was as painful as the injury. "I'll do it meself."

"*Bollocks* to that! The last time, it took ye three tries, when ye know I can set it right in one."

"Bugger it! I don't want yer help."

The glint in his cousin's eyes should have warned him. Flahertys never gave in. "Fine, then. I'll just sit here and watch ye make a bloody fool of yerself in front of our men. That will add spice to the talk already circulating that ye're one of the smugglers plying yer trade along the coast."

Finn knew better than to turn his back on his cousin. One minute he was on his feet striding along the path to their quarters, the next he was spitting out a mouthful of dirt and cursing a blue streak as Flaherty had indeed put his arm back where it belonged in one try as he knocked him to the ground.

He glared as his cousin helped him to stand. "Ye could have waited and had me lie on a bench like before."

Flaherty shook his head. "We haven't the time. Ye need to send word to His Grace."

Finn drew in a steadying breath, picturing the curtain wall in his mind as it had been hours before. "Aye. The wall was solid last night when we discussed the number of stones required to lay the last two courses needed to finish the wall." He turned to assess the damage.

Flaherty moved to stand beside him. Together they waited for the last of the rubble to settle before walking back toward the remains of the scaffolding and the ruined wall. Waving the dust from in front of his face, Flaherty asked, "Do ye think Ruan had a hand in it?"

Finn's gut twisted at the mention of the infamous French smuggler who had connections throughout England and France. "He'd be my first guess," he admitted. "Though to tell ye the truth, Buxton and his lackeys have had it in for me from the start."

Flaherty cursed, *"Feckin'* crooked excise men. They should be on the side of the law—not the lawless."

"Aye, anyone who holds an office for His Majesty should be honor-bound to do his duty. Those that collect the excise—the taxes—are just as important as those who work for the customs office."

"'Tis easier to be stationed in Cornwall than at the Excise Office in London. He can line his pockets with the coin he collects from ignoring his duties without fear of being caught."

Finn agreed. "He'd stand out in London. Here in St. Ives, half the people are involved in illegal activities. Buxton knows there is a greater profit to be made collecting a fee from the locals who purchase tariff-free goods. There is no coin if Buxton tracks down the goods he knows are being offloaded into the caves beneath Penwith Tower and turns them over to the customs officials."

"Sure and the lure of coins jingling in yer pockets is sweet, but at the expense of a man's honor?"

"Buxton doesn't know the meaning of the word."

Flaherty nodded. "Our patrols are cutting into their profits."

"We've had confirmation from those on the midnight patrol of the perimeter," Finn reminded him. "At least three of Buxton's men were seen entering the caves carrying crates."

"Working both sides of the law—he knows ye aren't one of the smugglers or bloody wreckers who ply their trade in the dark of night. What ails the man?" Flaherty asked.

Finn replied, "I work for the Duke of Wyndmere, who has interfered with his crooked ways."

"Wouldn't stop a man like Buxton," Flaherty scoffed. "What is the real reason?"

Finn slowly smiled. "Might have been when I knocked into him a sennight ago. He dumped a tankard of ale on his crotch. The lovely lass he was flirting with laughed at him. Ah, 'twas worth his feeble attempts at retribution."

Flaherty's bark of laughter soothed the chink in Finn's pride at having to admit to an old shoulder injury. His cousin would stand beside him or defend his back in a fight. The years spent testing one another in feats of strength and sparring had honed their bare-knuckle skills. It was just their way. The cousins were too closely matched in skill otherwise.

Needling each other added another level to their competition. When either of them won their bouts, with their aim *and* their words, the other had to acquiesce and buy the next two rounds of ale at the tavern.

"Couldn't have happened to a better man."

Finn grinned. "'Twas Eileen, the wench who has been casting her lures your way. When are ye going to reel her in?"

Flaherty put a hand over his heart and sighed. "I need a moment—ah, Eileen Doonan, the loveliest of the fair wenches working at the Mermaid's Glass tavern."

Finn shook his head, knowing his cousin was taken with the lass. It would be up to Flaherty to decide if he was interested in more than a tumble. And far be it from Finn to give his cousin advice about courting a woman, when the one he'd left behind filled his thoughts and his heart. He shoved them back into the box where they waited...until he was alone and could allow himself to relive the last night they'd spent in one another's arms.

He turned from the wall to where the men waited for the signal to return. "Let's have a word with the workmen before we let them examine the damage and give us their advice."

His cousin agreed and offered a hand to Finn.

Finn shoved his cousin with his good arm. "I can walk on me own. Mayhap ye should return to the tavern and see if ye can ply Buxton's whereabouts last night from one of the lovelies' lips."

Flaherty grinned. "'Twill be me pleasure. Ye'll tell His Grace yer suspicions?"

"Not until we have proof. For now, I'll let him know what happened today."

"What of the missing tools, and the destruction of the wagons we used to haul the stones to the tower just three days past?"

"We have our suspicions," Finn said, "not the proof we need."

"It should be enough to warrant consulting with Coventry or King," Flaherty grumbled.

Finn sighed. "I've been thinking the same. As the duke's trusted London man-of-affairs, Captain Coventry's connections are far-reaching. And Gavin King and his Bow Street Runners have eyes and ears everywhere."

"I'd suggest it to His Grace."

"'Twould be best if it were His Grace's idea," Finn said.

"If ye wait much longer, ye'll be standing on a different type of scaffold altogether—one where there's a rope around yer neck! Buxton will convince the local magistrate sooner or later that ye're working with that French bastard, Ruan."

Finn absently rubbed his neck, unable to dismiss the possibility. "We'll get the proof we need. We know Buxton is guilty. He'll be the one standing beside Ruan when they stretch their scrawny necks!"

LATER THAT AFTERNOON, Finn unrolled the hundred-year-old map of Cornwall. The duke had entrusted it to him when he was promoted to head of the duke's personal guard stationed at

Penwith Tower. The map listed the ancient *hundreds of Cornwall*—administrative shires designated from the year 925 to the present. After carefully smoothing the edges of the map, he placed rounded stones along the perimeter to hold it flat.

"What do ye need the map for, when all ye need to do is stand by the edge of one of the outcroppings to the village beyond?" his cousin mumbled. "Ye'll see where the locals live."

Finn glanced up from studying the layout of the villages nearest to the duke's estate—a manor house built in the latter part of the fourteenth century nearly a mile or more from the shadow of Penwith Tower.

"A missive arrived from His Grace with an addendum to his list of stonemasons and craftsmen from the village."

Flaherty snorted. "The first lot are probably wondering if the tower is as cursed as it's long been rumored to be."

Finn had to agree. "Half of the men are no doubt planning to hand in their notice in the morning. There have to be a few men on the duke's list worthy of hiring to handle the repairs to the footings, shoring up the curtain wall."

His cousin shook his head. "These Cornishmen are a bit like our neighbors back home in Ireland…mayhap a bit more apt to believe in dark spirits and the like roaming the moors in the *tween* times—just before dawn and dark."

"Don't forget when the clock is at half past."

Finn turned his attention to the map once more. Studying the duke's property, he traced the perimeter. The duke's holding ranged to the north of the manor house all the way to the cliffs overlooking the Celtic Sea. The map indicated a honeycomb of caves beneath the cliffs. They'd only had the time to search half of them. To the south, the property encompassed vast moors—dotted with circles of standing stones, and the remains of ancient hill forts—to the English Channel just beyond. With the tip of his finger, he followed the well-worn path leading all the way to the western tip of the peninsula—the very edge of the Cornwall. The village of St. Ives and Penwith, and most of his headaches, lay to the east, where Buxton, and his excise men, mingled daily with smugglers and wreckers—some frequenting the Mermaid's Glass tavern, while others preferred the seedier Randy Cock.

He splayed his hands on either side of the map and attempted to lean closer, but his shoulder protested. He bit back the groan and abruptly sat on the three-legged stool. The rough-hewn stool and battered oak table had been prized finds in one of the dilapidated outbuildings on the property. Finn didn't need fancy—he needed sturdy. His mind drifted toward Wyndmere Hall and the lovely Mollie…

"Ye should wear the sling I fashioned for ye."

Flaherty's words brought Finn sharply back to the present. "*Bollocks* to that!" He studied the list again. "We need at least six more men if we are to finish the necessary repairs in a timely manner."

Flaherty stared at him. "Timely manner? Since when do ye care when we finish the tower?"

Finn nearly blurted out, *Since the last night I spent in an angel's arms.* He managed to stop himself from bringing shame down upon Mollie's head—and his own. Aye, the shame would be his for tempting a maiden to toss her virtue and inhibitions to the four winds for a night of pleasure he would never forget, nor those that followed whenever he returned to Wyndmere Hall. Did she think of him, too?

"Well?" Flaherty demanded.

Finn pushed to his feet. "I'm not wearing a bloody sling."

"And?" his cousin pushed.

"And what?"

"Why do ye care when the tower is completed?"

"I don't," Finn said.

"Sure and Aunt Eileen—your sainted mother—would take a switch to ye, even at yer advanced age, for lying."

Finn's sharp bark of laughter broke the tension between the cousins. "Ah, but she'd have to catch me first."

Flaherty's look of superiority slid under Finn's skin like a sliver of wood. "A muscular block of granite such as yerself? Yer ma's not even five feet tall and barely weighs ten stone! She'd catch ye before ye tripped over yer own big feet."

The words hit their mark. Instead of his normal response—punching Flaherty—Finn controlled the need to level his cousin and let his anger show. He wouldn't be goaded into speaking of what was between Mollie and him. "Mind yer business," he warned, "and I'll be minding me own."

Flaherty's gaze met his. "Ye'll tell me when whatever is weighing heavy on yer mind begins to pain ye?"

Finn gave in. "Aye, Fenton. Not a minute before then."

"'Tis all I ask."

"And more than I can grant at the moment."

CHAPTER THREE

RUAN, THE FRENCH smuggler who *ruled* the free trade along the coast of Cornwall, stood on the foredeck of his ship, spyglass to his eye. The plume of dust and following rumble had him smiling. "It is done! The Irish dog who protects the English duke will have no choice but to give up."

With a lift of his chin, and the aid of his high-heeled boots, he looked down on his lackey—the grizzled man he paid handsomely to see that his cargo was smuggled safely ashore—and into one of the duke's many caves beneath the cliffs. "Well, Buxton?"

The excise man held out his hand, annoying the Frenchman. "You will accept my word, as O'Malley must accept my victory over him. The Duke of Wyndmere will never finish rebuilding. His men will flee in fear of the ghosts of the past haunting Penwith Tower." Buxton then surprised him by grabbing the spyglass and putting it to his eye. "Bloody hell!"

"From the cloud of dust, you have achieved what I asked. The scaffolding has collapsed."

Instead of the reply Ruan expected, the man shoved the glass at him. "See for yourself! Take a look at the footings of the blasted curtain wall!"

Unease sprinted through the smuggler. He knew how to aim and blow a stone wall to bits with a single cannonball, but not how to loosen the stones at the base of the wall to make it collapse—as Buxton has promised would happen.

He pulled the glass away from his eye, squinted at the tower in the distance, then put it back. The image did not waver. *Merde!* The wall stood! The top two courses of stone had toppled over, and there were a few stones missing at the base of it, but it stood.

Ruan had the blade against Buxton's neck before the man could blink. The urge to kill him was strong—but the realization that he needed Buxton stilled the blade in his hand. "I shall leave this nick to your throat as a reminder." He deftly adjusted the blade so the cut wasn't deadly or deep. "Do not fail me again."

Buxton's gasp of shock deepened to a groan of pain as he clamped his hand to the wound.

"Do not fail me again."

Eyes wide, the English dog stared for a heartbeat before nodding.

Though the excise man was still useful to Ruan—for the moment—he could not stand the sight of him. Ruan shouted to one of the men on deck, "Deposit *les déchets*—this trash—on shore.

Without a word, his man lifted Buxton over his head and tossed him into the Celtic Sea.

"*Imbécile!* Take him ashore in the dinghy!"

His man shrugged, put his leg over the side of the ship, and descended the rope ladder.

Ignoring the cries for help, Ruan turned his back on the two men he'd given orders to. They would either do as they were told or feel the sting of his blade right before he gutted them.

BUXTON HELD OUT his hand to the smuggler and let himself be hauled halfway into the small boat. It was a struggle, but he grabbed hold of the bench seat and pulled himself the rest of the way in. Cold, wet, and bleeding, he cursed when he should have been thankful Ruan had not slit his throat from ear to ear. He'd threatened to do just that more times than Buxton could recall, but this was the first time he'd actually felt the sharp edge of the Frenchman's dagger on his throat.

"It is not like *mon capitaine* to spare anyone who displeased him."

Buxton lifted his head to meet the other man's gaze. "It was not my fault."

The man continued to row toward shore in smooth, even strokes. "That is but a small matter to *mon capitaine*." He stared at Buxton without speaking for long moments. "Once you are of no use to him, you are dead."

The excise man refused to cower before the bloody superior frog facing him. He knew what Ruan was capable of. Buxton had lasted longer than any of the others employed by the Crown to rid the village of those who dared to ply their trade along the coast of Cornwall. He flinched remembering the last official the smuggler had bribed, used, and left hanging from the lamppost outside the excise building—with the man's bloody entrails spilling from his abdomen.

Ruan considered anyone who failed him a traitor—deserving of the Frenchman's version of a traitor's death.

Buxton leaned toward the larger man. "I could make it worth your while. I know Ruan's been sitting on his last cargo. If you'll send word when it's scheduled to be picked up and distributed…"

Without missing a beat, the Frenchman inclined his head. "Tomorrow. Two o'clock in the morning. The cave directly beneath Penwith Tower."

"How do I know you will not double-cross me?" Buxton demanded.

"Ah…and have you not planned to do the same to *mon capitaine*?" the Frenchman sneered.

Buxton knew then his time had nearly run out. *So be it.* He'd stand his ground, reap what he could, and slip away before either Ruan or his lackey were the wiser.

"If you double what you plan to offer," the smuggler continued, "I will double my efforts *not* to turn you over to be gutted and hanged from the gibbet outside your excise building."

"Done!" Buxton spat on his hand and offered it to the Frenchman.

The other man did not miss a beat rowing as he snorted with disdain. "Filthy English habit. You take my word, or you take your chances, *mon ami*."

Buxton had no other choice. "I shall take your word."

"*Bien*."

CHAPTER FOUR

MOLLIE WILLED HER hands to stop shaking. She had suspected...but had not been ready for the truth. She bathed her face with cool water from the ceramic pitcher in her bedchamber. Lifting her gaze, she stared at the face of a woman she no longer knew.

The woman she used to be had been raised to save herself for marriage.

The pale-faced woman staring back at her had tossed caution to the winds and tasted paradise in Finn O'Malley's arms. She thought she understood what a man and a woman shared in the marriage bed. But the moment he slipped her chemise over her head and looked his fill—his brilliant green eyes had glowed with the depth of his desire—she suspected her mother had not told her the truth. There was much more to the marriage bed than closing your eyes and praying it would be over soon.

God help her, she did not regret one moment—one caress. She'd cried into her pillow night after night after he left, knowing he had a duty and a vow to fulfill. Finn O'Malley would not return until his four-month rotation was up. By then, she'd be begging on the streets of London for a crust of bread to feed the babe growing in her belly.

Tears filled her eyes, for all that could have been if Finn had declared his love for her before he left—in front of at least one witness. She blinked them away as her mother's words echoed in her head... *Be careful what you wish for—it just might come true!* She'd wished Finn would love her enough to stay, and had thrown herself at him until he gave in to the desire that blazed to life between them every time they were in the same room.

He'd never said the words to her, though she'd told him more than once that night. Words hadn't been necessary when he could convey his thoughts with a glance, a touch. Hand to her breast, she remembered the tender way he taught her to open her heart, mind, and body to him, while he showed her with each caress, and every kiss, that he loved her too.

The cook and housekeeper had been keeping a close eye on her since Finn had left for Cornwall three weeks ago. Even the duchess had broken her normal routine to seek Mollie out to ask her how she was feeling. Did everyone expect her to make an announcement any day that she carried Finn's babe?

"Mollie? Are you coming?" Francis' voice broke through her daydreams.

Good Lord above, the last thing Mollie needed was Francis poking her head in the door before she'd had a chance to hide the chamber pot! She'd make an excuse and come back to empty it as soon as she got rid of the maid she shared duties with—her nosy friend.

Once Francis knew, Mollie may as well shout it from the rooftops. Her stomach ached from wondering how severe the duke and duchess' reactions would be. She could not imagine they would permit any of their staff to remain under their roof once they discovered she was with child...and unmarried.

Mollie clenched her jaw and squared her shoulders. Malloys never quit, but they knew when it was time to leave. She'd give her notice now—before she began to show. Their Graces were known for their generosity, and glowing recommendations, for those who left their employ. With a little luck, she'd land a position close by and wait for Finn's return.

A dark thought had her reconsidering. "I'm through waiting

for Finn… I waited for over a year!"

She placed a cloth over the chamber pot and carefully slid it beneath her bed—out of sight, until she could empty it without anyone being the wiser.

One last glance at the looking glass revealed the determined woman she used to be. "Better," she told her reflection. With a plan for their future—herself and Finn's babe—she lifted her chin, turned her back on the looking glass, and yanked open the door.

⫸⫷

FRANCIS CAUGHT HERSELF before she tumbled into Mollie's room and knocked into her friend. The sour expression on her face did not deter Francis from her goal one bit.

"How are *we* feeling this morning?"

Mollie glared as she swept past her into the hallway. "We're late."

Francis had dealt with her friend's mercurial temperament for the last few years working alongside her. As scullery maid under Constance, the Duke of Wyndmere's cook, promoted to lady's maid to the duchess—after the attack on Wyndmere Hall—and more recently in the nursery to relieve the nanny.

Closing Mollie's door, Francis rushed after her friend. "We're not that late. We have time to grab at least one scone or buttermilk tart—either one would sit well, given your…" Hand to her mouth, she realized what she'd said. It was too late to take back the words.

Mollie whirled around, a protective hand to her belly, confirming what Francis—and the other ladies employed by the duke and duchess—had suspected since Finn O'Malley returned to his post at Penwith Tower.

"How could you know when I've only just realized it myself?"

Francis sighed. "The signs were there."

Mollie narrowed her eyes. "And you are an expert."

Francis bit back what she wanted to say. Constance had advised her to speak in a calm tone for Mollie's sake—and her babe's. "When I noticed the change in your temperament and eating habits, I thought you were ill, so of course I told Constance I was worried."

"Constance knows, too?"

Francis watched her friend lose every ounce of color and sway on her feet. She wrapped an arm around Mollie, steadying her. "Don't worry. I've got you." As she watched, a lone tear escaped Mollie's eye. Francis knew then how much her friend had been holding inside. "It's better to let your feelings out than keep them to yourself."

"I'll never be able to keep going if I set even one emotion free," Mollie whispered. She looked at Francis and confessed, "Finn doesn't love me—he's not coming back."

The sorrow in her eyes cut Francis to the quick, and her friend's words slashed through her heart.

Needing to get to the heart of the matter, Francis asked, "Will you tell him about the babe?"

Another tear escaped, and Mollie wiped it away. "No."

"But he's the father! He deserves to know!"

"He didn't stick around long enough to find out if he would be," Mollie snapped.

Appalled, Francis grabbed Mollie's hand and held tight. "Finn would move heaven and earth to be with you if he knew you carried his babe! He is honest as the day is long. Once he gives his word, he keeps it!"

Mollie pulled her hand free and shoved Francis' arm from around her waist. "You don't know half as much as you think you do."

Francis watched her friend stomp toward the door to the servants' staircase and quickly followed. It would be her fault if, in her anger, Mollie tripped and fell.

She slapped her hand against the door at the same time Mollie's hand reached for the knob. "I'll go first," Francis said. "If you fall, you'll land on something soft…instead of your hard head."

Mollie's shocked look was worth the silent treatment she would no doubt mete out once she got her gumption back.

Using those few moments to her advantage, Francis opened the door and slipped in front of her friend. "Watch out for the laundry pile one flight down—and the tray near the bottom." To her surprise, Mollie thanked her. Turning to ensure her friend didn't get her feet tangled in the linens, Francis held out her hand. "Here, let me help you." Again, her friend surprised her by taking hold.

"I have a plan, you know," Mollie confided.

Francis glanced over her shoulder. "You wouldn't be Mollie Malloy without one."

"Thanks for saying that." When Francis remained silent, Mollie asked, "Don't you want to know what it is?"

"You'll tell me when you're ready."

"I'm giving my notice this afternoon."

Francis jolted to a halt, swinging her arm out to prevent Mollie from toppling into her. "You're what?"

"I cannot stay here! If Constance knows, then she'll tell Merry. Our housekeeper will feel obligated to confide what she knows—she'll likely tell the nanny, who will tell the duchess! Can't you see that I have to leave before that happens? Without Their Graces' recommendation, no one will hire me."

"And do you plan on telling your new employer that you are pregnant, or will you let them find out when you start to show?"

"That would be *my* business," Mollie reminded her. "Not yours!"

Francis narrowed her eyes at her friend. Without another word, she continued down the stairs, pausing to wait for Mollie before opening the door to the lower level. "Do you intend to tell anyone, or will you leave the friends you've made at Wyndmere Hall without a word?"

Mollie's look of indifference slipped to reveal that of a scared young woman. A heartbeat later, her mask was firmly back in place. "No one will miss me once I'm gone."

Francis held Mollie's gaze for a few moments. She drew in a calming breath and exhaled to curb the irritation bubbling dangerously close to the surface. "If you think that, it probably is best that you do not tell anyone what you are about. You are right—no one will miss you." With that, she opened the door and strode toward the nursery without looking back.

Mrs. O'Malley greeted them at the door with a finger to her lips as she motioned them inside. Francis entered and glanced over her shoulder in time to see Mollie's feigned shock as she said, "I forgot something. Be right back."

Francis knew Mollie was going back to her bedchamber to retrieve the chamber pot. She thought she was so clever and that no one had observed the pattern of the last sennight. It was the staff's *job* to observe everything. Constance, Merry, Mrs. O'Malley, and the duchess all noticed—they'd simply chosen to wait until Mollie was ready to confide her news before speaking to her.

Francis was not about to let her friend hand in her notice and leave Wyndmere Hall! If she had to ask Patrick to send word to Finn about Mollie's condition, then she would. Sorrow filled her. Breaking her silence might very well mean the end of the friendship between herself and Mollie.

Digging deep to firm her resolve, she made her decision. Mollie and Finn's unborn babe was more important than the friendship Francis treasured. She would sacrifice anything if it meant Mollie and Finn would finally realize what they shared was precious, and not to be set aside for pride. But more, she would speak to the head of the duke's guard for the sake of Finn and Mollie's unborn babe. Their little one deserved to grow up knowing he or she was loved.

CHAPTER FIVE

MOLLIE FELT AS if she were being watched. The feeling had steadily increased over the last few weeks, but seemed to come to a head when she was ascending the servants' staircase and nearly plowed into the head of the duke's guard.

"Mind yer step, lass," Patrick O'Malley cautioned. "These stairs can be treacherous if ye don't."

The depth of his voice, so like Finn's, had her heart leaping before she schooled her expression to meet his questioning gaze. Tongue tied, cheeks hot with her embarrassment, she couldn't speak. She nodded.

Still the man did not step aside. Like the rest of the O'Malley clan employed by the Duke of Wyndmere, Patrick had massive shoulders. Unless he turned to the side to allow her to pass, she had to wait for him to get out of her way—or turn around and retrace her steps—before attempting to ascend again.

"Somethin' on yer mind, lass?"

In her embarrassment, Mollie had not realized he'd been waiting for her to speak. Unsure if her voice would be steady or crack with emotion, she shrugged.

He snorted out a laugh. "Workin' for Their Graces, even *I* have learned a shrug is not an appropriate answer."

The tightness in her chest eased and the tension in her throat relaxed. "Her Grace is waiting for me."

Staring at her, as if willing her to confess the secret she carried, he finally inclined his head and turned sideways. "Well now, we cannot keep Her Grace waitin', can we?"

"Thank you." She lifted her skirts and hurried up the steps, not daring to glance over her shoulder to see if he was watching her. There was no need—she could feel his gaze drilling into her back.

How long would Patrick wait before he demanded the truth from her?

Good Lord, she could not tell him! Finn may never forgive her if his older brother found out he was going to be a father before Finn did.

She opened the door and quietly closed it behind her. Though the twins were known to sleep soundly, if they were close to waking up, the bang of a door or loud voices could set them to screaming.

Mollie smiled thinking of the little ones she and Francis had been charged to care for whenever the nanny or the duchess asked for their help. Unconsciously resting her hand to her belly, she wondered if she would have a boy or a girl. Would her babe have golden hair and brilliant green eyes, with a heart-stopping smile, like his—or her—father?

She shook those thoughts aside. It wouldn't do to be caught daydreaming when on duty. Lifting her hand, she gave three swift knocks and waited for the door to open.

"Ah, there you are, Mollie." The duchess motioned for her to enter before closing the door behind her.

Ever since the duke and duchess had mended the breach between them, the duchess was smiling—at all hours of the day or night—as if lit from within. Mollie knew from watching Their Graces that it was their love and admiration for one another that got them through difficult situations. Plots casting aspersions on the duke and duchess' reputations. Attempts to silence the duke and duchess—permanently! Kidnapping attempts on the twins— she shuddered remembering the fear that dogged her heels until

Patrick O'Malley and the duke's guard had ended it by catching the culprits.

Though she hadn't ever been to London—or the duke's town house there—she had heard whispers of the attack that occurred during the duke and duchess' first ball. The duels and attempts on the duke's brother's and cousins' lives. How did the duchess manage to keep going forward without falling apart?

She'd asked the question aloud without realizing it.

"I daresay because I know my darling duke has assigned the best of the best—the men of his guard—to watch over us and protect us," the duchess answered.

She held Mollie's gaze for long moments before taking hold of her hands. After squeezing them gently, encouragingly, she released them and asked, "Is there something weighing on your mind, Mollie? You seem distant as of late…troubled."

Her Grace had given Mollie the perfect opening. "Yes, Your Grace, there is."

"Since Richard and Abigail are still sleeping, we have a few moments to talk." The duchess motioned for Mollie to sit in one of the matching rocking chairs. Once they were seated, she said, "There now, isn't that better? Sometimes having the opportunity to sit is just what is needed."

Her warm and gentle smile soothed the edges off Mollie's fears. "Your Grace, you know that I consider it an honor to be one of your staff."

The duchess inclined her head.

Mollie's belly clenched as fear tried to take hold of her.

As if she could sense what her maid was going through, the duchess patted Mollie's hand. "I have found it is often best just to get it said."

Mollie nodded. "I have loved every moment working for Your Graces. Humphries, Merry, Constance, Francis, and the others have become like family to me." Before she lost her nerve, she rasped, "I'm giving you my notice, Your Grace. I'll be leaving your employ."

Instead of the shock she'd expected, the duchess nodded. "I've been expecting you to do so."

"You have? Why?"

"You have not been your normal sunny self, Mollie. Either something is at the root of the change in your disposition...or *someone*."

Tears welled up, but she refused to let them fall. She would not cry! "I had not realized it affected my work. I am deeply sorry."

"I have never complained, have I?"

Mollie met the older woman's direct gaze. "Nay. You have not."

As they rocked, the duchess peppered her with questions. Had Mollie received troubling news from home? Was there an issue she was unaware of with a member of the staff? Had something occurred when she had been running errands in the village?

Mollie answered no to all of the questions, dreading what she knew the duchess would ask next, but knowing she would have no choice but to answer honestly.

"I believe we have narrowed it down from something troubling you...to some*one*. Have you received a letter from Finn O'Malley recently?"

Mollie's snort of laughter caught her by surprise. She cleared her throat. "I beg your pardon, Your Grace. I have not received *any* letters from Finn O'Malley, though I never expected to."

"I see. Then my assumption that the someone troubling you is is indeed Finn."

She nodded.

"Sometimes it helps to confide in another," the duchess said. "Would you like to talk about it? I am a very good listener."

Mollie needed to get it off her chest but, at the same time, knew it was not fair to Finn to hear the news through the grapevine. He had the right to hear from *her* lips that he was going to be a father.

Richard's wail interrupted them. "I'll get him, Your Grace." As Mollie reached into the cradle and lifted the unhappy babe into her arms, love filled her. Love for the babe she was partly responsible for, love for Finn…and love for their babe sleeping in her belly.

She changed him and settled him back into his cradle. "He should go back to sleep for at least another hour."

"You know our babes' schedule, their likes, and dislikes," the duchess said. "Anyone with eyes can see the love you have for Richard and Abigail. You will make a wonderful mother."

Mollie's vision grayed as she felt the floor move beneath her.

"Steady now, Mollie."

The firm command had her struggling to fight the dizzy spell. The arm wrapped around her waist was comforting, something she could concentrate on while she waited for the spinning to stop.

"Sit."

She started to protest, then remembered to whom she was speaking. "Yes, Your Grace." Hand to her head as the dizzy spell subsided, she whispered, "I am so sorry. I don't know what came over me."

The duchess's steady gaze held her captive. "Don't you? It is obvious to those of us who have been blessed with babes of our own what your symptoms may be."

A tear escaped Mollie. "Your Grace, I—"

The duchess handed her a lace-edged handkerchief. "Wipe your tears, Mollie. I have a question to put to you."

"Another one, Your Grace?" Mollie hadn't meant to ask that. "Forgive me. I shall answer whatever questions you have."

"Do you love him?"

"Who?"

The first sign of irritation flicked across the duchess' features. "I will forgive you for being difficult, as you have just weathered one of what seems to be another of your dizzy spells."

"I don't have—"

"You most certainly do. Shall I tell you the dates and times of the last three that you have suffered?"

Heat seared Mollie's face. "No, Your Grace."

"Botheration, Mollie! A woman brave enough to show the man she loves just how much by gifting him with her virtue should be brave enough to tell him he is going to be a father!"

Mollie could no longer hold back her tears. "I am sorry. I never meant to disgrace a member of your household, or yourself and His Grace."

The duchess chuckled. "I would venture to say the very last thing you thought of before giving in to the devastating charms of Finn O'Malley was eventually finding yourself giving your notice and expecting me to accept it."

"I don't understand."

"What goes on between a man and a woman in the marriage bed? Oh dear," the duchess murmured. "And here one would think a man as charming as Finn would be adept at—"

"Not that," Mollie interrupted. "The part where you said 'expecting me to accept it.'"

"Well, I haven't accepted your notice. Have I?"

"Not yet."

"I do not intend to. You are feeling sorry for yourself and the circumstances you find yourself in."

Mollie sighed. "It is a bit of a shock, Your Grace."

"Ah, my dear, it should also be celebrated as a blessing. Children are a gift, you know."

Mollie's smile wobbled. "Yours certainly are."

"Yes, they are, but we are discussing yours. From what I have observed, you are a very strong young woman. In heart, mind, and faith. Did you ever think that mayhap you and Finn anticipating your marriage vows and finding yourself with child is all part of God's plan?"

Eyes wide, heart hammering, Mollie shook her head.

"Bloody hell! You should!"

"I beg your pardon?"

The duchess blew out a frustrated breath. "As well you should. You've made me lose my temper. I should be the one apologizing."

"You're a duchess—you do not have to apologize to someone so far beneath you."

"*Bollocks!*"

Mollie could not contain her laughter. When she caught her breath, she said, "You sound just like Finn and Patrick."

"Such a wonderful expression, is it not?"

"I...er... You do know what it means?" Mollie asked. "Don't you?"

"Yes. Precisely why it comes in handy to use it sparingly, else my darling duke tries to take me to task for uttering such a foul expletive." Mollie fell silent, and the duchess continued, "You do know that the duke gave Finn his permission to court and marry you over a year ago."

Mollie sighed. "I do."

"I have noted that Finn began his courtship, then left for Cornwall."

Mollie stared at her hands. "He changed his mind about me."

"I doubt that, if I know Finn—and I believe I do, as he is similar in temperament to his brother Patrick, and my husband."

"Why did he leave if he didn't have a change of heart?"

"Men like Finn, Patrick, and my husband are honest, have integrity, and will fight to the death to protect their vow of honor."

Mollie had to agree. "Aye, they will."

"Both brothers took a vow to protect my husband, myself, and our family. You distracted him until he had no choice but to ask my husband to send him to Cornwall."

"But I never—"

"I did not say you *intentionally* distracted him. He was distracted by your sunny personality, dedication to His Grace and myself, and willingness to jump into the fray and render aid to those injured when that madman attacked our home."

"I was so worried when Patrick carried Finn inside—I thought he was…" Mollie could not finish the statement. Her heart couldn't take even the *mention* of a world without Finn O'Malley in it.

"And that is why I cannot accept your notice. You are a vital part of our staff. I depend upon you, as do Constance, Merry, and Francis."

"Once I start to show…people will talk."

"Of course they will." When Mollie started to speak, the duchess held up a hand to stop her. "However, you and Finn will be married by then. With one glare from him, all talk will cease."

Mollie slowly smiled. "Do you really think he will ask me?"

"He loves you, Mollie. When he learns he is going to be a father, he will have to accept the responsibility."

"I do not want him to marry me to appease his sense of guilt."

The duchess laughed. "My dear, I do not believe Finn O'Malley has ever felt guilty about anything."

But Mollie knew Finn better than the duchess. "He does, Your Grace. He hides it, but he does."

"Shall I have Patrick send word to him, or would you prefer to write to him?"

"I will write to him," Mollie replied.

Abigail started to fuss. They both rose to see to her.

When Richard started crying, the duchess smiled. "He's hungry, poor thing. At least he waited until we finished our conversation."

"Thank you, Your Grace. I shall do my best not to let you down again."

The duchess sighed. "You have not let me down at all. Best change Abigail, while I feed Richard."

Mollie turned her attention to the little one staring up at her. Eyes so like her father's—a brilliant blue. As she held the child in her arms, she wondered what color eyes her babe would have. Finn had green eyes; her own were a lighter shade of blue.

A dark thought speared through her. Would Finn be angry with her that she found herself with child? She would be the reason he would have to forsake his vow to the duke.

What kind of a future would they have together if he blamed her?

God only knows…

CHAPTER SIX

PATRICK STARED AT Mollie's retreating form. She'd been avoiding him for the last few days. It wasn't obvious, unless one's duty was to be aware of everyone and everything in one's surroundings. It was his duty to know all that went on in and around the duke and duchess. Their lives—and the lives of their babes—depended upon it.

Irritation had him mumbling to himself as he opened the door and strode into the kitchen—the heart of Wyndmere Hall, and his ready source of information, due to the female staff members working for Their Graces.

Constance looked up and smiled as he crossed the threshold into her domain. "What brings you to my kitchen when I know you are due to relieve Rory Flaherty on the roof?"

"Faith but ye have me there, Constance. I have a few minutes spare and need to speak to you about a troubling matter."

The duke's cook could not hold his gaze. She looked away, but not before he saw what he suspected he'd find—Constance knew something. "Do you mind if I continue to work? I have to set these loaves of bread to rise and start on the rest of the day's baking."

"To stop ye would be to deprive meself and the others. Yer bread and baked goods are the finest I've ever tasted." He paused, looked over his shoulder, and leaned close to whisper, "And if ye tell anyone I said that, I'd swear 'twas a bold-faced lie. Me ma has far-reachin' connections—it'd break her heart to know she's not the only one with a fair hand at making bread and such."

Constance's trill of laughter filled the room and felt like a hug.

Grateful that she understood, he got right to the point. "I've just run into Mollie on the servants' staircase. She hasn't been herself since Finn left. Lately, I feel somethin' is different. The lass is quiet, and 'tis as if she's strugglin' under a heavy burden."

Constance didn't agree or disagree. So Patrick added, "More often than not, she's pale and has dark circles beneath her eyes, and a haunted expression on her face whenever ye catch her unaware." When Constance busied herself covering the loaves of bread with a linen cloth before setting them off to the side, he added, "If ye think I don't suspect there's more to her exhaustion than her duties, I'm not doing me job."

The cook's eyes filled. "She hasn't said a word—doesn't need to. The girl has not confided in anyone, not even Francis—and those two have been thick as thieves from the day the previous duke hired them to work as my scullery maids."

"I've sent word to Finn, as he requested." Patrick should not have said as much as he did, but his worry for the lass' condition was great. "Though I know for a fact he cannot leave Penwith Tower unless we shift men around and ensure we have sufficient protection at the duke's other estates."

Another of the duke's guards, Darby Garahan, burst into the kitchen. "O'Malley!"

"What ails ye, Darby?"

In answer, he nodded toward the long hallway that led to the rear entrance. Patrick followed. When they were far enough away that the cook wouldn't hear their conversation, Darby told him, "A messenger has just arrived from Penwith."

"Urgent?"

"Aye," he replied, opening the back door. "The stable master and one of the lads are taking care of his horse."

Their long strides ate up the ground between the duke's home and the stables. Patrick's thoughts raced back and forth between issues he knew his brother currently faced, and the mental list of those who were available at a moment's notice to join the ranks of the duke's guard in Cornwall. "If it's urgent, mayhap Finn finally has the proof we need to clean out the nest of traitors aiding the smugglers and wreckers in the village."

His cousin didn't bother to add his thoughts. In their weekly meetings on the situations in and around the duke's many holdings, his guard discussed the urgent need for intractable proof in order for the duke to use his position to demand the Excise Office clean house in Cornwall...specifically in the village of St. Ives.

Patrick paused with his hand on the door to the stables to signal to Rory Flaherty. His shrill whistle was immediately answered. Turning to Darby, he said, "Rory'll hold his position for a bit longer." He didn't let thoughts of what could have happened take hold of him.

They only had two members of the duke's guard in place at Penwith Tower. There hadn't been a need for more than that, as they'd hired on men to add to their guard as well as workmen from the village. As of late, rumblings that more than one local excise official was in league with free traders had increased. Finn had not asked, but Patrick knew his stubborn brother needed help—now!

"Should I advise the duke?" Darby asked.

"I'll speak with the messenger first." Patrick opened the door to the stables. "Finn may have sent word to His Grace's London man-of-affairs."

Darby agreed, "Captain Coventry has a growing number of former military men at his disposal."

"Aye," Patrick said. "Add in whomever Gavin King of the Bow Street Runners can lend the duke, and we may not have to shuffle the guard. They are due to move on to their next assignment in their quarterly rotation of the duke's estates in a fortnight."

They found the messenger speaking with the stable master. One of the stable lads was taking care of the young man's horse. From the look of it, the missive no doubt contained bad news.

Patrick hailed the stable master. The older servant met his gaze and said, "Here's O'Malley now."

Patrick nodded to him and asked the messenger, "Ye have word for me from Finn O'Malley?"

The messenger seemed relieved to hand it over. "It's urgent, Mr. O'Malley. I'm to wait for your reply and head out immediately."

O'Malley broke the wax seal and asked, "Back to Penwith?"

"Nay," the younger man replied. "I've two messages to deliver in London."

"Cook is preparing a meal to warm yer belly," Patrick said.

"Thank you, sir."

He read the missive. As was Finn's way, it was curt, advising of the damage to the curtain wall surrounding the tower, but never mentioning what he no doubt knew his brother suspected—sabotage. *Damn! Months of work, destroyed?* The missive briefly noted minor injuries sustained, without mentioning how many or to whom.

Making certain to school his features so no emotion showed, Patrick read on. Finn hadn't gone into detail as to the extent of the destruction. From the first, Patrick had advised the duke that missives between members of his guard and his family were not to mention names, unless absolutely necessary. Pertinent information relating to His Grace's holdings were not to be mentioned. The potential for missives being intercepted before reaching their destination was high.

His brother did not have to spell it out for him—they both knew the French smuggler, Ruan, was behind the destruction. What Patrick needed to find out was whether his brother had secured proof that the free trader had assistance from the handful of crooked officials Finn had previously identified.

He folded the missive and slipped it into the pocket of his waistcoat. "I'll show ye to the kitchen. While ye eat, yer horse will be pampered and have a chance for a brief rest. How far is it to your next change of horse?"

"Another ten miles." Giving his horse one last pat on the flank, the messenger said, "This boy's not ready to put up for the night, but he'll enjoy the attention—and the snack of oats."

"I have a few questions for ye," Patrick said as they walked toward the rear entrance to Wyndmere Hall. "Ye need only to nod if the answer is yes."

The messenger looked from Patrick to his cousin and back.

"I take it the missives ye're deliverin' to London are for Captain Coventry and Gavin King."

The messenger gave a brief nod.

Darby opened the door and motioned for them to precede him into the large anteroom just off the long hallway leading to the kitchen. "We have been known to grab a quick meal here. Constance, the duke's cook, has a meal ready at a moment's notice for weary messengers."

"Aye," Patrick agreed. "'Tis a hard ride—most often at hours when the rest of the world is asleep, but not meself and the rest of the duke's guard." Holding the messenger's gaze, he added, "We share a similar purpose, lad. Ye deliver urgent missives…and we protect those who receive them."

The man removed his cap when Constance walked into the room carrying a tray with a steaming bowl and mug, a plate of bread, and a crock of butter.

"You must be starving," the cook said. "Sit, eat, enjoy."

"Thank you, Mum."

Constance smiled. "You are most welcome." With a nod to the men, she left.

"Stay with the lad, Darby," Patrick said. "I need to speak with the duke."

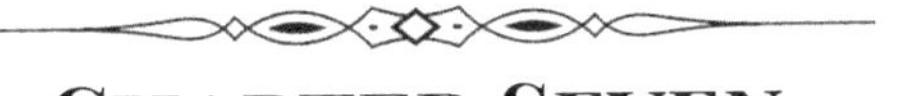

CHAPTER SEVEN

F INN TENSED AT the sound of hoofbeats rapidly approaching, then relaxed. Being braced for trouble at all hours of the day was exhausting, but necessary. The men *expected* to be attacked guarding the stonemasons that worked nonstop to shore up the footings nearly destroyed a sennight ago.

"Flaherty!"

His cousin did not respond—he had his head tilted toward the sound, listening. Finn knew he'd heard the rider too.

Flaherty walked toward him. "What do ye think took Patrick so long to reply to yer missive?"

They both recognized the rider from his horse and the way he rode, leaning forward as if he whispered to his horse—he was one of the duke's messengers.

"Our guard is spread a bit too thin for me liking," Finn said. "I've no doubt that between Patrick, His Grace, Coventry, and King, we'll soon have reinforcements."

"Aye," Flaherty agreed. "'Tis a veritable nest of vipers yer man in St. Ives uncovered."

Frustration had Finn raking a hand through his hair until it stood on end. "At last count, nearly half the village of St. Ives was involved—either in the smuggling or the wrecking."

Flaherty's gaze narrowed on the rider who was headed toward them at a fast trot.

"Bloody bastards, wreckers," Finn continued. "They seem to offer a hand to those aboard a ship that's floundering…and then kill to steal their cargo."

"'Tisn't stealing if no one aboard the ship remains alive," Flaherty reminded him.

"Their deeds reserve their spot in the fires of hell."

"Ye don't have to convince me of that, Finn."

Finn clapped a hand to his cousin's shoulder. "Aye, the buggers know they cannot take the cargo of a sinking ship unless all those aboard perish."

"Profiting from murder should carry the sentence of a traitor's death!"

Finn agreed. "With Coventry backing us, I hope we can convince His Grace to stand up in the House of Lords and suggest such a change."

"The lords from Cornwall would never stand for it."

Finn snorted. "Aye, that would be the end of them living like kings as they, too, line their pockets with their share of the bloodstained coin."

The rider pulled back on the reins and dismounted. "Message for you, O'Malley."

"Thank ye, lad." Finn accepted the sealed note. Breaking the wax seal, he asked, "How is your da's injury faring?"

The younger man sighed. "His temper is up and his mood foul."

Finn and Flaherty shared a look before Flaherty said, "Me da and Finn's—when he was alive—would be on the mend by the time they were in a foul mood. Couldn't stand the thought of sitting on their arses, waiting to heal, when there was work to be done."

The messenger chuckled. "It's good to know my father is in good company."

Finn closed the missive and tucked it in his waistcoat pocket. "If ye'll follow me, there's a round of bread, block of cheese, and ale in our quarters. Ye'll have a meal while we have one of the village lads rub down and water yer horse. He'll appreciate a handful or two of oats along with some sweet, fresh hay."

"Why is it that you and the other members of His Grace's guard are the only ones concerned with a messenger's empty belly, or that of his horse?"

Finn grinned. "'Tis well we know how hard ye work, doing the duke's bidding. Me brothers and cousins come from a long line of farmers—and rebels. We're used to working from sun up till well past midnight, as the work of a rebel only begins once darkness falls."

Flaherty chuckled. "And well we know it. A meal and a pint go a long way to fill a man's belly, while oats and hay do the same for his horse." He waved Finn and the messenger toward the lane leading to their quarters. "I'll stay with the men."

A look of understanding passed between the cousins. Flaherty understood that Finn needed to question the messenger privately.

The group of men hired to deliver messages to and from the duke's many estates were keenly observant—part of the reason Coventry had hired them on behalf of the duke. The young men were fiercely loyal to Coventry and the duke, both of whom looked beyond their desperate circumstances, understanding the men hired would do anything to feed the families that depended on them.

Their fathers had either served in a branch of His Majesty's military forces and were forced to muster out, due to injuries received in their service, or had given the ultimate sacrifice—their lives for king and country.

Finn would glean pertinent information from the messenger's observations—after he read the missive from his brother at Wyndmere Hall.

"MORE ALE?" FINN asked.

The young man shook his head. "One cupful refreshes a man—two could muddle his head."

"Wise words. Yer da's?"

The messenger chuckled. "Mum's. She's fierce in her insistence that we do not overindulge our taste for ale and strong spirits."

"Sounds like a woman after me ma's own heart. Now then, what did ye note about me brother?"

"He was stiff with tension. Could he have had an argument with one of your cousins?" the young man asked. "I know if I had to work with family, I'd be tense most of the time."

"Ye have the right of it, lad. As well ye know ye can trust family to have yer back—no matter what."

The young man agreed. "If I were to guess, I'd think it had to do with what's been happening in and around Penwith Tower. It's hard not to worry when there are smugglers as apt to take your coin as slit yer throat."

"Was the duke with me brother when ye accepted the missive?" Finn asked.

"Nay, although one of the maids was waiting with him—she asked if I would deliver a verbal message to you."

"Well now, why did ye wait so long to tell me?"

The messenger grinned at Finn. "She said I was to wait until we were alone, as it is a private message."

Finn slowly smiled. *Mollie-lass.* He should have written to her before now, but between the repairs to the tower—and the curtain wall—and keeping an eye on the free traders, he hadn't had a moment to spare. "We're alone. What did Mollie Malloy have to say for herself?"

"Just two words. I asked her twice if she wanted to say more, but she declined."

Finn felt worry coursing through his veins. Patrick's missive had ordered him to return to Wyndmere Hall as soon as their cousin James Garahan arrived with two of the men working for Coventry—but didn't tell him why. And now this! "Best get it said."

The messenger locked gazes with Finn. "She had tears in her eyes when she said, 'Hurry home.'"

It took every ounce of Finn's control not to react to the message. Something was definitely wrong. Was she ill? Had she been injured? Had something happened to Patrick's wife or their babe? "How did my brother react to her words?"

"He seemed satisfied, as if he had been expecting it."

"I see. Thank ye for the message. Will ye be returning to the Lake District?"

The young man shook his head. "I'm to report to Captain Coventry in London."

"If ye've eaten yer fill, I'd best see ye on yer way."

FLAHERTY APPROACHED WITH the messenger's horse. He waited until the young man mounted and rode away to ask, "Trouble at Wyndmere Hall?"

"Aye," Finn replied.

Flaherty stared at him. When Finn did not elaborate, he asked, "Is it one of the duke's twins? Her Grace?"

Finn clenched his jaw and slowly relaxed it to answer, "Nay. 'Tis Mollie—she bade me hurry home."

"Don't borrow trouble."

Finn snorted. "Ye sound like Ma."

"Sure and me own ma said it to me brothers, and meself, more times than I could count. 'Tis sound advice, just the same. When do ye leave?"

"As soon as Garahan arrives with Bayfield and Tremayne."

Flaherty gave a brief nod. "Both men I'd be honored to have at me back."

"I've heard Captain Bayfield carries scars from burns he received when his ship caught fire," Finn said. "He tries to hide the scars, though I cannot think why—they're badges of courage and honor."

"Aye," Flaherty agreed. "He doesn't like to speak of what happened. Those he meets underestimate him. The lace he wears at his cuffs, and the elaborate cravat he wears, are to hide the scars."

"Coventry told me Bayfield nearly died from the burns."

Flaherty nodded. "I'm told they cover his back and arms."

Finn clenched his jaw. "I'm thinking I'd rather be shot."

"Ye have more than once," Flaherty said. "Don't be tempting fate. As to Tremayne, I've heard he's a brilliant tactician. Former lieutenant in the Royal Dragoons."

"Our cousin Michael O'Malley swears if he had to have someone—not a brother or cousin—at his back," Finn added, "it would be Gryffyn Tremayne. I hear the lieutenant rallied after a near-fatal saber wound to the face."

Flaherty was listening intently. "Bloody hell—wounds to head and face bleed like a stuck pig."

Finn sighed. "He bears a scar from forehead to chin where the blackguard slashed him."

"He's lucky to have survived."

"Ye have the right of it." Finn stared at the water in the distance, the Celtic Sea, wondering what could be behind Mollie's request that he come home—and hurry. *"Bollocks!"*

"What ails ye?" Flaherty asked.

"I think I know why Mollie sent for me."

"Knowing the lass, she wouldn't send word unless she had no other choice."

Finn shoved his cousin. "How would you know?"

"Did ye forget that I met the lass when we converged on Wyndmere Hall to protect the duke and his pregnant duchess from that bastard Hollingford?"

Finn sighed. "I did, yes."

"As I recall, the other scullery maid was fair of face as well."

"Francis," Finn replied, meeting his cousin's gaze.

"The sooner Garahan arrives with the others," Flaherty said, "the sooner ye can be on yer way."

Finn didn't have to say anything more. There was no doubt his cousin would remember how tenderly Mollie had nursed Finn back to health when he was injured in the battle to protect the duke and duchess and their home.

Flaherty nudged his cousin to get his attention, asking, "When do ye expect Garahan?"

"Midday tomorrow," Finn answered.

"Any instructions ye can think of that I don't already know?"

Finn frowned. "None."

"Well then," Flaherty said, "ye'd best be packing yer things—"

"I won't be staying long enough to need anything more than a change of shirt and extra rounds of ammunition."

"Spoken like the hardheaded cousin I love like a brother."

Finn grinned. "I know I'm yer favorite O'Malley."

Flaherty barked with laughter. "Aye, ye're not as annoying as the rest of them."

CHAPTER EIGHT

MOLLIE COULDN'T STOP wringing her hands as she waited for Francis to join her in the garden. Her heavy woolen shawl kept the worst of the chill from seeping into her bones. She wished spring would hurry up and get here!

"Mollie!"

She turned at the sound of her friend's voice, and relief swamped her. "I thought you'd never get here."

"Some of us have a few extra duties as of late."

Mollie hung her head. "I swear I had no idea Her Grace was going to lighten my duties—or give them to you!"

Francis reached for Mollie's hand and squeezed it briefly before letting go. "I was teasing you. You know I'd do anything for you. Besides," she said, "the duchess is right. We cannot have you overexerting yourself. It isn't good for you or your babe."

Mollie felt tears well up and angrily dashed them away. She was frustrated that her emotions had either been extremely high—or very low. "Lord, I hate to cry!"

Francis handed Mollie her handkerchief and tugged on her arm. "Let's see if there are any bulbs coming up."

"It's too early," Mollie protested.

"Not in the very back of the garden. Have you forgotten the protected spot where the snowdrops always come up—even in the snow?"

Mollie frowned. "I hope we aren't due for any more snow."

"It does make our trips to the village more arduous," Francis remarked. "I don't mind when it's just a dusting, or mayhap an inch or two, that melts as soon as the sun comes out."

Mollie smiled at her friend. "Thank you, Francis."

"For what?" Francis asked. "Dragging you through the chilly air, searching for signs of spring, when we could be having a cup of tea and lavender scones warm from the oven?"

Mollie jolted to a stop. "Constance baked lavender scones?"

"They are Her Grace's favorites," Francis reminded her.

"Mine too."

Francis tried to hide her laughter but couldn't keep from smiling. "I had no idea. Oh! Look, there they are!"

Mollie rushed after her friend and dropped to her knees beside her. She brushed one of the slim white petals with the tip of her finger. "Faery flowers."

"My gran used to call them that too."

"I used to have a special name for my grandmother," Mollie said. "It wasn't Gran."

"Oh? Was it Nan?"

Mollie shook her head. "*Ghra.*"

"Doesn't that mean hope or something like that in Irish?"

Mollie shook her head. "It means love. When I was small, I couldn't say grand or grandma—it came out as *ghra*, which pleased my mum and grandmother no end."

"That's a lovely memory to have of your grandmother. You must miss her," Francis said, then added, "My grandmother could always use another granddaughter. I'm happy to share."

Pushing to her feet, Mollie linked her arm with Francis'. "You are the best of friends. What say we go beg a few lavender scones and clotted cream from Constance?"

"If we hurry, we should be able to convince Constance to brew a pot of tea and share it with us. The more the merrier."

Feeling lighter in spirit, Mollie grinned. "Race you back!"

The two arrived at the back door, more than a bit breathless, disheveled, and giggling. "Constance, could you please, please spare just two small lavender scones?" Francis asked. "We're feeling a bit peckish."

The cook shook her head at the two young women as if they were children—instead of nearly twenty years old. "What have you two scamps been up to? From the roses in your cheeks, and brightness in your eyes, you've had a bit of fresh air." She tilted her head to one side, studying them. "Unless you were on the roof—and I know you weren't—you had to have been running."

Mollie and Francis shared a look and shook their heads.

The cook's expression changed to one of concern. "Mollie Malloy, don't you know better than to run in your condition?"

Mollie's mouth fell open as fear for her babe—the one she just remembered she carried—swept up from her toes. The room grayed, and the floor shifted beneath her feet as she reached out for something to steady herself.

"Mollie-lass!" an all-too-familiar deep voice called from behind her.

She whirled around and put a hand to her head to stop the spinning. "Finn?"

He swept her into his arms and frowned at her. "Who else calls ye Mollie-lass?"

Hand to his cheek, she stared into the blazing green of his eyes and whispered, "You're back!"

"Aye. 'Tis time we had a private conversation."

His warmth seeped into her bones, and her head now felt light for an entirely different reason. The man admitted he'd never answer her letters...but she'd summoned him home—and he came!

"Mollie-lass."

She glanced up at him. Nerves bubbled to the surface and tangled with the myriad emotions spiraling through her. When he frowned, she remembered his statement. "What conversation would that be?"

Instead of being irritated with her, he grinned. "Ma's going to love ye, Mollie. Almost as much as I do."

The shock of his declaration had her drawing in a breath, unable to exhale. His face and form disappeared behind a veil of black.

⫸⫸⫸✦⫷⫷⫷

"WELL NOW," PATRICK drawled as he strolled in behind his brother. "I see ye've not lost any time telling the lass the two of ye are to wed."

Finn shook his head and patted Mollie's face, trying to bring her out of her faint. "Why in the bloody hell did she swoon?"

Patrick shrugged. "If ye didn't tell her ye're here to marry her, what did ye say to her?"

"Mollie's made of sterner stuff than to fall into a faint because of a few words," Finn protested. "She must be ill."

Patrick's lips twitched as he tried to hide a smile.

"What?" Finn demanded. "'Tis yer job to know everything that goes on around here. What's wrong with me bride?"

"Does she know she's going to be your bride?" his brother demanded.

"And why not? The lass told me she loved me."

"And then fainted?"

"Bloody hell! She told me before."

"Before you told her?"

"Aye…before I left for Cornwall."

"And ye left without declarin' yer intention to marry the lass… Are ye daft?"

Constance intervened before the brothers butted heads. "Why don't you take Mollie to the back room and lay her down on the cot? She'll be more comfortable there."

With a grunt, Finn turned and retraced his steps down the hallway to the room just past the pantry. Worry speared his heart. He did not want to let go of Mollie, but knew she needed to rest. He settled her on the cot. "She looks so pale. Have ye been overworking her?"

Patrick poked him in the back. "Did ye not read the missive I sent to ye?"

"Aye—Garahan, Bayfield, and Tremayne arrived, as ye said. I left Flaherty in charge and came as ye asked." Patrick punched Finn in the shoulder. Pain shot from his injured shoulder to the tips of his fingers and back. *"Feckin' eedjit!"*

"Bollocks! Why didn't ye say ye were one of those injured when the scaffolding collapsed?"

"And take a chance the missive would be intercepted?" Finn glared at his brother. "Ye're an arse!"

"Ye've accused me of the same...more than once," Patrick said.

Finn rolled his aching shoulder, hoping to work out the worst of the pain. "Ye punch me in the shoulder that's just been realigned, and I'm the *eedjit*?"

"Aye. Ye know I meant the other missive."

"I only received the one," Finn insisted.

"How is that possible?"

"Only one way that I know of."

"Bloody—"

"Hell," Finn finished for his brother. "Anyone with half a brain would know the men riding to and from Penwith Tower were the duke's personal messengers."

"Have you had word that one of the duke's messengers is missing?"

"Nay," Finn answered. "Each of the lads have routes with more than one stop along the way before they return, so no one has mentioned anyone missing." He looked at Patrick. "Ye need to alert the duke."

"I need to speak to the duke," Patrick said at the same time.

They locked gazes, and Finn inclined his head. "I'll wait here with Mollie while ye speak to His Grace. Ye'll need to send word to Coventry in London, and Flaherty in Cornwall."

"Tell the lass I'm sorry me brother is an *arse*," Patrick said, leaving.

Finn was laughing when Mollie's eyes fluttered and slowly opened. "I'm not dreaming," she said.

"'Tis a boost to a man's ego to know the woman he loves dreams of him."

Tears welled in her eyes, magnifying their soft blue.

"Are ye in pain?"

"Nay," she whispered. "Surprised."

"Ye sent a message—two words. Not the letter I was expecting, mind. Why in the bloody hell wouldn't ye expect me to be here?"

"I know how important your position is within the duke's guard—and your vow to protect the duke and his family. I overheard what happened recently in Cornwall. You are needed there, Finn." When he just stared at her, she added, "You never send word that you are coming—you just appear. You could be here because of an important missive you received."

"I am, lass—yours." He brushed a lock of sunshine silk off her forehead. "Is there something ye wish to tell me?"

She sighed at his touch. "I've missed you, Finn O'Malley."

He rolled his eyes. "Try again, lass."

She frowned at him. "I'm happy you are here."

"Bloody hell, Mollie! Tell me why ye asked me to hurry!"

"I… Well, you see… The truth is, I have been suffering from fainting spells."

Finn's frown deepened. "I'm here to marry ye!"

She couldn't speak—every ounce of moisture in her mouth dried up. Eyes wide, she tried to summon enough to unstick her tongue from the roof of her mouth. When she finally managed, she asked, "Why?"

Finn shoved to his feet and paced from where she lay on the cot to the open doorway and back. Towering over her, he asked, "Why do ye think?"

"I'm not feeling up to a battle of words with you, Finn. Why would you arrive expecting to marry me when you haven't had the courtesy to ask?" When he stared at her as if she'd lost her mind, she asked, "And why is today the first time you told me you loved me?"

Finn scrubbed a hand over his face. "Are ye going to be this difficult after we're married?"

She sat up and swung her legs over the side of the cot. "I haven't accepted your proposal because you haven't asked me yet!"

"Would either of you care to explain why you are shouting at one another?" the duke said, entering.

"Yer Grace!" Finn said.

"I am so sorry, Your Grace!" Mollie added.

Patrick stepped into the room behind the duke. "As ye can see, me knot-headed brother has returned."

"Why did I go to the trouble of procuring a special license for the two of you to marry if you are so at odds with one another?" the duke asked.

"Thank ye, Your Grace," Finn said.

"Special license?" Mollie asked at the same time.

"It seems we need an interpreter," the duke mumbled. "Shall I send word to the vicar to wait until tomorrow to marry you?"

"I didn't realize," Mollie began, only to shake her head in disbelief. "I'm grateful, Your Grace, and apologize. I had no idea…"

"Not to worry, Mollie. It is becoming clearer by the moment that you were unaware of Finn's intention to marry you the moment he returned." He turned and glared at Finn. "I do believe you should try asking your intended in a more civil tone—and for God's sake, at a lower volume, so you do not wake the twins!" The duke shook his head and glanced at the head of his guard. "I shall leave you to mediate, Patrick." Before either of them could answer, the Duke of Wyndmere strode from the room.

Patrick glared at his brother. "Do I need to remind ye what ye did for me when I was ready to walk away without asking

Gwendolyn to marry me?"

Finn shook his head.

"I'll ask ye to be kind to me brother, Mollie, and hear him out. There's more here to be considered than yer pride—or his."

With that, Patrick spun on his heel and followed in the duke's wake.

"Mollie," Finn rasped. "Forgive me for anticipating yer answer." He reached for her hand and got down on one knee. "Ye'd make me the happiest of men if ye'd marry me."

Her silent tears tore at his heart and had him worrying she'd refuse.

"I thought ye loved me?"

"I do."

"Then why are ye crying?"

"I cannot marry you."

"Why in the bloody hell not? His Grace went to the trouble of getting the special license so we can marry immediately."

"You are only asking me to marry you out of obligation. You only said you loved me so I would agree."

Finn's face lost all expression. "When were ye going to tell me ye're carrying me babe?"

She could not meet his gaze.

"Did ye think to leave without a word? Me babe in yer belly and me heart in yer hands?"

She gasped in shock. "I do not have your heart—"

"Good God, lass! Ye've had it since the moment I opened me eyes and saw yer angel's face hovering above mine, tears in yer eyes, and prayers for me on yer lips."

"Why didn't you tell me?"

He blew out a breath. "'Tisn't easy for me to speak of such things. I thought you knew the night we spent together." He pulled her to her feet and held her to his heart. "I would never have let ye get past me defenses if I didn't love ye."

"I would never have thrown myself at you if I didn't love you with every ounce of my being, Finn."

"Well then, now that we've cleared that up, can ye be ready to wed this evening?"

"I haven't agreed to marry you."

Finn grabbed hold of her upper arms and gently set her away from him to watch her eyes as he asked, "And why in the bloody hell haven't ye?"

"You don't want to get married to anyone," she reminded him. "Your words, not mine."

"I've changed me mind."

"Why?"

"If ye don't know the answer to that simple question, I'll not be telling ye."

"What kind of marriage would it be, if you only asked me to marry you because I carry your babe?"

He brushed the tip of his finger along the curve of her cheek to beneath her chin, tipping her face so he could line up their lips. "An honest one. We've professed our love, and ye've given me yer virtue and yer heart. I'm asking for the same when ye pledge before God, the vicar, and witnesses tonight." He pressed his lips to hers in a featherlight kiss. "Will ye, lass? Will ye marry me?"

Mollie sighed and leaned into him. "Aye, Finn O'Malley. I'll marry you."

"Tonight?"

She lifted on her toes and pressed her lips to his to seal her vow. "Tonight."

He scooped her off her feet and whirled her around. "Faith, ye won't be sorry, lass. Marriage to me will be an adventure. Ye'll see."

A FEW HOURS later, they exchanged vows before the vicar. Their vow-taking was as unconventional as those who stood to bear witness to the ceremony that would bind them together for the rest of their lives: the Duke and Duchess of Wyndmere, Patrick, and his wife, Gwendolyn. Three of his cousins, along with the butler, housekeeper, cook, and Her Grace's other lady's maid, Francis, waited to wish the couple luck.

"A toast!" Patrick raised his glass. "To me brother Finn, and his lovely bride Mollie."

Everyone raised their glasses.

Sincerity rang in Patrick's voice as he said, "May yer days be long and filled with laughter."

"May ye know no strife," their cousin Eamon O'Malley added.

Darby Garahan lifted his glass. "May ye remember not to let the sun set on an argument."

Rory Flaherty grinned as he added, "And may ye be blessed with at least a dozen children."

Mollie was laughing as Finn's lips claimed hers. When he eased his hold on her, he whispered in her ear, "The adventure's only just begun."

CHAPTER NINE

"WHERE DID YOU hear this?" Buxton demanded.

The man he questioned lifted his chin and met him glare for glare. "I'm not a free trader. If you wish to know more, it'll cost you."

The king's excise man had paid the Cornishman for information before. The man would never reveal his sources, but his information had always been reliable. Knowing he had no hold over the man—or his family—Buxton agreed and handed over the extra coin.

"The Randy Cock tavern." He dropped another coin in the man's outstretched hand. It disappeared along with the rest of the coins before the man added, "O'Malley is expected to return with his bride in a fortnight—if not before."

Buxton motioned for one of his men to open the door. Once his informant left, he digested the news. If anyone were present, they would note the look of unadulterated glee shining in his eyes—but as he preferred it, he was alone. He rubbed his hands together in anticipation. At last, he would be able to force Finn O'Malley to talk!

He needed a diversion that would have the duke's guard at Penwith Tower stretched thin...and he had just the thing. Fires strategically set at points to the north, south, east, and west of the duke's manor house would guarantee the duke's men would be busy for hours dousing the flames. While they were putting out the fires, one of his men would swoop in, kidnap O'Malley's bride, and hold her for ransom.

GARAHAN WALKED ALONG the top of the renovated curtain wall. The inner walkway afforded an excellent view in all directions. No one would be able to take the tower that stood within the walls by surprise.

"When do you expect O'Malley to return?" Bayfield asked.

Garahan and Coventry's men had spent an hour with Flaherty, getting the lay of the land. The excise men looked the other way for a price. The wreckers murdered for profit. The smugglers who were part of Ruan's wide network and the locals were happy to pay the Frenchman's cut-rate prices for the duty-free goods.

"Within a fortnight—mayhap a few days earlier," Garahan replied.

Tremayne stood on the other side of Garahan, his gaze fixed on a point below them, near the first of the caves they regularly patrolled. "We have company."

The men were immediately on alert, prepared to act.

"Where?" Garahan asked.

Tremayne pointed to the tiny pinprick of light far below them. It winked out, then reappeared. "Someone is signaling a ship out on the water."

"Aye," Bayfield, the former navy captain, agreed. "There'll be a longboat out there, ready to offload their cargo into the caves below us."

"We'd best alert Flaherty," Tremayne added.

The sharp whistle had Garahan smiling. "Never mind, lads. Himself already knows. We just might be able to roust a few free traders tonight after all."

Tremayne, a former lieutenant in the king's dragoons, drew

his pistol from his waistband. Moonlight reflected off the barrel. "Ready."

In a swift movement, Bayfield whipped the handle off his cane, brandishing a deadly-looking stiletto. "Ready."

Garahan's rumbling chuckle had the men grinning in response. "Nothing like a bit of action on a brisk evening with a hint of spring in the air."

"Thought you preferred using your fists?" Bayfield remarked.

"I do love going a few rounds with me fists. After we've hauled away this small band of smugglers, I'd be happy to have ye test yer skills against me own."

Tremayne inclined his head. "You're on."

"Happy to," Bayfield added.

"Let's catch up to Flaherty," Garahan said.

The men descended the newly constructed staircase and headed for the postern gate that would lead them to the narrow, winding path through the brush and rocks to the caves below.

Flaherty was waiting for them on the other side of the gate. "I've a handful of men stationed on either side of the caves."

"And two who've infiltrated one of the free traders working for Ruan," Garahan said with a grin. "I've been paying attention, cousin. It helps to have some of the locals on our side."

"Aye," Flaherty agreed. "Half of them ply their trade for Ruan and his minions, while paying the crooked excise official we spoke of to look the other way."

"Buxton," Garahan said.

"And the other half?" Tremayne asked.

"Decent folks working to keep their families fed," Flaherty told him. "'Tis to those good men we owe our thanks."

"Their lot has improved with the duke pouring his coin into his family's crumbling tower—" Garahan began.

"Newly renovated," Bayfield interrupted him.

The hoot of an owl sounded below them. "'Tis time," Flaherty said. "Bayfield, come with me. We'll circle around behind the cave and come in from the west. Tremayne, you and Garahan follow that path, stand guard, and wait for my signal."

"And come in from the east," Tremayne said with a nod. "Excellent plan."

"We'll slip in behind the guards," Garahan said, "while the others are storing their cargo inside the cave."

"How many guards?" Bayfield asked.

"Two," Flaherty answered.

"Bold, aren't they?" Garahan said.

"They used to be," Flaherty replied.

Tremayne understood what Flaherty implied. "After tonight, they'll be wondering if they'll live to see another sunrise."

"The gibbet in front of the excise building won't be empty for long," Garahan predicted.

"Ye reap what ye sow, cousin," Flaherty said.

"Aye, Flaherty. Ye reap what ye sow," Garahan echoed.

The plan worked like clockwork. Flaherty and his men, aided by Bayfield, had the guard bound and gagged, waiting for Garahan's signal. It came a few moments later. Together the men stationed themselves on either side of the cave, waiting to jump the men as they came out.

They picked them off one at a time, using only silence and their brawn as weapons. The sound of a pistol being fired would tip the smugglers carrying cargo ashore off to the fact that trouble awaited them at the mouth of the cave.

"How many more are inside?" Tremayne asked.

Flaherty glanced behind him, counting heads—they had captured six men. "Half a dozen more."

"Do you have a wagon nearby?" Bayfield asked.

"Aye," Garahan answered. "They'll be waiting for me cousin's signal. They'll load up our prisoners and take them into the village."

Thankful for the full moon, they used hand signals as they waited for their quarry to emerge. Once again, the element of surprise was on their side.

The next smuggler slinking from the cave was facedown in

the sand before he could reach for his weapon.

Five more followed, each taken down from behind before they uttered a sound.

"Well now," Flaherty said. "Seems we've captured an entire crew. Which one of ye is the captain?"

Garahan snorted with laughter. "Did ye forget ye had us gag them?"

"Faith, I don't need to hear their reply. The one who looks the most worried is our captain." Flaherty pointed to the shortest of the twelve-man crew. "Him."

Garahan met the man's gaze. "He'll be the first one to hang."

Flaherty kicked the man's left foot. "Unless ye tell us what we want to know. Ye may be useful to us as a way to get to Buxton. If not…ye'll hang with the others."

At the mention of the excise man's name, the captain and his crew stilled.

Garahan sighed. "It was worth a shot, Flaherty. Signal yer wagon. I'd like to get a few hours of sleep before I'm on guard duty again."

The wagon arrived with a driver and three men in the back. "Kelly," Flaherty greeted the driver. "We've a fine haul tonight."

"How many?" Kelly asked.

"An even dozen," Garahan said.

"I've brought men to stand guard in front of the caves."

Flaherty nodded. "Thank ye. We may need the three I brought with me to lend a hand in case any of the prisoners get the notion to try to escape."

"Will one of you accompany Buxton when he retrieves the cargo stashed in the cave?" the driver asked.

"Tremayne and I will," Garahan said with a nod to the man at his side.

"See ye in an hour or so, men," Kelly said. Turning to Flaherty and the others, he asked, "There's no room in the wagon—do you plan to walk to the village?"

"Nay," Flaherty said. "We've men waiting with horses for

us." He glanced at the men flanking him and said, "We'll ride."

Kelly asked, "Do you think Buxton will try to hold on to the cargo and collect the payment?"

"I'm counting on it."

"You have a plan to catch him in the act?"

"We'll let him think he's slipped through our fingers tonight," Flaherty answered. "We've witnesses planted at each of the shops where the cargo is expected to be delivered. When Buxton has his men make the rounds tomorrow night, as is his custom, he'll be sealing his fate."

"He'll think he succeeded," Tremayne said.

Flaherty agreed, "We'll have him dead to rights before Finn and his bride return."

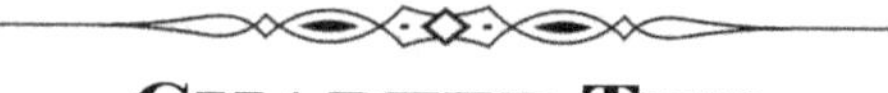

CHAPTER TEN

MOLLIE OPENED HER eyes and gasped.

"I thought it was a dream, too."

Finn tucked her into his arms and rolled over so she was beneath him, staring up at him with wonder in the depths of her soft blue eyes.

"Now where were we?" Finn asked as he left a trail of kisses along the edge of her jaw. He lifted his head, meeting her gaze. "No, that wasn't it. Ah…I remember now."

He dipped his head and trailed the tip of his tongue along her collarbone, pleased when she squirmed beneath him. He paused to inhale the scent that was uniquely Mollie's—rain-soaked roses—before pressing his lips to the hollow of her throat. "I'm feeling a bit peckish, lass. Mind if I sample a bit more of ye?"

Her strangled moan of pleasure was a balm to his soul. He'd nearly lost her, believing he could only keep one pledge at a time. He should have remembered the hell his brother Patrick went through before realizing he did not have to choose between his vow to the duke and the one he wanted to make to Gwendolyn.

Praise God for his brother…and the duchess, for their timely interference, convincing Mollie to stay.

Sampling rose-scented flesh with delicate nibbles and sensuous kisses, he forged a path to the valley between her beautiful breasts and lingered. Suckling and nibbling, driving her higher, then pulling away to blow gently on the flesh he'd so thoroughly tasted.

Pinning her to the mattress with his hips, he held her captive. "Ye're a feast fit for a king, Mollie-lass. Mind if I sup a bit more of yer sweetness?"

The need in her eyes called to him. When she lifted her hips, he accepted her silent invitation like a man possessed.

He claimed her lips in a ravenous kiss, while his fingers followed the curving path from the night before to the treasure she'd given only to him. He found her more than ready for him. "Tell me ye want me, lass."

"Hurry! Please, Finn?"

Though it cost him—need had him by the throat—he would not take what he craved until she gave him the words. "Tell me."

"God, Finn! Now!"

Her passion had him aching with need, ready to burst, but still he held back. "I can wait," he crooned as he slid lower and pressed his lips to her hip, before moving across her belly to her other hip.

As she writhed beneath him, the sound of her moans urged him lower. He traced a path with his tongue from her navel to the very heart of her. Taking his time, he traced the softness he'd plumbed just hours before burying himself to the hilt. The memory of her warm, wet heat had him growling low in his throat. He shuddered with the effort it cost him to pull back from her. "If ye cannot give me the words, I'll be forced to stop."

He watched her eyes, waiting.

"I'M ON FIRE, Finn, from wanting you. Make love to me now!"

Finn's rumbling chuckle should have irritated her, but Mollie needed him to end his torture. She slid her hand around his waist and pinched his firm buttocks. The surprise in his eyes had her laughing...before he lowered his head and probed her depths with his tongue until she sobbed out his name.

"Say my name again, lass."

Dazed from the pleasure he wrought from her, she met the intensity of his gaze. "Finn O'Malley—the love of my life."

He grabbed hold of her hips and rasped, "Mollie O'Malley— the love of mine," then plunged into her welcoming warmth over and over, wringing every last drop of pleasure from her, while giving her pleasure in return. When her arms slid from around his back, he buried himself to the hilt and pressed his lips to her heart.

They flew over the edge of madness into the abyss of pleasure, wrapped in one another's arms.

⊱⊰

MOLLIE WOKE WITH a start, sweat beading on her brow as her stomach roiled ominously. She moaned as the familiar feeling washed over her.

"Lass, what ails ye?"

Hand to her mouth, she dashed out of bed and reached the chamber pot in time to lose the contents of her stomach—three times—before she felt herself being lifted high. Cradled against Finn's broad chest, she tucked her head beneath his chin. Her acute embarrassment was a bit easier to handle when she couldn't see the expression on his face. She just knew he would be repelled by what he'd witnessed.

Without a word, he helped her into her nightrail and placed her in the middle of the bed, drawing the covers up to her chin. Hand to her forehead, he frowned. "Ye're warm."

"I'm—"

"Don't tell me ye're fine when I just watched ye puke up yer guts—three times!"

"Finn, I'm not—"

"Not what? Ill? Anyone with eyes could see that ye are. Have I worn ye out? *I'm a bloody feckin' eedjit!* Forgive me, lass. I was so desperate to make love with ye again—now that we are man and wife and don't have to hide what we are doing—that I lost me head and forgot about yer delicate condition."

She giggled at his choice of words.

"Do ye think me worry is funny?"

"Nay." But she snorted with laughter, negating her reply.

He leaned over the bed, his frown ferocious. "I never took ye to be a heartless wench."

That had her smile turning upside down. She bolted upright and shot to her feet. "How dare you call me heartless!"

"If ye had one, ye wouldn't laugh at yer husband when he's worried sick that ye're ill with consumption—or worse!"

The fight abruptly left her at the inflection in his words, and the baffled expression on his face. Finn was *never* baffled. She had only seen his confidence. This was a new side to the man she'd pledged to cherish for life. He must truly be worried.

Moved at the depth of his caring, she sat back down and asked for a cup of water. When he turned to get it without a word, she waited for him to return.

He handed her the cup and waited for her to drink.

When she emptied it, she lifted her head and looked at him. "It's apparently common for expectant women to suffer through bouts of sickness—either in the morning, or sometimes all day."

"Do ye think me daft that I'd believe that?"

Crossing her arms beneath her breasts, she huffed, "Know many pregnant women, do you, husband of mine?"

He leaned in close enough their noses almost touched. "Nay, wife of mine. Ye're the only one."

"Then you'd best pay attention and not expect me to be up and about fixing your breakfast until the sickness passes. The midwife has been to see me twice now and assured me everything is normal, and to expect the sickness to pass in another month or so."

He sat down heavily and leaned forward with his head in his hands. "I'm to be greeted by me wife with her head in a chamber pot for the next few weeks?"

Though the image—and the reality—was not amusing in the least, she laughed softly. "Believe me, I'd much rather it was *you* relieving the contents of *your* stomach," she confessed. "It's exhausting."

"Aw, lass, I'm sorry. I had no idea a woman suffered so."

"Haven't you spoken to Patrick about what Gwendolyn went through when she was expecting?"

"Nay. Me brother was consumed with worry over the possibility that she'd lose their babe as she lost her first."

"Those were extreme circumstances," she reminded him. "Gwendolyn's situation is nothing like what happened when her first husband was found murdered. Gwendolyn is a strong woman, and proved it giving birth. Patrick should have had more confidence in her."

Drawing her into his arms and onto his lap, Finn wrapped his arms around her. "He masked what he kept close to his heart, fearing it would add to Gwendolyn's own worries. Best speak about something else, lass, else ye'll upset yer delicate constitution."

She snorted.

"Do ye find that amusing, too?"

"You think I'm delicate?"

"Aye, ye're a little bit of a thing. It's plain for all to see me babe is draining yer strength."

"I suppose *any* man would be able to carry a babe to term and then go through the birthing process without a hitch—or wince of pain?"

Finn's sharp bark of laughter was what she'd hoped to hear. The last thing she needed was him worrying about her health in the months ahead of them until their babe was born. He'd probably follow her around and hover. The duke had hovered before the duchess had their twins.

"Faith, I doubt it. I bow to yer superior stamina and strength, wife of mine."

She pressed her lips to his cheek. "Thank you, husband of mine."

"Why don't ye rest for a while longer? I'll see if I can bring up a tray with something to tempt yer appetite."

Lord only knew what he'd find tempting. She warned him, "Certain smells make me nauseated."

He donned his trousers before slipping his arms into his shirt sleeves—careful not to aggravate his healing shoulder. Sitting on the edge of the bed, he pulled on socks and boots. "What would you like me to bring?"

"Some weak tea would be nice."

His expression left no doubt he was working through a problem in his mind. "What would ye like to soak up the tea? I won't have ye puking again today, if I can help it."

She hid her smile, not wanting to upset him. Apparently, *she* was the problem. "Mayhap Constance will have some day-old bread."

"Ye aren't joking?"

"Nay. If she doesn't, I could try nibbling on a scone or two."

Finn leaned over and kissed her forehead, cheeks, and the end of her nose. "Rest."

"I'll try," she promised.

He frowned at her for good measure, stepped across the threshold, and closed the door behind him.

She released the breath she'd been holding and murmured, "What have I gotten myself into?"

Finn's words after they said their vows reverberated through her head: *The adventure's only just begun.*

CHAPTER ELEVEN

FINN STRODE INTO the kitchen. "Constance, I need yer help."

The cook looked up and smiled. "Well, I must say, it is a surprise to see you up and about this early. Didn't His Grace give you the next three days away from your duties?"

"Aye. Mollie's asking for a bit of weak tea and day-old bread, if ye have such lying about. Can't imagine ye would, with the number of people ye feed daily."

Constance set down the knife she was using to slice bread and brushed her hands on her apron. "Can you wait for a few moments while I summon one of the footmen? The maids are busy with duties elsewhere, or else I'd ask one of them."

He'd never admit his insides felt as if they'd be clawed by a wild beast if he waited. "Why not ask me to help? I'm the one interrupting yer morning duties."

"I would appreciate that. Please, hand me the small serving tray from the sideboard while I prepare the tea for Mollie."

When he set the tray on the large oak table in the center of the kitchen, she thanked him then said, "Now, if you'd be kind enough to refill that large pail with water, I won't have to wait for one of the footmen to see to the task."

The need to have a woman whose opinion he trusted assure him that his precious Mollie was not risking her own health carrying his babe had him hesitating by the back door, pail in hand.

Constance added tea leaves to the pot and placed the lid on it, then looked up and noticed him standing there. "If it's the nausea that has you worried, don't let it. It is more common than one might think. Her stomach upset should assure you she will be fine and deliver a happy, healthy babe."

"What kind of thinking is that when 'tis obvious she's suffering?"

"Midwives that practice the old ways—of the wise ones—worry when the mother feels nothing. When the woman feels ill, some say it is a sign that her body is accepting the babe. It takes longer for some than others for the body to acclimate itself."

He inclined his head and opened the door.

"Finn?"

He looked over his shoulder to answer, "Aye?"

"She has Her Grace, Merry, Francis, the midwife, and me looking after her. We will not let anything happen to her."

"I'm beholden to ye."

She smiled and said, "Fetch the water, Finn."

Relief speared through him. "Aye, Constance."

When he returned with the full pail, Constance had the tea tray ready for him. "What is all this?" he asked.

"Day-old bread, as she requested. I have added a few sweet treats, and savory ones. To be on the safe side, leave the tray on the small table beneath the window. That way, the scent will not overwhelm her."

"Does the babe affect a woman's sense of smell?"

"It can. Sometimes, just one or two seem to trigger a bout of nausea—in others, it can be a multitude of scents."

"In other words, ye don't know which ones bother me wife yet."

"I did not say that. She cannot stomach eggs prepared in any way, nor can she handle the thought of mutton, let alone the smell of it cooking—especially simmering in my stewpot."

He sighed and lifted the tray. "I'll see that she stays clear of your domain until she's more accustomed to dealing with things I never would have imagined would be a problem for the lass."

She shooed him toward the door. "Go feed your wife."

"What if she's asleep?"

"She has always been a light sleeper—see if you can rouse her. She needs to eat. An empty stomach becomes nauseated more easily than one that is full."

Finn thanked her one last time before retreating to the servants' staircase. Making his way to the top, he only bobbled the tray once. "How do the servants manage not to spill the bloody thing when they take the stairs?"

No one was about, so no one answered.

He didn't bother to knock, but he did open the door slowly. Mollie was waiting for him.

"Well now, lass. Ye're looking a mite better." He set the tray on the table as Constance had bidden him to do. "Now then, do ye need me to tell ye what's on the tray to tempt yer appetite?"

She grimaced and turned a ghastly green. "Uh...no thank you. If you wouldn't mind taking the tray into the hallway...?"

Quick to respond, he put the tray on the floor in the hall and returned. His gaze met his wife's, and guilt tore through him. The angelic lass who had stolen his heart—and twisted him into randy knots with her passionate response to him—suffered because of their lovemaking. Did this happen to all women, or only the lusty ones? Would the nausea plaguing her, and the prospect of the birthing, change the passionate woman she'd become after he unlocked the desire burning inside of her? Would she ban him from their bed?

Bollocks! He would never understand women, no matter how hard he tried. He needed to clear his head before guilt and worry drove him stark raving mad!

Patrick would be on the roof at this hour of the morning. He'd assigned himself that shift after his daughter was born, explaining he was already awake, so why not greet the sunrise from the rooftop?

"Finn?" Mollie asked.

He buried his worry and schooled his features. "Aye, lass?"

Her eyes were bright and her cheeks rosy once more. "May I please have a cup of tea?"

"Let me fetch it for ye."

"Did Constance have any dry bread?"

"Left over? Aye, lass. Said she saves it just for ye. Will one slice do?"

"Yes, thank you."

He returned with the teapot, cup, and saucer, placing them on the table. "I couldn't carry the blasted cup without spilling yer tea."

She tossed the covers aside. "I'm fine now, Finn, and can serve myself."

He jabbed a finger at her. "Ye'll get back in that bed and find a bit of patience for yer husband while he fetches yer poor excuse for a meal."

Her lips twitched as she smoothed the covers on top of her legs. At his pointed look, she bit her lip before saying, "If you pour a half cup of tea, and carry the pot with you, you won't spill it and can fill it the rest of the way once I'm holding it."

"And take the chance I'll scald yer lovely legs if I can't get the bloody tea in the bloody cup?"

⪻⪻⪻⪻⪻⪻

SHE CLOSED HER eyes and slowly opened them. "Please be patient with me this morning, Finn. Tomorrow, you can rise early and go find Patrick. He's on the dawn shift…usually the roof. It gives Gwendolyn quiet time to feed their daughter."

"Who will take care of ye, if I don't?" he demanded, frustration rolling off him in waves.

"I managed before you came strolling back into my life. I supposed I shall manage if you cannot bring yourself to deal with what is far worse for me than it is for you."

His face paled and his jaw tensed. "If ye have need of me, ye know how to find me."

She sagged against the pillows as he stormed out. "Hardheaded, stubborn mule of a man!"

She felt better having tossed the words out—even though he didn't stay long enough for her to hurl them at him, she knew in the future, she would have to bite her tongue and not say whatever popped into her head. Men were, after all, fragile creatures. Always needing to be told how brave and strong they were.

Hah! But they did not birth babes—women did! He did not suffer through the nausea; she was the one who dealt with the stomach upset. But she did admit—at least to herself—that her husband was trying to accept her condition. The notion that there was nothing he could do to prevent her from suffering through the nausea was obviously eating at him. There was only one solution…and it was unacceptable to her, now that she'd experienced another night of ecstasy in her husband's arms.

There was no way in heaven she would give up making love to the man who'd taught her so many ways to give and then revel in the pleasure to be found in one another's arms.

This would be a discussion she did not relish having with the stubborn Irishman she'd married. Mayhap she could ask Gwendolyn's advice. She and Patrick had seemed to settle into a happy relationship after he got past the fact that he could not *fix* her. Even the formidable head of the duke's guard had had to wait for their babe to arrive, and his wife's body to adjust to being a mother, with patience heretofore unknown to the man.

If *Patrick* had managed to keep his frustration to himself, then by all that was holy, Finn would learn to do the same.

Feeling much better after resolving how to deal with her husband's reaction to the all-too-obvious effects of her carrying their babe, she nibbled on the dry bread and emptied the first cup of tea.

The soft knock on her door roused her from her troubled thoughts. "Come in."

Francis peeked around the edge of the door, and her eyes widened. "Whatever is wrong? Are you still feeling ill? Didn't the tea and bread settle your stomach?"

"I'm fine—"

"Botheration!" Francis exclaimed.

Mollie giggled. "You sound just like Her Grace."

Her friend grinned. "Did I? Good! I meant it. I heard from the horse's mouth—"

"Which horse?"

Francis tilted her head to one side. "The one you married."

"Don't you mean the horse's arse?"

"Is that any way to speak about the man you've been pining for since Patrick carried him in over his shoulder bleeding from a head wound?"

Mollie shrugged. "He's acting like a bear with a thorn stuck in his paw."

"More like a new husband struggling to realize the lovely woman he left behind is now more than a handful with her rioting emotions and uneasy stomach."

"Shouldn't he have stuck around to find out if I needed him? What if I got dizzy, fainted, and hit my head on the corner of the table before landing face-first on the floor?"

Francis bit her lip to keep from answering.

"Well?" Mollie demanded. "Are you on my side or Finn's?"

Her friend sighed audibly. "If you must know, Finn's."

"What? Wait! Why are you not on *my* side? You are my friend, not his!"

Francis' broad smile had Mollie realizing her friend was teasing her when she answered, "He's bigger."

Mollie took a halfhearted swing at her friend's arm and missed. "You should know better than to tease a pregnant woman."

"You'll forgive me."

"Will I?"

"You have to," Francis insisted.

"Oh, and why is that?"

Francis sat beside her friend on the bed and wrapped an arm around her. "Because you love me."

"I *used* to."

Francis shook her head. "Nay, you always will because we're sisters of the heart. And unlike siblings, we will always have one another's back through thick…and thin. Good times and bad."

"Sounds like you're rewriting marriage vows."

"Friendships are a bit like a marriage—both involve two people who care about, even love one another."

"But marriages don't always last forever," Mollie whispered.

"They do if you are raised in the Catholic faith like we were," Francis reminded her.

Mollie leaned her head on Francis' shoulder. "Do you think Finn will shy away from me now that he's seen how I spend my mornings?"

"Bent over the chamber pot?" Francis asked.

"Aye."

"I don't. He had to get the worry—notice that I didn't call it what it really was, fear—off his chest. He'll spend most of the morning outside on patrol with his brother and their cousins. Being among men—who are quite simple in makeup, if you ask me—will restore his faith in his ability to handle any situation with aplomb."

"If that does not work, do you think he'll return to Penwith Tower without me?"

"Have the two of you spoken to the duke, or had a chance to discuss expectations of where either of you want to live?"

"No, but I suppose he'll have to go back to Cornwall. I haven't heard otherwise—have you?"

Francis shook her head. "I haven't."

"Well then, I'd best start packing, since I do not have any duties until the end of the week."

"Why not rest for a bit? I'll help you after my shift in the nursery is over." Francis stood and straightened her skirts. "I'll ask Constance to prepare a nice luncheon tray—bland, as it seems to be what you need midday—and we can share it in your room upstairs."

Mollie got to her feet and sighed. "I do feel a bit uncomfortable staying in such an opulent room. How does it not bother Finn?"

Her friend's smile was mischievous, her reply risqué. "I daresay your darling husband was too busy admiring something other than the counterpane on the bed—mayhap what was waiting in the middle of the bed."

Mollie's face flamed before she dissolved into hysterical laughter. When she caught her breath, she scolded her friend, "Francis, you should be ashamed to even suggest such a thing!"

"A girl can dream, can't she?"

That last comment had Mollie's full attention. "And just who would this girl be dreaming of?"

It was Francis' turn to blush, encouraging Mollie to push to have her friend confess whether it was the new footman the duke had hired on—or if it was one of the duke's private guard.

Francis finally gave in when Mollie feigned having a dizzy spell. "You do not play fair!"

"All is fair in love and war," Mollie reminded her. "Now tell me. Is it Eamon O'Malley or Darby Garahan?"

"Neither," Francis grumbled.

Hands to her mouth to cover her gasp of surprise, Mollie said, "Oh, oh! It's Rory Flaherty! I should have known—you get this odd look in your eye whenever he passes through the kitchen when we are delivering or retrieving Her Grace's tea trays."

Francis dropped her head in her hands and groaned. "I can't help it. It's the wave in his auburn hair and the way it's always slipping into his eyes. My fingers itch to smooth it off his forehead, then trace the line of his strong jaw and—"

Mollie grabbed hold of her friend's hands and tugged on them to get her attention. "You'd best stop daydreaming, or else we'll be hearing from my husband that *you* were on the rooftop with Rory when Finn relieved him at dawn."

Francis slowly returned to her senses and sighed. "My heart knows what it wants."

Mollie squeezed her friend's hands and released them. "And what of Rory's?"

Francis shrugged. "I haven't spent enough time in his company to say more than hello or goodbye to him."

Mollie narrowed her eyes and stared out the window, lost in thought. "We'll have to see if we can arrange for the two of you to have a conversation of at least two sentences."

Francis was smiling when she left with the promise to return after her shift ended.

Mollie was too excited at the prospect of matchmaking her friend with her husband's cousin Rory to sit still. She folded what few items of clothing someone—probably Francis—had brought to the guest room the day before. A few articles of Finn's clothing were draped over the back of one of the chairs. She folded those, too.

That done, she was ready to sit for a few moments. Tired from the morning's uneasy start, she decided to sit on the bed for—just for a few minutes.

The brush to her cheek woke her. She slowly opened her eyes and stared into eyes the color of polished emeralds. "How are ye feeling, lass?"

She took silent stock and then said, "Better. And you?"

Finn frowned. "I'm fine. Why?"

She sighed and closed her eyes, feigning sleep so she did not have to answer him.

"Shall I send for the midwife?"

The worry in her husband's voice bothered her, but she guessed it would take more than one day for him to accustom himself to her daily ups and downs.

Before she could respond, he was apologizing. "I'm sorry for sounding harsh with ye. Forgive me?"

She opened her eyes and held his gaze for long moments. "Of course. I'm not the only one who has a new role to fill. It will be hard on you too, Finn—just in a very different way than it has been for me."

"Oh? And what way might that be?"

She slowly smiled. "You'll have to temper your brash responses with sweetness, or else you'll find I've become a watering pot."

He blanched at the suggestion. "I shall do me best not to upset ye, lass."

"And I shall try to explain what I'm feeling and ask for help, even though I do not think I really need it."

"You do."

"I know. Thank you, Finn."

He leaned close and brushed his lips across hers. "Ye're welcome, lass. Now rest."

Her eyes closed of their own accord as she drifted off to sleep.

CHAPTER TWELVE

MOLLIE WOKE WITH a start, disoriented as she brushed the sleep from her eyes. *I must have dozed off.* She waited a moment or two before sitting up—she'd learned the hard way that swift movement upon rising wreaked havoc with her sensitive stomach.

Pleased not to feel even a twinge of dizziness, she slid from beneath the covers and dangled her legs over the edge of the bed. The quiet knock on the door had her smiling. She knew it would be her friend, ready to help her pack for her journey to Penwith Tower.

"Come in."

"Oh good," Francis said, entering the room. "You're awake."

"Only just. Please tell me I did not sleep for two hours."

"You know I don't like to lie. My shift in the nursery is over, and Her Grace agreed that it was important for me to help you gather your things, as Finn plans to leave at midday."

"Has something happened? We still have two more days to ourselves."

"Finn received a missive," Francis replied.

Mollie's belly clenched. "Trouble?"

Francis shrugged. "You know how tight-lipped the duke's men can be."

"If there was trouble, Finn would want to leave right away—

not midday."

"Your husband is being very considerate," Francis replied. "He's obviously noted you are not your best upon rising."

Mollie should agree, but it irked her to. Instead, she smoothed her nightrail and walked over to the washstand. Pouring the cool water into the bowl, she washed her face and hands, and the temperature of the water helped to clear her sleep-addled brain. "I'll just be a moment. Why don't I meet you upstairs?"

Francis slipped her arm through Mollie's. "Someone has to button you up." Without asking, she gave Mollie a nudge toward the dressing screen. "Which gown would you prefer to wear? The green or the blue?"

"I left my gowns upstairs."

"Her Grace had me bring two down and place them in the wardrobe while you were sleeping." When Mollie huffed instead of answering, Francis cheerily said, "Can't decide? Well then, blue it is! If you ask me, it will show off your auburn hair and matches your eyes."

"Finn won't notice what I'm wearing," Mollie protested. "He'll be pretending not to watch me, while he waits for me to cast up my accounts."

Francis giggled. "Lovely image. He'll adjust to your morning routine eventually."

Mollie was soon laughing along with her friend. "What a rude awakening for the poor man—the joys of impending fatherhood."

Francis had Mollie's chemise and gown draped over her arm as she joined her friend behind the screen. "Turn around, if you don't want me to see your naked self."

Mollie snorted, as she knew Francis expected. It had long been their way to tease one another to lift their spirits. She stood still while Francis helped her don her chemise. "He'll become accustomed to it," she said, more to assure herself than her friend.

Francis paused with the gown hovering above Mollie's head. Lips quirked, she asked, "To your naked self?"

Mollie snorted and smiled at Francis. "You do wonders for my changeable moods, Francis. Would you consider asking Her Grace if you could accompany me to St. Ives?"

Francis hummed beneath her breath while helping Mollie with her gown. "Turn your back to me." She quickly did up the buttons and patted her friend's shoulders. "I cannot leave Her Grace just yet. You and I are the only maids who have acted as the duchess' lady's maids—and nursery help. If you and I both leave, she'll have to start training two new maids at the same time!"

"We are not indispensable," Mollie reminded her friend as she smoothed the miniscule wrinkles from her gown.

"I know." Francis stepped out from behind the screen. "The time it would take to train the maids currently handling our old jobs as scullery maids would be exhausting."

Mollie sighed, moving to stand beside her. "You are right. I wouldn't want to heap more troubles on Her Grace. Not when she seems to be so happy now that the difficulties between she and the duke have been ironed out."

"It was a worry," Francis said. "According to Constance, confiding in one another would have avoided the situation."

"Do you think Finn has been avoiding confiding in me?"

She sighed. "Mayhap. It is hard to say—the duke's guard as a whole keep their innermost thoughts to themselves."

"Aye, and all seem to have mastered unreadable—or is it unapproachable?—expressions."

"Now you understand why I cannot go just yet, even though I would love to see you settled."

Mollie gathered the few things she had in the bedchamber and slipped her arm through her friend's. "Her Grace is lucky to have you, Francis. Remember, you will always be welcome in our home."

Francis opened the door with her free hand and urged Mollie along. "Time to pack the rest of your things."

FINN WISHED HIS brother would cease rattling off advice. He had months before Mollie gave birth! "I appreciate hearing yer advice, but I have other more pressing issues on me mind."

"What could be more urgent than the well-bein' of yer wife?"

"Her safety."

"Bloody hell!"

"Aye," Finn agreed. "That's where I'll be, if I do not find a way to convince the local excise official to mend his thieving ways and capture the smugglers! 'Tis past time he levied taxes on their goods, instead of taking coin and looking the other way."

Patrick frowned. "How many men does this Buxton have working for him?"

"He has a dozen in St. Ives."

"Are all of them collectors of tax?"

Relieved that his brother was discussing the problem of smuggling beneath Penwith Tower—and not the trials a pregnant woman faced—Finn answered, "Four of the men patrol on horseback, four are stationed at points along the coastline—"

"Beneath Penwith's cliffs?" Patrick asked.

"Aye."

"And the others?"

Frustration bubbled close to the surface as Finn remembered the latest tales involving Buxton's men. "They mete out punishment for those who think to betray Buxton—or get in his way, like the duke's messengers."

"And?"

"Flaherty found the lad clutching his messenger's pouch."

Patrick's gaze locked on Finn. "Was he in time?"

Finn shook his head. "The poor bugger bled out before Fenton could save the lad."

"Lad?"

"Couldn't have seen more than six and ten summers."

"Have ye spoken to His Grace about this?"

"Flaherty sent a missive. It should have arrived before I did."

The brothers tensed. Patrick said, "That's the second time this happened. Someone is interceptin' the duke's messengers before they arrive at their destinations."

"We thought it was just the missive ye said ye sent, telling me about Mollie's suspected condition."

"I'll speak to the duke while ye pack. Ye'd best be leaving at once—Mollie should remain here for her own protection."

"I'll not have ye dictate what I do, or not do, with me wife."

"Bugger it, Finn! It's herself, and yer babe, I'm thinkin' of—not yer bloody pride."

Finn fought to control the anger surging through him at his brother's words. "I'll think it over and speak to Mollie."

"You'd ask the woman carryin' yer babe if she wants to accompany you through what will amount to the gauntlet? Ye have no idea how many men will be standing on either side of the two of ye, ready to whip ye with their cat o' nine tails! This isn't one of our brothers or cousins travelin' with ye. 'Tis yer wife—and she's in fragile condition!"

Finn's snort of laughter surprised his brother.

"What in the bloody hell do ye find amusin'?"

"Mollie does not think she's fragile or delicate. It'd be to yer benefit not to mention either of those words when speaking to her."

Patrick slowly smiled. "Ma was right. We've both found women strong enough to stand beside us through thick and thin, good times and bad."

"That we have," Finn agreed. "Ye'd best be speaking to His Grace. I'm off to pack and have a chat with me wife."

"Good luck!"

"Good luck, yerself!"

A FEW HOURS later, Finn was standing feet spread, arms crossed, frowning at his wife. "Have ye not heard a thing I've just told ye?"

She lifted her chin, meeting him frown for frown. "Every word. Are we going to stand here all afternoon arguing, or will you be reasonable and agree that the safest place for me is by your side?"

"There is unrest at Penwith Tower," he explained. "'Tis a far cry from the life ye've been accustomed to, working with the duke's staff here at Wyndmere Hall, running errands and chatting with those who live in the village."

"I can adapt to change as easily as you. In fact, probably better than you."

He took the direct hit to his pride and rolled with it, firing back, "Oh, aye. I saw how well ye were handling things this morning, when ye were bare-arsed, bent over the chamber pot puk—"

Incensed, she clapped a hand to his mouth.

He placed his hand over hers and held it there while he traced her lifeline with the tip of his tongue before pressing a swift kiss to her palm. "Before ye ask, the answer is no."

What in the world is he talking about? "No what?"

"Nothing is sacred when it comes to protecting ye."

She did not know whether to be relieved that he had read her thoughts, or worried, so she sharply reminded him, "I'll not have you speaking of what happens behind closed doors, Finn O'Malley!"

He yanked her against him and had the temerity to growl at her! "What have I done to give ye such a low opinion of me character, lass?"

Righteous indignation swept up from her toes. "It must have been the bare-arsed—"

"I beg yer pardon."

The couple turned as one, and Mollie felt every ounce of blood rush from her face at Patrick O'Malley's knowing look.

One glance at them, and his expression changed from a smirk

to anger. "Ye'd best not irritate yer wife. 'Tisn't good for the babe." He pushed Finn out of the way and wrapped an arm about Mollie. "Here now, lass, have a care for the babe and rest for a moment. While ye're fighting to accept that the babe ye carry has more control over yer life than ye do, know that ye aren't alone in your battle. It took Gwendolyn a bit of time to understand the way of things and agree that I know best."

"Leave off, Patrick!" Finn thundered. "Go bother yer own wife."

Patrick didn't bother to turn around when he jabbed an elbow in Finn's gut. "Now then, lass, why don't ye put yer feet up and have a bit of a rest?"

Incensed with his brother—and worried about his wife—Finn scooped her into his arms, kicking his brother in the side of his knee as he passed him on the way out of Mollie's bedchamber on the third floor. At Patrick's sharply inhaled breath, he said, "Be a good lad and bring me my wife's bag."

Finn smiled at the curses his brother mumbled, knowing if they'd been alone, he would have shouted them. "Me brother means well," he told Mollie. "'Tisn't entirely his fault he's bossy. As the eldest, he was tasked with watching out for the rest of us."

Mollie snuck a peek at the man still muttering. "He takes his responsibilities as seriously as you."

"Runs in our blood, ye know."

"It runs in Malloy blood as well. We fight to the last breath."

Finn pressed a kiss to the top of her head. "Is that a warning, lass?"

She poked him in the chest. "Aye. Will we be riding to Cornwall in a carriage or on horseback?"

Her question had him chuckling. "A delicate lass such as yerself should ride in comfort. We'll be borrowing one of the duke's many carriages."

She sagged against him.

"Even if ye prefer riding on a horse, lass, I cannot in good conscience allow ye to be out in the elements in yer condition."

"I know."

She sounded resigned…and forlorn. "What is it, lass?"

"You'd best pack a chamber pot."

It killed him to hold back the snort of laughter that almost escaped. He debated if he should tell her the truth before finally admitting, "I've asked the stable master to borrow two of his largest buckets for our journey."

Instead of ringing a peal over his head, his firebrand of a wife brushed a kiss to his jaw. "Thank you for planning ahead."

"I thought of the extra blankets and cushions for yer comfort. 'Twas Patrick who mentioned the duke's sister-in-law suffered nausea riding in a carriage—reminding me our cousin Michael's wife suffered the same."

"I'll have to remember to thank him before we leave."

"No need—I'll take yer thanks now."

She giggled and looked over her shoulder. "I didn't realize you were right behind us, Patrick. Thank you for your thoughtfulness."

"'Tis just a bucket," he grumbled, following them down the staircase.

"Without it, I'd worry that I'd be sick all over the interior of His Grace's carriage."

"In that case, I'm happy to have relieved yer worry." He paused for a moment before asking, "Are ye sure ye won't change yer mind and stay."

"Patrick!" Finn warned.

"I'm not askin' yer hardheaded self. I'm askin' yer wife."

"I'm sure," Mollie said. "Thank you for worrying about me."

"'Tis me job."

"As the oldest O'Malley brother," Mollie asked, "or as the head of the duke's guard?"

"Both," he answered. "When ye married me brother, ye became me sister. 'Tis an honor to watch over ye."

Finn reached the bottom of the stairs and had his hand to the doorknob, but didn't turn it.

"What are ye waitin' for?"

Finn looked over his shoulder at his brother. "I'll be thanking ye now for including Mollie in yer long list of those ye feel responsible for."

"She's me sister now."

"Only recently. While I've been away, ye were me eyes and ears, worrying about her," Finn said. "Take me thanks and be grateful before the urge to put me fist in yer gob has me doing something ye'll regret."

"Wait a moment, while I consider yer generous offer...yer thanks or yer fist in me mouth..."

Finn was laughing when he opened the door. "Faith, I apologize for me arse of a brother, lass." He set Mollie on her feet in the hallway that led to the kitchen. "Would ye like to have a quick bite to eat before we leave? His Grace wants to have a word with me before we leave."

"That would be wonderful. I missed midmorning tea and scones."

With his hand to her waist, they walked into the kitchen and were greeted by Constance and Francis.

"We were about to send someone to fetch you," the cook said, ushering Mollie to a seat at the huge kitchen worktable. "You missed your teatime. If you don't want to suffer unduly from nausea, you'll need to remember to have small meals more often during the day."

"It eased the worst of me wife's stomach upsets," Patrick said, tossing Mollie's bag at Finn. "Don't forget yer wife's things."

Finn caught the bag and clapped his brother on the shoulder. "Thank ye—for everything, Patrick."

His brother rolled his eyes and turned to leave.

"Patrick?"

He glanced over his shoulder. "Aye, Mollie?"

"Thank you."

He flashed a grin. "Ye're welcome, lass. If ye're through blatherin', do yerself a favor and eat."

She smiled and, to Finn's surprise, did as she was told.

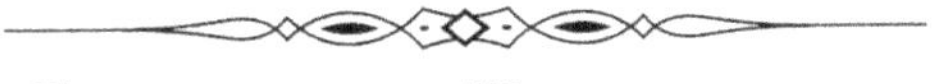

CHAPTER THIRTEEN

THE DUKE OF Wyndmere entered the kitchen and all talk ceased.

Finn shifted to stand behind his wife's chair and place a hand on her shoulder. "Yer Grace, do ye need to speak privately with me?"

"Sorry to be late," the duchess said as she swept into the room. "Have you told them yet?"

The duke reached for her hand and pulled her close to his side. "I was waiting for you, my dear." He smiled at the couple. "In keeping with our new policy, you will be excluded from the quarterly rotation of the guard."

"New policy?" Finn asked.

"It started when Patrick married Gwendolyn," the duchess said.

"When your cousins Sean and Michael married, they too were removed from the rotation," the duke added.

Relief filled Finn. He'd planned to request the change in his status. Now he wouldn't have to. He gently squeezed his wife's shoulder. "Thank ye, Yer Grace."

"That's not all, Finn," the duchess said. "Tell him, darling."

The pair were smiling when the duke said, "I've sent word ahead to ready one of the cottages near the manor house."

"I shall be happy to help get it ready for guests," Mollie said.

The duchess shook her head. "As you and Finn are married now, we wanted you to have your own quarters at Penwith Tower."

"We plan to refurbish the manor house," the duke said. "Neither Persephone nor I wanted to add the duties of caretaker to those you perform as head of my guard in Cornwall. The cottage is our wedding gift to you."

Finn was momentarily at a loss for words—though, truth be told, his ma and da would never believe it—before he was able to thank the duke and duchess. "We never expected such a gift, Yer Graces. Thank ye."

Mollie rose from her seat and moved to stand in the shelter of her husband's arms, fighting to hold back her happy tears. "Thank you. Thank you both."

"You are a young woman of courage and fortitude with a giving heart. You will be greatly missed, Mollie."

Mollie's eyes filled at the duchess' words. "What will my new duties be?"

The duke lifted a brow in silent question, before he lowered it and said, "Won't the duty of seeing that the head of the Penwith Tower arm of my personal guard is well fed and his numerous injuries will be seen to enough?"

"Surely with the long hours I expect your men will spend on patrol, I will have plenty of time to help out at the manor house."

"If you can spare the time," the duke said, "mayhap you could lend a hand cooking for the rest of my guard there."

"Of course, Your Grace. It would be my honor, but surely that won't take up all of my time."

Finn put his arm around his wife's shoulders and chuckled. "I think that's enough duties to begin with. We'll add to them if and when the need arises."

"But—"

"Your health, and that of your babe, comes first," the duchess reminded her. "Promise me you will not do anything to tax your strength."

Without missing a beat, Mollie replied, "What could possibly be more taxing than an overprotective husband?"

Patrick roared with laughter, and Finn shoved him backward into the wall. Turning to his wife, he rasped, "Ye shouldn't taunt fate like that, lass."

His brother immediately apologized. "I wasn't thinking, Finn. Ye're right." He stared down at his sister-in-law and urged, "Ye'd best be watching over yer shoulder, lass, until yer challenge has been answered."

"What challenge?" she asked.

"Faith, as Irish as me wife's roots are, she was raised in England," Finn said.

Patrick inclined his head in agreement. "She needs a holy charm to protect her."

Finn agreed. "Ye'll wear this," he told Mollie, pulling a silver chain over his head. "Never take it off," he warned, slipping it over her head.

"St. Christopher is the patron saint of travelers," Patrick said. "He'll protect ye when Finn or Flaherty are on patrol."

Mollie grasped hold of the warm medal. Worry filled her. "What of you, Finn? Who will protect you if you've given me your holy medal?"

"Yer love, lass. That's all I'll be needing."

They left for Cornwall an hour later.

BUXTON TOSSED A bucket of water on his captive.

The young man sputtered and opened his eyes but didn't cry out—he was staring at the body of another of the duke's messengers lying beside him covered in blood from the fatal wound to his throat.

"Who is Mollie Malloy?"

Unable to look away from the carnage, he shrugged.

Buxton hauled him to his feet by his throat. While the duke's messenger struggled to break free of the hold, the excise man threatened, "You tell me or you die." He released his stranglehold and watched the young man collapse at his feet, gasping for breath.

"She must work at Wyndmere Hall. That's where I was summoned and tasked with delivering O'Malley's message to his brother here at Penwith Tower."

"Then she's connected to the Duke of Wyndmere and his guard?"

"Aye."

"She must be a servant," Buxton mused aloud. "The duke's sister married and moved to the borderlands—the only familial connection to the duke is his duchess, and her name is Persephone." The young man's worried expression amused the excise man. "Don't worry—you will not have to suffer expulsion from the duke's exalted messenger squad."

"I won't? Why?"

Buxton bent, withdrew his dagger from his boot, and slit his prisoner's throat from ear to ear. He laughed uproariously at the surprised expression on the dying man's face.

"You'll be dead."

Turning his back on the men he'd murdered, he motioned for one of his men standing guard at the mouth of the cave. "Dispose of their bodies."

"I'll row them out to sea and toss them overboard."

Buxton shrugged. "Be sure to row out far enough that the tide will not deposit the bodies along the shoreline."

The man wasn't quick enough to hide his revulsion as he bent to haul the first body over his shoulder.

"Oh, and Richards?"

"Aye, sir?"

"There is always another who will be willing to take your place and pocket your share of the coin we collect from our French benefactor."

The man paled and nodded that he understood.

Buxton had already planned the man's demise, the moment Richards showed his weakness. Every man who served under him knew: Buxton did not make threats—he made promises.

Chapter Fourteen

"Two bodies washed ashore last night during the storm."

Flaherty stared at Tremayne's closed expression and knew it was not due to someone foolish enough to be out on the Celtic Sea. Those that lived along the coast of Cornwall knew the many moods of the waters that could give life—with its bounty of fish—or take it away from those who sought to test their strength against it.

"Did ye move them?"

"Aye," the lieutenant answered. "Both had messenger's pouches wrapped around their throats."

Flaherty understood what the former dragoon did not say. "Strangled."

"Postmortem."

"How in the bloody hell would ye know?" Flaherty demanded.

"Their throats had been slit from ear to ear," Tremayne said. "The leather pouches knotted around their necks would be a swift and efficient message if their bodies ever made it to shore."

Flaherty hesitated, his gut roiling with unease. He hoped he was wrong. "I may be able to identify the bodies, if they weren't bashed against the rocks during the night."

"The leather pouches…" Tremayne trailed off as they made their way along the winding path to the beach below.

Flaherty knew the man had something to add. "Aye?"

"They have the duke's crest burned into the inside flap."

Flaherty held back from the need to bash his fists into something—or someone—to relieve the anger and frustration twisting inside of him. "Bloody buggering hell!"

Tremayne paused at the bottom of the path. "It will be my pleasure to send whoever did this straight to hell."

Flaherty nodded. Coventry would have informed his men of the constant battle the duke's guard waged against those who sought to discredit the duke—or cause him harm before sending them as reinforcements. He owed it to Tremayne and Bayfield to tell them his suspicions. "'Twas a message for Finn and meself— from Buxton."

"The crooked excise official?"

"Aye. The man's fond of the efficiency of a slit throat."

"Leaves a bloody message."

Flaherty held back the rest of what simmered inside of him, saving it for the battle ahead. "Lead on."

Tremayne headed toward the smallest of the caves carved beneath the duke's tower. "We put the bodies in here."

"Good choice. There is no sign that it's been used in the last decade," Flaherty said.

"From what you and your men have told us, we'd best move the bodies before nightfall, or risk discovery."

Flaherty curled his hands into fists, imagining they were wrapped around Buxton's throat. "Striking out at the duke, murdering two of his messengers, just made this personal. We'll put an end to Ruan and Buxton's operation if we have to go to Hell and back again to track them down!"

Tremayne squatted beside the first body and lifted the flap on the leather pouch.

The Irishman acknowledged the symbol. "For the duke's sake, and that of his family, I had to see the proof with me own eyes before making me report."

Tremayne moved to the other body and lifted the flap—again

showing the duke's crest. "How do you plan to deliver it?"

"Well now," Flaherty said. "I'm thinking to deliver it wrapped in Buxton's entrails." When the lieutenant slowly smiled, Flaherty sighed. "Faith, I knew ye would agree it's an effective way to deliver the missive, but I'm thinking ye'll press me to come up with another way to send the news to His Grace."

"Why not send one of the workmen instead of a messenger?"

"Yer idea has merit, but we'll have to disguise him so he looks like a wealthy lord—otherwise, he'll be stopped and hanged before he can explain why he's on a horse worth a king's ransom."

"Excellent notion."

"I'll put the question to me cousin. Finn should be arriving in the next day or so."

"We'll hold on to the proof," Tremayne said. It wasn't a question.

Flaherty agreed, "Aye. We won't be burying the evidence with the bodies."

"Will you alert the constable in St. Ives?"

Flaherty rubbed his chin. "I'll consider it."

"You don't trust him."

"Ye remind me of me cousin, Finn."

"Do I?" the lieutenant asked.

"Aye, ye're built like a bull—as is Finn. Ye've a sharp mind, are courageous, and have a soldier's heart."

"I've only met your cousin once, though I've heard tales of him from Coventry. I'm looking forward to working with him. It's always a pleasure to meet another man worthy of His Majesty's Dragoons."

"Ye agree, then? Not to bring the constable into our problems?"

Tremayne nodded. "We hold off telling the constable until O'Malley returns. We'll need the wagon."

"I'll send one of the men after Kelly. He usually has two or three men accompany him wherever he goes."

"A cautious man."

"Saved his life more than once in the last year, but that's a tale for another time—when I have the leisure to sit and raise a pint while telling it."

Tremayne grinned. "When you do, I'm buying."

"Are ye certain ye prefer working with Captain Coventry? We could use a man with yer skills here at Penwith Tower."

"I owe the captain my life," Tremayne said. "Though I do not mind being on loan to His Grace."

"We'll see how long Coventry deigns to let ye stay. We'd best gather the men and let them know what ye've discovered." They walked up the path, and Flaherty swore.

"What is it?"

"Are ye a betting man?"

"At times," Tremayne answered. "Why?"

"Finn won't be arriving alone."

"Is he bringing reinforcements?"

"Nay," Flaherty replied. "A distraction."

FINN STOPPED COUNTING when the coach stopped—again—so he could empty the contents of one of the buckets they'd brought as a cautionary measure. God help him, he never thought his wife would react to the motion of the carriage as Patrick warned she might!

"Ye're a warrior queen, love," he soothed as he pulled his wife onto his lap. Her body trembled from the aftereffects of retching. "Is there nothing that will help?"

Mollie was quick to respond, "Stopping the coach and letting me walk the rest of the way."

"'Tis five miles more, lass."

That seemed to perk her up. "Is that all? Coachman! Stop the coach!"

The carriage slowed and came to a halt. Finn turned to his wife and demanded, "What in the bloody hell do ye think ye're doing?"

In answer, she slipped off his lap and bolted out of the carriage.

"Mollie Catherine Malloy!" Finn thundered, reaching for her, but she was as swift as a rabbit being chased by a pack of hounds. "Have ye lost yer sense?"

She ignored him, walking past the horses stamping their feet, anxious to continue moving. "I'll arrive in due time. Do not concern yourself."

He overtook her with but a few of his long strides, burying the need to shake some sense into his wife. Wasn't the motion of the carriage what turned her stomach inside out in the first place? Hands on his hips, he frowned—in his mind, he was glaring at her.

"I'll have yer explanation now, wife."

"I should think it would be obvious—especially to a man of high rank within the duke's personal guard."

Finn noted the dark circles beneath her sky-blue eyes and her pale-as-parchment skin. "Ye'll be fine once we reach Penwith Tower, lass. I'll fill the tub waiting for ye meself, so ye can wash the disaster of a trip here from yer mind."

She sighed. "I'll be dead by the time we arrive."

Finn wrapped her in his embrace and pressed a kiss to the top of her head. "Ye won't ever speak of such things again. Ye're me wife, the mother of our babe. I vowed to love ye and treasure ye till we breathe our last."

He couldn't make out what she murmured beneath her breath. He eased his hold on her and stared down at her. "What was that ye said?"

"If you insist on dragging me back and putting me in that coach, I'll be dead by the time we arrive!"

The fire in her eyes and conviction of her words shot through him. He swept her off her feet and started back toward the carriage.

"Finn, I'm begging you."

"Ye don't have the strength to walk for five minutes, let alone five miles, lass, and ye know it."

"So, you'll use your superior strength, and misplaced sense of knowing what is good for me, to force me to get back into that bloody coach?"

He clenched his jaw and silently blasted the difficult woman with the whole of his vocabulary of curse words. When they were close enough, he hailed the coachman. "I need ye to unharness one of the lead horses. Me wife and I shall be riding the rest of the way."

"How will you ride without a saddle?" the coachman asked.

Finn grinned. "Ye don't need a saddle to ride a horse."

The coachman tied off the reins and stepped down from his driver's seat. With a shake of his head, he warned, "His Grace will not be pleased when I tell him what happened."

"His Grace won't question ye," Finn said, setting Mollie on her feet beside him. "Ye'll tell him it was a direct order from the head of his Penwith Tower guard!"

"Aye, O'Malley."

Finn stalked over to the carriage, reached inside, and retrieved two blankets, while the coachman quickly unharnessed the horse and led him over to where Mollie waited. Finn nodded to the man and turned to his wife. "If ye think ye'll be warm enough wrapped in one blanket, I'll place the other on the horse for his comfort."

"One will be fine, Finn." She placed a hand to his forearm and leaned close to press her lips to his cheek. "Thank you."

He wrapped a blanket around her shoulders, then folded the other and draped it over the horse. "There's a lad," he said. "Ye won't mind carrying the two of us, will ye? Me wife weighs no more than thistledown."

Mollie was smiling when Finn lifted her onto the horse's back. "Thistledown?"

He mounted behind her, pulled her onto his lap, and answered, "Less after our journey from Wyndmere Hall."

WISELY, MOLLIE KEPT her mouth closed. She'd won their argument and did not have to set foot in that blasted doom machine! Just the thought of climbing into the coach had her stomach flipping over and nausea roiling in the pit of her belly.

She leaned back against her husband's broad and powerful chest, closed her eyes, and drifted off to sleep.

The crack of a rifle jarred her awake. "Finn?"

"Hang on, lass. We'll make a run for it!"

Something warm and wet seeped through the blanket onto her shoulder. She knew without asking that he'd been shot. Mollie slipped the blanket off her shoulder, folded one corner, and pressed it to his upper arm. Finn leaned lower, using his body as a shield against their attackers.

They rode like the devil was nipping at their heels, but Finn was forced to rein in their horse when a trio of riders blocked the road in front of them—rifles pointed at their hearts.

"Keep quiet," Finn whispered in her ear. "No matter what!"

She squeezed his hand in answer, and prayed they would live to see another sunrise.

CHAPTER FIFTEEN

MOLLIE CAME TO with a jolt. The memory of her husband being dragged from their horse and beaten by three men at once had her swallowing the bile rushing up her throat.

She clamped down the urge and willed her stomach to settle. Casting up her accounts would not help Finn. Cunning and careful calculation on her part would. It had to! She refused to believe that the lifeless, bloody lump the men had kicked to the side of the road—her husband—was dead!

Thin streams of light filtered through the broken window above her head. A tiny patch of light was visible beneath a door on the other side of the room. She would not sit still while her husband needed her! She struggled against her bonds, trying to free herself, but only succeeded in rubbing her wrists raw until they bled.

The gag tasted of sweat and desperation. Hers? She shook her head. Certainly not Finn's. She brought up the memory of the scent of his sweat and reveled in it. Honest, healthy, invigorating—as he had been when last they'd made love.

She inhaled, sending up a prayer of thanks. Whoever held her captive had not blocked off her ability to breathe through her nose.

God, if you're listening, don't let Finn be dead!

Footsteps sounded on the other side of the door. She braced

herself to fight, and a voice seemed to whisper from her heart, telling her to feign unconsciousness. She slumped to the floor.

A jangle of keys and the snick of a lock opening alerted her that she was no longer alone.

"You've done well, men," a cultured voice said. "Our captive will lure the rest of the duke's men out—while we lie in wait to cut them down."

Her gasp of shock had the swinging lantern moving closer.

"Ah, you are awake. Help Mrs. O'Malley sit up, men. She'll want to hear the rest of our plans. Tell her what you did with her husband's body."

She cursed at them through the gag as they manhandled her into a sitting position.

"Remove her gag."

A large man knelt and reached around her to loosen the knot and remove the foul bit of linen from around her face.

"It should be interesting to hear what she has to say when you describe the bones you broke and the dagger you left in his back."

Her captor's words, and soulless black eyes, had the bile rushing back up her throat. She threw up on his boots.

"Bloody hell!"

The crack of his hand to her cheek punctuated his curse, but cleared her head and loosened her tongue.

"Mark my words—Finn is *not* dead." She prayed her declaration was true as she warned, "He was feigning unconsciousness. He is on his way to unleash the wrath of his anger on each and every one of you! Not even God will help you then."

His boots forgotten, the man leaned over her. "Finn O'Malley is dead. No man could survive the beating he took—or the knife in his back." Nodding to the man still hovering near her, he said, "Gag her!"

She twisted to avoid the sweat-filled cloth but could not. Digging deep, she shored up her flagging faith and prayed with heart, mind, and soul.

God, please let my words be true. Finn is not dead!

A MOIST, WARM wetness covered his face once, and then a second time, rousing him. He slowly took stock of his injuries as the horse nudged him, reminding him of his duty…and his love.

"I have to go after them—they have Mollie!"

Grabbing hold of the horse's mane, he pulled himself to his knees and slowly rose to his feet. He swayed but managed to stay remain standing long enough to mount the horse. He pressed his knees to the horse's sides, urging his mount forward, while he hung on with the last of his strength.

"SIR! THERE'S A riderless horse headed this way!"

Flaherty joined the man on patrol and stared at the odd shape of the horse. "Either that horse has a hunchback—or someone is riding him."

Motioning for one of the guards to join him, he ran along the rampart and descended the stairs. The clicking of half a dozen guns above him, trained on the unknown rider and horse, did not ease his worry as recognition slammed into him.

"Finn!" He ran toward the horse and grabbed hold of the bridle. "Hold the horse while I help me cousin off his back."

"Mollie," Finn groaned.

Flaherty's legs bowed as he caught his cousin before he could fall to the ground. "What happened? Where is Mollie?"

"Ambushed us. Left me for dead." Finn's gaze bored into Flaherty's. "Fenton, they've got me wife!"

"Wife?"

Flaherty's mind raced, trying to piece together what had happened. He had an idea it had to do with his cousin's state of mind every time he returned from Wyndmere Hall. He would question Finn later. To do so now was pointless when his cousin had blood oozing from a number of injuries. It was a miracle he wasn't dead!

"Did they steal her horse, too?"

His question was answered a moment later when the sound of hoofbeats thundered toward them. "Carriage ride made her ill," Finn explained. "We thought to ride the last five miles on horseback."

"Double?"

"She's light as air," Finn said, the vacant expression in his eyes finally clearing.

"Ah, Mollie," Flaherty said, "the petite, fair lady's maid with auburn hair and blue eyes."

"Me wife," Finn reminded him.

Flaherty smiled. His cousin's irritation eased his mind. Finn would recover. "Let's get ye inside and see to yer wounds before ye fall flat on yer face."

"I have to go after them."

"Which direction?" Finn shook his head and moaned. Flaherty figured it was from the purple lump above his left ear. "Looks like they clocked ye with the butt of a pistol."

"I'll tell ye the whole of it, after we find me wife."

Flaherty grabbed hold of Finn's arm, intending to drag him along, and felt the warmth of his cousin's blood beneath his fingers. "Shot ye, too?"

"Paltry wounds," Finn scoffed. "Either come with me, or I'll go without ye!"

When his cousin stumbled, Flaherty steadied Finn with a hand to his back. "Ye'll bleed out before ye can find their trail," Flaherty said as he led his cousin to the kitchen.

"She's carrying me babe." Finn's voice broke saying the words. "Ye've got to help me save my family!"

"I'll bind yer wounds meself," Flaherty promised. "Then we'll ride out and track down the bloody buggers that stole yer wife.

We'll save her and yer unborn babe." Bracing his cousin's bulk, he quietly gave the order for the men to assemble.

He stanched the flow of blood from the lead ball that passed through his cousin's upper arm and the wound in his back. "These need threads."

"There's no time," Finn said. "Mollie, our babe—sear it; it'll be quicker."

Flaherty nodded and withdrew the knife from his boot, straightened and removed the flask from his waistcoat, and handed it to Finn. "You first, then a bit for me blade before I heat it in the fire." Finn took a healthy slug and handed it back to Flaherty, who doused the blade before looking at his cousin. "Don't try to be a hero. Yell if ye need to."

"I won't," Finn rasped, watching as his cousin heated his blade in the flames.

"Will ye need a bucket?"

"Nay. I'll not be puking up me guts. Just get it done or I'm leaving!"

"Sit!" Flaherty roared. He walked back over to the table and held the knife poised over the lesser of the wounds—the one from the lead ball. The one in Finn's back would be more painful.

"Ye have one minute more and I'm—"

"Shut yer gob!" Flaherty put the blade to Finn's flesh and dug deep to ignore the stench of burning flesh.

Finn never flinched…never made a sound.

"I need to heat the blade again," Flaherty warned.

Finn nodded.

Flaherty repeated the process. The wound wasn't as ragged as the one in Finn's arm…someone had stabbed his cousin in the back!

Finn sagged against the table, panting when Flaherty lifted the blade from his skin.

"Do ye want to—"

FINN SHOT TO his feet and stumbled outside. He bent over and emptied the bile he'd held inside while Flaherty cauterized his wounds.

Flaherty appeared with a damp cloth and handed it to Finn. "Wipe yer mouth and I'll hand ye me flask."

Steadier, Finn followed Flaherty back inside and submitted to his cousin's applying healing salve and thick bandages, then waited for him to wrap linen strips around his wounds to hold the bandages in place.

Finn held out his hand. "Thank ye, Fenton. I need to leave now…alone. Buxton and his men cannot know I've reached Penwith Tower and am bringing reinforcements. If they think I'm alone, they're more apt to bargain with me."

"Aye," Flaherty agreed. "They'll gladly trade yer wife for yer useless, battered body. Think, man! What do they want? Why have they taken her?"

Finn's gaze met his. "The duke's missing messengers."

"Aren't missing any longer."

Finn did not have to ask if they were alive—Flaherty would have said as much.

"The sea gave up her dead," Flaherty told him. "Tremayne found them."

"Tossed over the side of a boat in a storm?"

Flaherty stared at Finn and said, "Throats slit and their leather messenger pouches knotted about their necks."

Finn's hands curled into fists. "A warning."

"A message. They want us to know they captured two of the messengers and know what was in the sealed missives. Do ye have any notion what they contained?"

"Only the one. When I arrived at Wyndmere Hall, Patrick told me he sent word via messenger alerting me to Mollie's condition. Don't ye see, 'tis why they kidnapped me wife—to force me hand."

Flaherty's eyes widened. "Why would they leave ye for dead? What would they have to gain?"

"Finn!" Garahan burst into the kitchen, stopped, and stared. "Ye aren't dead!" He grinned. "I told Murphy it was a lie—after I clubbed him in the gob."

"Fighting at the Randy Cock again, were ye?" Flaherty asked.

"Wasn't it yerself who gave me the assignment to infiltrate the locals?"

Flaherty shrugged. "'Twas the best solution at the time, though I admit, I'd forgotten yer penchant for stirring up trouble once ye've raised a pint or two."

"'Tisn't trouble when someone insults yer family."

"Isn't it?" Flaherty asked.

Garahan flashed a grin. "'Tis justice." He shoved Flaherty aside to get a closer look at their cousin and held up three fingers. "How many do ye see?"

Finn swatted his cousin's hand away without answering.

Garahan leaned even closer, demanding, "Let me see yer eyes."

"I'll be blackening both of yers, if ye—"

"Leave off, the insults, lads," Flaherty ordered them. "At his insistence, I've patched himself up, cauterized his wounds with a hot blade, and bandaged him. We'll send word if we need ye."

"Bugger that!" Garahan got in Flaherty's face and shouted, "Ye'd leave me behind while the bloody buggering bastards that took sweet Mollie Malloy captive go free?"

Finn put a hand on Garahan's shoulder. "'Tisn't Mollie Malloy."

Garahan paused to meet Finn's gaze. "Oh God, 'tisn't the fair Francis, is it?"

"'Tis Mollie *O'Malley*."

"I don't know whether to congratulate ye or clobber ye in the head for taking the lass' virtue."

Finn swung at Garahan, but missed as his cousin danced out

of range of Finn's fist. "Ye vowed never to marry. 'Tis the only reason I'm thinking ye married her. God, Finn, couldn't ye leave sweet Mollie alone?"

Finn glared at his cousin. "'Tis the other way around. A man can only resist for so long."

Garahan slowly smiled. "Well then, congratulations are in order. 'Tis clear the lass could not help herself. Knowing Mollie, she must love ye, though Lord knows why." After a moment, he said, "Faith, there isn't a woman alive who can resist an Irishman in his fighting prime."

"We're wasting time," Finn barked. "The two of ye sort out who'll stay and head up the guard patrolling the tower, and who'll follow along behind me."

Finn could hear his cousins bickering as they vied for the honor of rescuing the fair Mollie O'Malley. Outside the curtain wall surrounding the tower, he looked up at the sky, raised his clenched fist, and vowed, "Ye'll not let anything happen to me wife or me babe, Lord, or ye'll face me wrath when I storm the gates of Heaven!"

"Sounds like the convoluted prayer of a desperate man."

Finn glanced over his shoulder. Tremayne stood with two horses saddled and ready to ride.

"If anything happens to me wife and unborn babe, I'll take me own life, if only to join them in Heaven!"

The lieutenant held Finn's gaze for a moment, then said, "If you take your own life, you forfeit Heaven and will end up buried at the crossroads with a stake through the heart."

"Me brothers and cousins would see to it that doesn't happen." Finn studied the man before him. "Have ye extra powder and lead balls?"

Tremayne ignored the question, mounted his horse, and waited for Finn to do the same.

"Ye aren't going to answer me, when 'tis clear enough ye were sent to act as reinforcements to the guard under me command?"

"I make my own decisions—no matter who is in command."

Finn inclined his head. "Ye sound as stubborn as meself. Faith, I'm glad ye're accompanying me, Tremayne."

They rode out together, returning to the place where the blackguards stole his wife and left him for dead. With Tremayne's military experience, and the Irishman's years spent avoiding trouble back home, they had no trouble finding the trail.

"A blind man could follow them," Tremayne said. "Why could they *want* you to find them, if they think you're dead." Before Finn could answer, Tremayne, said, "On the other hand, it is no doubt my superior tracking skills."

Finn studied the ground, "If they believe I'm dead, why go to the trouble of covering their tracks?"

Tremayne frowned. "I'm not convinced."

"Mollie will be holding on to the hope that I'm alive," Finn said. "She can be very convincing."

"Say I agree with you. They will be expecting you, and when you show up…" Tremayne let his words trail off.

Finn said, "They plan to kill me."

"And your wife?"

Finn's eyes filled, and a tear slipped past his guard. "They'll try to kill her too. I'm hoping the surprise of seeing me—when they thought me dead—will give me time to swoop in and save the day."

Tremayne said, "That will be a feat long remembered. Though who will tell of it, when the bastards who took her will be dead before they touch her?"

The former dragoon's words lightened part of the heavy weight Finn carried. Mollie and their babe would never have been in danger if he hadn't stubbornly ignored his brother's insistence that she remain at Wyndmere Hall.

"'Twill be me fault if they harm one hair on her head."

"From what Flaherty said, they shot you, nearly beat you to death, and stuck a knife in your back," Tremayne reminded him. "How could the fault be yours?"

"She wanted to come with me, and in me pride, I thought I could protect her. Patrick wanted her to remain at the duke's estate…I refused."

The dragoon inclined his head, understanding what O'Malley did not say. "Believing she'd only be safe if with you."

Finn wasn't surprised that the man had guessed what he was thinking. Having met Tremayne previously, he knew they were more alike in temperament and mind than Patrick and himself.

The bond between them solidified when Tremayne finally answered Finn's earlier question. "I have a supply of powder, lead balls, and wadding for four men."

"I'll be thanking ye after me wife is safe in me arms."

The lieutenant nodded. "And if she bears you a son, you'll name him Gryffyn."

"'Tis a Welsh name!"

"Aye. I was named after my father, a warrior of renown."

"When Mollie is free, I'll consider it as a middle name. Our son will have to have an Irish warrior's name."

Tremayne was laughing as they rounded a turn in the trail and spied three horses grazing near a small, dilapidated shack surrounded with brambles a short distance away.

THE TWO MEN reined in their horses, dismounted, and approached on foot. The roar of the sea drowned out their footsteps—and the sound of their pistols being cocked. With a nod, Finn indicated he'd take out the guard on the left, leaving the other guard to Tremayne.

"Too easy," the lieutenant whispered.

"Aye. Mollie must have been convincing. 'Twould seem they're expecting me—but not you. Stay here and wait for me cousin. I'll give a shout if I need help."

"You've lost a lot of blood and aren't thinking clearly. I'll go in and guard your back."

Finn grabbed the other man by the arm and growled, "'Tis me family they have, and me they want."

Tremayne's eyes widened as what O'Malley did *not* say hit him. "You don't plan to fight them at all."

Finn didn't bother to answer. "Follow me, and I'll kill ye meself."

"I'll see that your cousins know not to bury you at the cross-roads and will guard your wife with *my* life."

Finn nodded in silent thanks. He released the hammer and tucked his pistol into the pocket of his frockcoat.

Head high, he reached for the door and yanked it open. "I've come to make a trade, ye bloody buggering bastards!"

He knew he would be walking into a trap, and was surround-ed the moment he stepped over the threshold.

"Take me to Buxton," he demanded.

In answer, someone punched him where the lead ball had torn through his upper arm, while another man lashed Finn's hands behind his back.

He ignored the pain of the blow—it was nothing compared to the agony that tore through his heart when his eyes locked with Mollie's. He vowed to make them pay for the bruise on her cheek, and the pain he glimpsed in the depths of her eyes. The lass was terrified.

"Ah, O'Malley. Glad you could join us," Buxton crooned. "I've just been telling your wife my plans for your public execution. Care to hear what I have in mind for you?"

Finn's gaze clashed with the excise official's. "Ye can do whatever ye wish to me—as long as ye set me wife free before-hand."

Finn expected Buxton's surprise—he counted on it—and wasn't disappointed.

"Why would I? When I fully intend for her to have a front-row seat when I gut you and hang you by the neck until you're dead."

Finn's mind raced while he taunted Buxton, "Faith, even I know gutting a man brings on death faster than hanging him." There had to be a way to prevent his wife from watching the bloody death Buxton planned for him. "I've amassed a small fortune working for the Duke of Wyndmere. 'Tis yers, if ye let me wife go now."

"There is a large shipment due in on the evening tide. After the goods have been inspected and stored in the caves below the duke's tower—which, by now, I am certain you have discovered—I shall consider your offer."

Finn kept his expression neutral as relief swept up from the soles of his feet.

Buxton glanced at Mollie and then back at Finn. "I'll have your fortune...and the pleasure of watching you die a painful death."

"Done." Thank the Lord, Mollie would not have to watch his grisly demise.

"And will enjoy it all the more with your wife standing beside me."

Finn lunged forward and rammed his head into Buxton's stomach. "Ye bleeding bastard! I'll kill ye with me bare hands!"

He was roughly yanked off Buxton and hit from behind. Pain shot through his skull, but he fought the enveloping black long enough to look into his wife's eyes and rasp, "Forgive me, Mollie-lass."

CHAPTER SIXTEEN

TREMAYNE CAREFULLY MADE his way through the thicket surrounding the cottage, hoping to find a window. The rude wooden structure was so small, it may not have one. But he rounded the far side and found what he was looking for. He prayed the lack of men standing guard outside meant they were all occupied inside the shack.

Waiting beneath the window to assess the situation, he listened. The conversation he overheard sickened him. The bastard Buxton planned to force O'Malley's wife to watch while he had her husband publicly executed. Tremayne took a chance that the men inside were concentrating on their prisoners and peered through the opening. Finn fought against his captors. Three men tackled and held him, while another clubbed him on the back of the head.

Finn's wife swayed but managed to hold on to her composure and remain standing. She had to be in shock from the gruesome picture the excise official had painted of the death he planned for her husband.

As long as Buxton and his men were preoccupied with Finn, Tremayne just might be able to rescue her. He had a plan for how to save O'Malley, but it would require at least a dozen men and would have to wait until the day of his execution. From the information the duke's guard had relayed about the crooked excise official, Tremayne would wager the man would want to announce to all and sundry of his plan to execute the head of the duke's Cornwall guard—he would expect a large audience for Finn's execution.

He waited while the men—and it took four—hauled Finn's unconscious bulk from the building. Buxton kept shouting orders to his men while they loaded the big Irishman into the waiting wagon.

The driver glanced over his shoulder, and Tremayne recognized him. *Kelly!* All hope was not lost if the man driving the wagon was one of those on the duke's payroll. He nodded to Kelly, who immediately started an argument with Buxton and his lackeys, creating the diversion Tremayne needed.

Tremayne silently thanked the man while he tried to blend into the shadows, then slipped in through the shack's open door.

Mollie jolted in surprise when she saw him walking toward her. He lifted his hands to show he held no weapons. "I came with Finn to rescue you." He slipped the gag off her mouth and watched while she moved her jaw from side to side. He released her from her bonds, saying, "I'm one of Captain Coventry's men. Lieutenant Tremayne."

Mollie ran her gaze across the scar slashing one side of his face, from forehead to chin, but did not show any reaction to it. "You can rescue me later. We have to save my husband!"

"I gave O'Malley my word that if I had the opportunity, I would whisk you away to safety."

Her eyes welled with tears, but she blinked them away. "He's planning to sacrifice his life in exchange for mine. We have to stop him!"

Tremayne owed Finn's wife an explanation. "And we will, but not now. We're leaving."

An unholy light changed her soft blue eyes to hard-as-iron midnight blue. "Not if I have anything to say about it."

"Keep your voice down," he warned. "I have to get you out of here, or else you will not have a say at all." He looked at her, glanced at the window, and back at Mollie. "Have you ever climbed out a window before?"

"Years ago, to meet one of my friends at dawn near the faery hillfort back home."

He nodded. "Try to land on your feet, or your bottom—not your head!"

She snorted. "I'd be more concerned with how you'll fit through the window," she said, taking in the width of his shoulders. "You're built like my husband."

"You first." He gave her a boost and waited until she disappeared through the opening before walking to the door. Keeping an eye on the men still gathered by the wagon in a heated debate, he slipped away undetected. The shouting suddenly stopped. With one thought in mind—escape—Tremayne swept Mollie into his arms as he leapt over the low tangle of brambles and ran as if the hounds of hell were after him.

When they were far enough away, he felt her hot tears on his neck. He slowed to a stop and set her on her feet, then bent from the waist to catch his breath. Finally straightening to his full height, he vowed, "I promise you, we will not leave Finn at the mercy of that bastard Buxton."

"But that's what you've done!" She glared at him before slipping around him to run back the way they came.

"Mollie Catherine O'Malley!"

She skidded to a stop. "How did you know my full name?"

"Finn told me on our way to rescue you. He insisted I keep you and his babe safe. I gave my word, and if you know your husband, you know he'll be depending on me to keep it. Otherwise, he will believe you do not love him enough, even after he's traded his life for yours."

She stood dry-eyed with her hands stiff at her sides. "I cannot lose him."

"You won't. Now follow me." He slipped his arm through hers and looped back around the way they'd come. Keeping the low-lying brush and brambles between them and detection, they made it back to where they'd left the horses hidden. He linked his hands and bent so she could use his hands as a step to help her mount her horse.

From where she sat perched atop the horse, she pleaded, "Promise me you will go after Finn."

He swung up behind her. "You have my word."

It was the last words they exchanged until they met Flaherty halfway to Penwith Tower. Flaherty took one look at her red-rimmed eyes and shook his head. "When?"

Mollie snapped to attention and shook her head. "Your stubborn cousin willingly traded his life for mine. But that wasn't enough for the bastards. They hit him on the back of the head and tossed him into a wagon."

Flaherty listened and then turned to Tremayne. "Did you see who was driving the wagon?"

Tremayne smiled. "Aye. Kelly."

Flaherty's snort of laughter seemed to baffle Mollie. "My husband's life depends on the whim of an unbalanced, crooked excise official—and the two of you are pleased?"

"Aye, lass," Flaherty said. "Kelly's a part of the duke's guard in Cornwall."

Her relief was so great, she collapsed—and would have fallen off her horse if not for Flaherty's quick reflexes. "Have a care, lass. Ye need to stay strong for me cousin and yer babe."

"I will. Now, what can I do to help rescue Finn?"

The two men rounded on Mollie. "Rest!" Flaherty ordered her.

"Rest!" Tremayne said at the same time.

The men were chuckling again, while she frowned at them. "Not until I see more than the two of you riding after those fiends."

"I already gave you my word," Tremayne reminded her.

"And I see you have not made one move to follow after those men."

"I have to see you safely back to Penwith Tower first."

"Nay. I'm coming with you."

"Mollie, now is not the time to argue with the lieutenant," Flaherty said. "We have to see ye to safety."

"Finn got his way when he traded his life for mine. *Now it's my turn*. I'm going after him, with your help…or without it!"

"Fine, then," Flaherty grumbled. "But ye'll do as Tremayne or I say, or we'll gag ye and tie ye up ourselves to keep ye from harm. Understood?"

She inclined her head but did not give her word. The men frowned at her but did not make any other demands of her as they headed toward the cliffs and the paths that would lead to the caves beneath Penwith Tower.

GARAHAN WALKED INTO the Randy Cock tavern with an attitude. He looked to be spoiling for a fight—and several of the customers seemed ready to give him one.

Just an hour before, he'd fought against the plan Flaherty and Tremayne came up with when they returned with Mollie. The lass was dry-eyed when she shared the news Finn was being held prisoner in one of the caves below Penwith Tower.

The memory of the pain in the depths of her pale blue eyes when she told of Finn trading his life for hers and their unborn babe's slashed through him. He had to release the anger and frustration churning inside to think clearly when they returned to rescue Finn.

He slugged the first man who moved to block him from reaching the bar, elbowed the second, and kicked the feet out from under the third.

Garahan grinned at the crowd gathered. "I'm having a pint before I agree to go a round with any of ye."

The ragtag group of men cleared a path for Garahan. He lifted his chin, slapped his coin down on the bar, and ordered his first pint.

Two pints later, he set the empty tankard down, turned, and knocked the closest man off his feet with a right cross that had the man crumpling to the floor. "Who's next?"

He showed no sign of recognition when Coventry's man, Captain Bayfield, got to his feet and challenged, "I am."

Garahan threw the first punch, but Bayfield surprised him by evading the blow, countering with a solid hit to Garahan's ribs. Garahan grinned as he returned the favor, landing an uppercut to the captain's chin.

Those gathered in the Randy Cock broke into cheers when they realized the men were evenly matched. Garahan silently cursed the day he'd agreed to Flaherty's plan. Wagers were placed, and the din of the crowd increased.

He grabbed Coventry's man in a chokehold and rasped, "Any news?"

Bayfield leaned in and punched him in the kidney. "Reinforcements are coming."

Garahan grunted and grinned when his fist connected with the other man's cheekbone. "When?"

Bayfield smiled and delivered a jab to Garahan's ribs. "Tonight."

Garahan stiffened, then countered with a blow that knocked the other man into the trio of tables. "Ye'll pay for that, ye cur!"

The crowd roared when Garahan dove and landed on top of the other man. Wood splintered as the tables collapsed beneath the combined weight of the men. And that was when the Randy Cock's patrons gave a shout and joined in the brawl.

Once the others were pounding each other, Garahan and Bayfield slipped out the back door. "Faith, yer jab reminds me of me cousin Finn's," Garahan said.

"Your right cross is a thing of beauty."

"Didn't knock you out, though," Garahan said. "Yer chin is as hard as granite."

Bayfield shrugged. "Let's get moving before anyone realizes

we're not under the pile of wood that used to be the Randy Cock's tables."

They vaulted into their saddles and rode off in the direction of the coastline.

"What's yer plan until reinforcements arrive, Bayfield?"

"Don't die."

Garahan's snort of laughter lightened the heavy burden they both carried. Until reinforcements arrived, the nest of vipers in their midst could not be fully exposed and made to pay.

But, by God, Buxton and his cohorts *would* pay!

CHAPTER SEVENTEEN

T HE DUKE OF Wyndmere's face was grim when they stopped
to change horses. Captain Coventry nodded to the men who
rode with them—four were on loan from Gavin King of the Bow
Street Runners, and two were Coventry's, former military men
who'd been injured and forced to retire. "Quarter of an hour—
and no more."

The duke waited until the men were out of hearing range,
trusting Coventry—who had been his mentor and friend for more
than a decade—to ask, "What if we do not reach St. Ives in time?"

The intensity in Coventry's gaze relieved the sharp edge of
the duke's worry. And his words reaffirmed what the duke knew
to be fact. "Your guard is the best of the best. King's men have
fought admirably alongside your guard whenever called to do so.
Two of my men, Bayfield and Tremayne, accompanied Garahan
a sennight ago and are already in Cornwall. Masterson and
Hennessey ride with us. Between King's men, my men, and the
members of your guard stationed at Penwith Tower, we will not
fail."

The duke clenched his jaw, then relaxed it. "I thought the
worst was behind us after dealing with the last slanderous attack
against my family—this time involving my brother and his wife's
reputations."

"As long as there are those who feel slighted that they don't have the wealth and title they feel they deserve, and feel compelled to take aim at those who have it—"

"There will be a need for my trusted guard," the duke finished. "Wise decision, adding to the number of men stationed to London."

"Aye," Coventry agreed. Motioning to one of the inn's stable lads, he said, "See if the innkeeper has our meat pies and ale ready, lad."

"Right away!" The boy ran to do his bidding.

"We'd best make use of the facilities, too."

The duke inclined his head and sighed. "I gather you shall accompany me again and wait outside the privy while I relieve myself."

Coventry snorted to cover his laughter. He pitched his voice low so as not to be overheard. "I gave Her Grace our word that I would guard your back to and from Penwith Tower—and that you would allow it."

The duke raised an eyebrow. When Coventry patiently stared back, the duke acquiesced. "We'd best hurry."

The half a dozen men riding with the duke and Coventry ate the proffered meat pies with relish and downed their tankards of ale, all the while keeping an eye out for trouble. When they were finished, the men mounted and rode off in formation: Masterson in the lead, two of King's men flanking the duke and Coventry on both sides, with Hennessey bringing up the rear.

It was full dark when they reached the outskirts of the village of St. Ives. As agreed upon ahead of time, the group split up— King's four men guarding the duke, and Coventry riding with his men.

Coventry's group rode ahead, slowing down as they approached a seedy-looking tavern boasting the name the Randy Cock. Masterson mumbled something to Hennessey that had the two men snickering.

The group riding with the duke had a similar reaction. As arranged, the groups joined together again once they reached the outskirts of town. Back in formation, they followed the road that led to the top of the hill, where the duke's tower stood in all its glory on the cliffs that faced the Celtic Sea.

"The curtain wall appears to have been fully repaired," Coventry said, signaling to the men who watched their approach from the ramparts high above them. The group rode through the archway into the courtyard, where the men dismounted.

Flaherty strode over to greet them. "Yer Grace."

"Any change, Flaherty?" the duke asked.

"Nay, Yer Grace. Finn is alive and being held in the largest cave beneath our feet."

"How many men are watching the cave?"

"Four. We discovered an opening at the back of the cave. Two of our men were able to slip through the narrow opening and stand watch without anyone being the wiser."

"The few times my brothers and I were able to sneak away to explore the caves, we never uncovered any openings from above," the duke said.

"Did ye make yer way to the very recesses of the cave?"

The duke's wry smile gave away the fact that he did not. "We were quite young—and though stout-hearted, we were too busy playing pirate to fully explore the cave."

"We're thinking we may be able to hoist Finn up through the opening."

"But you're not certain that his shoulders would fit," the duke said. "Are you?"

Flaherty reluctantly agreed. "We may have to go with our original plan."

"And that would be?"

"We wait until the day Buxton plans to execute me cousin."

"That would be cutting it too close," the duke said.

"It would," Flaherty admitted. "Buxton will be sure that his plans will be carried out. When the French smuggler, Ruan, hears of it, he will be satisfied that St. Ives and the other towns dotting the coastline will remain under his command, with Buxton's aid."

The duke considered the possibilities, but worried that leaving it to the last moment may not be wise. "I'm sensing a caveat."

"We have a man who's infiltrated Ruan's men stationed in St. Ives and another working under Buxton's nose."

"I don't like waiting until the last moment—anything could go wrong."

"Aye. 'Tis why we've been widening the opening leading down into the cave."

"How soon do you believe Buxton will start bragging about capturing O'Malley?"

Flaherty met the duke's direct gaze. "He already has."

The duke's stomach knotted. "Then time is running out. You'll take me to the cave."

"I'm thinking we'll have ye stop in the Mermaid's Glass tavern in a few hours so the locals can see the Duke of Wyndmere has finally made an appearance."

"What do you hope to accomplish by my being seen there and not the Randy Cock?"

Flaherty's expression was grim. "Word will reach Buxton. He may demand a ransom for Finn."

Two young men approached, and Flaherty nodded to them. "Lead His Grace's horse and the others to stables, lads. Be sure to give them a good rubdown, then water and feed them."

Watching the horses being led away, the duke asked, "Where is Mollie?"

"Stirring a huge pot of stew over the fire."

"She's not resting at the cottage my wife and I gifted to them as a wedding present?"

Flaherty could not hide his pained expression. "As long as Finn is being held prisoner, she refuses to budge from the tower. Every time we insist she rests, the stubborn woman glares at us."

The duke slowly smiled. "So much has happened in such a short time. When I received your missive, Persephone warned that Mollie may be resistant about taking the time to rest while Finn is in Buxton's clutches. Mayhap I can sway her to put her feet up and rest."

"She'll listen to you, Yer Grace," Flaherty said.

The duke didn't bother to mention that women did not always do what one would expect them to do—or say—especially when pregnant, as he'd learned when Persephone was carrying their twins. He wondered if he could expect more of the same with his wife's pregnancy this time around. Rather than worry about what she was doing—or not doing—while he was in Cornwall, he followed Flaherty to the building that housed the kitchen.

"There you are, Mollie."

The large spoon she held clattered to the floor as she whirled around, hand to her heart. "Your Grace! I would have been on hand to greet you, had I known you were expected." He bent to retrieve the utensil and hand it back to her. She set it on the table and wiped her hands on her apron. "Are you hungry? I just took a batch of scones from the fire. I've learned how to cook them in a covered pot at the edge of the coals so they don't burn. It's a bit different than using the cookstove Constance uses at Wyndmere Hall."

Sensing the woman needed to keep busy to distract herself and not worry about her husband, he noticed the kettle. "Mayhap a scone or two with tea would hold us over until the stew is ready."

"Us?" She glanced behind the duke. "Who is us?"

The duke answered, "Captain Coventry, two of his men, and four of Gavin King's men."

Tears welled in her eyes, and she quickly brushed them away. "Are you here to rescue Finn?"

"That is the plan, Mollie. Persephone is adamant that you do not worry yourself into such a state that it will harm your babe. I gave my word that I would see to it you got enough rest each day. Would you do that for me?"

At the mention of the duchess, she agreed. "After I serve up tea and scones for six."

The duke chuckled. "Let me check with Coventry—the men may already have joined the others on patrol."

Mollie wrung her hands as she said, "I'm afraid there are no furnishings inside the great hall in the tower. Would you mind taking your tea here in the kitchen?"

"That would be fine, thank you. I shall be back directly." Satisfied that he had accomplished part of the instructions received from his duchess, the duke went in search of Coventry.

CHAPTER EIGHTEEN

R UAN LISTENED TO the latest report and frowned. "And you witnessed this fight at the Randy Cock?"

"*Oui, mon capitaine.*"

"How many rode into the village with the one sporting a black eyepatch and sling?"

"Just two."

The smuggler mulled over the information. "The duke rode with four men in red coats? Military?"

"*Non, différent.* Alike in color and quality, but not of the English regiment."

Ruan inclined his head. "Ah, Bow Street Runners."

"*Exactement!*"

"Our excise official has outlived his usefulness."

"What about his prisoner?"

"O'Malley? He is one of the duke's guard, no?"

"*Oui.* Buxton plans to execute him in front of the excise building."

"The fool! To do so would jeopardize our entire operation, now that the duke has arrived."

"What will you have me do, *mon capitaine?*"

"Put an end to the English dog."

Fear had the other man glancing about him before asking, "The duke?"

Ruan snorted. "Not this time, *mon ami*. The crooked tax official, Buxton."

"I shall see it done at once." The man turned and strode to the door.

"Wait," Ruan said. "Let us see what Buxton will do once he learns the duke has arrived. Then I shall decide where and when the man's life will end. Go now and spy on him. I want to hear what the man's reaction is when he learns the duke has come to bargain for O'Malley's life."

FINN WOKE DISORIENTED, and for a moment could only remember being beaten and left for dead at the side of the road. The inky darkness surrounding him was too dark to see his hands in front of his face—if they weren't bound behind his back. Even with no moon, the sky would have dozens of stars—even if it were cloudy. He must be inside somewhere.

All at once, his thoughts cleared. He remembered his precious Mollie standing before him, sporting a purple bruise on her cheekbone, as he offered his life in exchange for hers. The bloody bastard who'd struck her accepted the exchange—but he lied. He now had the both of them captive. His lovely Mollie was being held prisoner at the shack, and himself somewhere dark and dank. *The cave!*

Thank God he knew where he was. Sensing no movement or sound, he tugged against his bonds to no avail—they were secure. He would have to escape first…then he would find his wife and free her. Then and only then would he be able to put an end to the man who'd kidnapped his wife and struck her—Buxton.

"So many different ways to choose from," he muttered aloud. "A lead ball to the brain—no, too quick a death for the likes of him." The distraction of trying to come up with a number of ways to kill the man would keep the worry for his wife from driving him insane. "Ah…a lead ball to the gut—he'll bleed out...slowly."

He fell silent as his mind raced to another option. "I could tie him to me saddle by the feet and drag him through the village." Finn paused to consider who might be watching him mete out justice to the man who'd tried to kill him twice, and planned to publicly do so with Mollie watching.

Would other wives or children see *him* dragging Buxton behind his horse?

"*Bugger it!* I can't take the chance any lads or lasses would witness me deed. I should just hobble the man in private and be done with it!"

An answering raspy chuckle had his gut churning.

"Who's there?" When no one answered, he wondered if he'd imagined it was a chuckle, when it could have been the scraping of a bat's wings rubbing together, or some cave-dwelling creature scuttling across the rocks and sand inside the cave.

Alone, with his hands and feet lashed together, Finn contemplated a plan to separate his mind from the excruciating pain the excise official would inflict with his dagger when he sliced Finn's belly open.

His thoughts churned until something occurred to him. "Mayhap Buxton will be using a sword when he flays me gut open. Nay—wouldn't the blade be too long then?" He grunted in agreement with his own line of reasoning. "A long-bladed dagger or short sword. Aye. That's what the man would use."

⇻⇺

"WELL? HOW IS me cousin?" Garahan demanded as he bent over the widened opening at the top of the cave and pulled Bayfield free.

The man was smiling.

"What in the bloody hell do ye find amusing?"

Bayfield shook his head. "O'Malley was talking to himself."

"Aye. We all do, if ye must know. Argue among ourselves as well." Coventry's man studied Garahan until he started to feel ill at ease. "'Tis a family trait. What was he saying?"

"I believe he is planning to kill someone."

Garahan snorted. "His captor, no doubt. That crooked excise official needs killing. What did ye hear?"

"O'Malley said something about a lead ball to the brain, and then the gut."

"Ah, the first would end a man's life quickly…the second, slowly," Garahan said. "What else did ye hear?"

"From what I could gather," Bayfield answered, "he had decided to drag Buxton through the streets behind his horse but did not want any young boys or girls to witness the deed."

"Well then, that's grand," Garahan replied. "He's distracting himself from worrying about his wife. He's planning how to kill Buxton—but as he's staring fatherhood in the face, he's considering how it would look if it was his own little one witnessing the deed. He'll not be dragging the man through the village. Depending on where he started, the man could be more bone than flesh by the time he arrived in St. Ives."

Bayfield shook his head. "I've seen it done. It is a gruesome sight."

"I have meself as well, when I was a lad. According to me da, it wasn't warranted. Da's always right," Garahan said.

Coventry's man nodded. "Fathers usually are."

"So ye fit through the opening. Do ye think Finn would?" Garahan asked.

Bayfield fell silent, and Garahan reasoned the man was considering the size of the hole and the width of Finn's shoulders. Finally, Bayfield answered, "Tremayne is roughly the same breadth through the chest and shoulders as your cousin. If he fits, then Finn will."

"He and one of King's men were headed to the tavern to meet with their contact," Garahan said.

"One of Buxton's men?" Bayfield asked.

"Nay," Garahan replied. "One of Ruan's."

"The smuggler?"

"Aye," Garahan answered.

"Do you plan to take him down along with the crooked tax official?" Bayfield asked.

Garahan narrowed his eyes and stared off into the distance before turning to reply, "We hope to enlist his aid."

Bayfield chuckled. "I understand if you feel the need to keep a part of your plans close to the vest, but—"

"That is the plan," Garahan said. "Word among the locals who offload the Frenchman's cargo is Ruan knows Buxton is taking a bigger cut than agreed upon."

"There is no honor among thieves," Bayfield said.

"Aye, but ye have to know who ye're thieving with—there are those who will look the other way when ye take advantage."

"But not Ruan," Bayfield added.

Garahan agreed. "Never Ruan. The man would sooner cut out yer tongue than listen to yer excuses."

"Aren't you taking the same risk by enlisting the man's aid?"

"Me cousins and I do not think so," Garahan said. "The end result will be a new excise official arriving to clean out those on Buxton's staff crooked enough to go along with him rather than report any wrongdoing to the higher-ups in London."

Captain Bayfield brushed the mixture of sand and dirt from his trousers and hands. "What do you plan to ask the smuggler to do?"

"Have his men hidden in the crowd to take out whoever wields the dagger or sword."

"I see. What of the rope that will likely be around Finn's neck at the time? Buxton may be expecting you and your men to attempt a last-minute rescue, and will open the trapdoor on the scaffold."

"Me men will be aiming for the rope above Finn's head—and whoever has their hand on the wooden handle that opens the trapdoor."

Bayfield nodded. "You would be cutting it close, but it could work."

"It *will* work," Garahan insisted.

"What do you plan to offer the Frenchman to entice him to help you?

"The ransom."

"Buxton is demanding coin to release your cousin?"

Garahan's gaze drilled into Bayfield's. "He's demanding coin not to force Mollie to watch."

"I thought she was safe at Penwith Tower."

"Last I knew, the lass was." Garahan sighed audibly. "She's a worry. Bound and possessed that she'll rescue her husband—with or without our help."

"You have her well guarded," Bayfield reminded him.

"Aye, but we never underestimate the determination of a stubborn Irishwoman in love."

"We'd best get back and see if Tremayne is available to try the hole in the cave's ceiling on for size."

⤞⤝

WHEN THEY ARRIVED back at the tower, Tremayne was dismounting. Garahan hailed him. "You're back soon. What happened?"

"Our contact never showed. We'll go back later."

"I'll be tagging along with ye."

Bayfield walked over to the men, saying, "We need your bulk, Tremayne."

The lieutenant smiled. "If only you were the sweet barmaid I chanced to meet down at the Mermaid's Glass."

"Ye'd best not be letting Flaherty hear ye speak of Eileen Doonan," Garahan warned from where he sat atop his horse.

Tremayne glanced over his shoulder at Garahan. "Does your cousin have an understanding with the beauty?"

Garahan shrugged. "I've been spending more time at the

Randy Cock, so I could not say for certain, but he's warned me away from her more than once since I arrived."

The lieutenant nodded. "Duly noted. I will not have time to dally with any lovely maidens until after we set Finn free. Do you need me to act as Mollie's bodyguard?"

"Not yet. We need to see if you fit inside a hole."

Tremayne snorted with laughter. "This is the first time any of my mates admitted beforehand that they planned to toss me in a hole."

Bayfield's lips twitched. "That hole was only three feet deep. We dug it ourselves."

Tremayne's gaze narrowed. "So you said, when you found me a few hours later with a sprained ankle from the six-foot drop into the hole you dug to keep me from meeting the lovely Sarah."

"Later!" Garahan ordered them. "We need to return to the cliffside now if we are to be at the Randy Cock in time to meet with Ruan's man."

Tremayne glared at Bayfield, mounted his horse, and followed the men riding through the archway.

They rode in silence toward the cliffs. When the path started to narrow, Garahan raised his hand in silent signal to halt. He dismounted, and the men did the same. "Bayfield, ye'll stand guard here with the horses."

The captain agreed, then asked, "And if I hear anyone approaching?"

Garahan glanced around at the sparse terrain before answering the question with a question: "Know any birdcalls?"

Bayfield nodded and gave a good imitation of a mourning dove.

"Aye, that's fine, then. Just once will be enough. Normally, I'd whistle to let ye know I heard ye, but being this close to the shore—and the chances of one of Ruan's or Buxton's men discovering us—I'll answer ye with an owl's hoot." Garahan demonstrated.

"What if you need me?" Bayfield asked.

"Ah, good point," Garahan said. "If Tremayne gets stuck, it'll be a two-man job to free him."

Tremayne scowled, then suggested, "Why don't you give three short hoots if we run into trouble?"

The men agreed. Satisfied with their plan, they separated—Bayfield to stay behind as guard. Garahan motioned for Tremayne to follow as he took the path that would lead them to the ledge where he'd discovered the hole to the cave below…the cave where his cousin was being held prisoner.

Garahan stopped, and Tremayne glanced around. "I don't see any holes."

The Irishman grinned. "'Tis hidden." He walked over to a pile of rocks and removed the three perched at the top.

Tremayne walked over to lend a hand. He removed the next three, then stared at the opening they'd uncovered. He looked at the hole, then glanced at Garahan out of the side of his eye. "Is it the same width all the way through?"

"Far as I know. Bayfield didn't say otherwise."

"He wouldn't," the lieutenant grumbled. Whether or not his shoulders would fit through the opening was vital to their plan to free Finn. "Let's get it done. Where's the rope?"

Garahan reached under a large, flat-topped boulder and pulled out a coil of rope. "I can loop it around yer waist."

"Toss me one end," Tremayne ordered him. He quickly fashioned a loop and a knot.

"Looks like the one Bayfield used—is it a sailor's knot?"

Tremayne snickered. "Any one of the King's Dragoons can tie a knot that'll hold as well as any sailor in His Majesty's Royal Navy."

Pleased with the response, Garahan watched the other man slip the loop over his head and beneath one arm. He walked over to the largest boulder and tossed the rope around it twice. The added weight of the boulder would steady him as he braced himself—and the weight of the man he planned to send in through the roof of the cave. "Ready?"

Tremayne lowered himself into the opening. Waiting with his arms above his head and both hands on the rope, he nodded.

Garahan eased his hold on the rope, allowing it to slack as the other man descended into the hole.

"Bloody hell!"

Garahan spread his feet wider and braced himself to hold his position. "Are ye stuck?"

The mumbled curses were all the answer he needed.

"Hang on, I'll signal to Bayfield." Garahan gave three short hoots, and a few moments later, Bayfield arrived.

"Where's Tremayne?"

"In the bloody hole!" Tremayne answered.

Bayfield's lips twitched as he listened to Tremayne curse roundly. "Here. Let me hold the rope while you see about freeing our friend."

Garahan approached the hole and knelt next to it. Peering over the side, he assessed the situation and called over his shoulder, "Brace yerself. I'm going to shift a few stones and see if we can pull him free."

"You'd bloody well better," Tremayne grumbled.

"Ready!" Bayfield said.

Garahan slipped the dagger from his boot, lay on his belly, and reached into the hole. He dug around the first stone and pulled it free. He studied the rest of the stones before choosing another. At the frown from the lieutenant, he dug out three more.

The last stone got stuck for a moment, and when he gave it a tug, he heard the all-too-familiar sound of a rib cracking and Tremayne's sharp intake of breath. Exposed as they were for longer than they'd planned, Garahan knew they needed to hurry. He called down, "Ready?"

"Aye."

"Start pulling, Bayfield, while I brace the rope on this end."

A few grueling moments later, Garahan saw the top of Tremayne's head—and the pained expression he wasn't quick enough to hide.

Garahan and Bayfield hauled him up and over the edge of the hole. Working quickly, Garahan lifted the rope from around Tremayne and untied the knot. The three of them stacked the rocks, then coiled the rope and hid it once again beneath the flat-topped rock.

Tremayne stiffened as he swung into the saddle. Garahan wagered the rib was broken—mayhap 'twas more than one.

"O'Malley wouldn't fit," the lieutenant grumbled.

Garahan motioned for silence until they were clear of the area. "Sorry about yer ribs."

"Cracked?" Bayfield asked.

Tremayne didn't answer. Garahan knew they'd be wrapping the man's broken ribs before they had to leave for their meeting later tonight. Hopefully their contact would show up this time. "Can ye lift yer arms above yer head?"

"Already did on the way into the hole."

Garahan shook his head. "We could use men like yerselves as part of the duke's guard."

Coventry's men just smiled. "We owe our lives to the captain," Tremayne said.

Garahan nodded. Their loyalty to Captain Coventry was part of the reason they'd be welcome among the guard. "Did the captain ever tell ye who gave him the idea to hire others such as yerselves to create his own guard?"

As if they knew what Garahan was looking for—their thanks for giving the captain the idea—they shared a glance between them before shrugging.

Garahan knew then that they were having a laugh at his expense. "Ungrateful buggers."

As they approached the archway to the courtyard, Tremayne nudged his horse closer to Garahan's. "No one needs to know about my ribs."

"If it'll keep ye from doing the task assigned to ye—"

"It won't," Tremayne insisted.

Garahan hesitated. How many times had he, or his cousins and brothers, hidden what would be considered insignificant injuries from one another? Too many to count. "I'll be watching ye. If I think ye'll be more of a hindrance than a help, I'll be telling the others."

Tremayne glared at him, but finally nodded. "Agreed."

"There's a supply of linen strips on one of the shelves in the tack room. Bayfield, we'll take care of yer horse, if ye'll tell the others we'll be along shortly."

"What excuse do I give them?"

Garahan shrugged. "None."

"They'll know one of you is injured," Bayfield said. "Won't they?"

"Aye, but they'll keep it to themselves until they think it will be a problem."

"It won't," Tremayne said as they stabled the horses.

"As I said, I'll be the judge of that."

Tremayne, having no other choice, agreed.

CHAPTER NINETEEN

MOLLIE'S HANDS TREMBLED as she measured flour into the mixing bowl and spilled it. "Botheration!"

Muttering the duchess' favorite expression when she was vexed had her missing those who had been her constant companions for the last few years. Shoving that thought to the back of her mind, she carefully scooped the flour back into the container and willed her hands to steady as she measured for the second time.

Instead of the desired effect, she spilled even more flour this time. She sank onto the stool next to the table where she'd prepared the last few meals for the duke's men. Exhaustion and worry had been draining the life out of her since she'd watched those men drag Finn's unconscious body away from the shack.

Since Tremayne and the others had not gone back to the cave to rescue her husband as promised, she would!

"Finn, I'm coming to save you."

The words seemed empty, as she knew her current jailors watched her like a hawk. They would no more let her leave on her own to go after her husband than let her put out a fire in the kitchen.

A fire in the kitchen...

The idea took hold as she glanced about her. The wooden building that housed the kitchen was far enough away from the stables to not be a threat to the horses. Given that half the men were on patrol, those remaining might not notice in time to contain the small fire she planned to set.

"The stables could be a distraction if I let the horses out of their stalls." Wiping her hands on her apron, she resolved to escape to the cliffs and slip down the hole she'd overheard Garahan and the others discussing earlier. She had memorized every word, from where the rope was stashed beneath a large, flat rock, to the fact that Tremayne had injured a few ribs trying to fit into the hole. She swallowed her fear, knowing if Tremayne—who was as broad through the shoulders as her husband—did not fit, it meant Finn wouldn't either. Her worry increased, but she managed to set it aside and think about what she could expect to find. Surely he would still be bound—she'd best bring a knife with her. The problem of how to escape past the guards was too much to think of right now. Fire first, horses second. On the way to the cliffs, she would pray for inspiration.

There *had* to be a way to free Finn.

She gathered bits of twig and small branches, breaking them into pieces that would fit into the cast-iron pot she'd just scrubbed clean. After lining the bottom of the pot with them, she used one of the knives to tear a wide strip off the hem of her chemise. Tucking the knife into the pocket of her apron, she added the fabric to the pot.

"Now, what would can I use to create smoke?" Mollie remembered the time she'd accidentally knocked over the container of tallow fat when Constance left her in charge of the kitchen. The fat soaked the pile of rags she had been using to wipe out the pots before scrubbing them. Worried that she would have to listen to another lecture, she wasn't paying attention to the candle that she'd set down on the table...too close to the rags. When she'd bumped into the table, the whoosh and flames that erupted horrified her.

Mollie didn't remember screaming, but she did remember Finn bolting into the kitchen, hauling her over his shoulder and out of harm's way, while Patrick smothered the fire to put it out. She'd had to listen to *three* lectures that day. One from Constance, one from Patrick, and the one that had her hanging her head from Finn.

This time, it would not be an accident.

She poured tallow fat onto the bits of fabric, then broke off a sliver of kindling and held it over the glowing coals in the fireplace and waited for it to catch fire.

Saying a silent prayer that no one would be injured because of her actions—or that the building would burn down—she touched the flaming bit of wood to the tallow-soaked cloth, and the kindling beneath it, and waited for it to ignite. Satisfied when it began to smoke and then burn, she let herself out the side door and ran to the rear entrance of the stables.

Quiet as a mouse, she tiptoed to the first stall, lifted the latch, and watched the horse whinny in delight before running toward the open door. She waited a few moments, then opened each one of the stalls until all of the horses had been set free.

She heard the shouts then, men calling to one another as the fire was discovered. Another cry rang out when the horses charged toward the archway and thundered beneath the men patrolling the ramparts.

In the confusion, she kept to the shadows and let herself out through the little used postern gate. The rusted hinges squeaked, and she hesitated. But between the shouts of the men putting out the fire and the others who gave chase hoping to catch the horses, no one would hear the protests of the ancient gate. She moved from the shelter of the trees to the shrubs that eventually gave way to the tangle of brambles as she drew closer to the cliffs…and the cave where her love was held prisoner.

She didn't bother to look over her shoulder—she knew someone would put two and two together and realize what she'd done.

Hands trembling, she prayed no one would stop her.

Coil of rope in her hands, she looked for something to tie it to. The only thing that looked as if it would do the job was a stump of a tree. After tying off the rope, she gathered the rest and carried it over to the pile of rocks. She removed them quickly, knowing at any moment that someone would catch her.

She tied the rope around her waist, prayed, then lowered herself into the black opening. Bouncing off the tight walls of the passage, she winced. Last night, the duke's men had reported seeing Finn propped up against the wall of the cave, but to avoid detection, they had been observing him from a distance. He did not know anyone was planning to free him. Not one of the duke's men had voiced the worry that slashed across her heart—he could die, and the bastards who captured him would leave him there to rot!

Bile rushed up her throat, but she clenched her jaws and willed it to recede. Nothing would prevent her from freeing Finn. Using the toe of her half boot, she tapped it to the sides of the passage again and again to keep from slamming into the rocks as she continued her descent. Wrapping one leg around the rope, she felt the fabric of her gown snag on it. Why hadn't she thought to borrow—well, appropriate—a pair of trousers from Flaherty or Garahan? She'd done that too many times to count growing up— trying to keep up with her older brother.

He never minded that she tagged along—he even showed her how to climb a rope, and hit a target dead center firing an arrow—and pistol.

The lower she climbed, the more she regretted not taking the time to plan for all aspects of Finn's rescue. She could have at least thought to wrap her hands with a linen strip or worn gloves. The skin of her palms scraped at first, then ripped and tore with each successive handhold. They would be raw by the time she climbed the rest of the way down.

If she had waited, someone would have been up at the top, lowering her to the bottom. Too late now to grumble over what-ifs. She should be more worried about whether she'd calculated correctly—if not, she would run out of rope before she reached the bottom.

Lord, please let there be enough rope—so I only have to fall six feet instead of sixteen!

FLAHERTY WAS THE first one to reach the kitchen. He stopped and stared at the smoke billowing up out of the cast-iron pot in the middle of the kitchen table. "Bloody hell! Mollie!"

His angry bellow was echoed by Garahan's from where he stood in the middle of the empty stables.

The duke calmly concluded that Mollie O'Malley had started the fire in the kitchen—reminding him of the near-disaster his guard and his cook had once regaled him with. Mollie had accidentally started a fire in the kitchen at Wyndmere Hall that could have burned the entire structure to the ground! He never questioned whether it had been an accident—the poor maid was horrified when he spoke to her on his return from London.

This time was no accident.

Setting the horses free was inspired. "A double diversion," he remarked as he strode toward the men gathered who were not due on patrol for another hour. "It appears as if Finn's wife has decided to go after him on her own."

The men's faces mirrored the expression he tried to hide—the overriding fear that Mollie would be caught trying to free Finn. There was no telling what the deranged excise official Buxton would do if he had her in his clutches a second time.

"Does she know the way to the caves?" the duke asked.

Flaherty nodded. "She stubbornly insisted on accompanying us there after we rescued her. Her sense of direction is keen— even in the dark."

The duke wished to God he'd heeded his wife's suggestion and ordered two men to guard Mollie. The young woman was as strong-willed as his Persephone. The memory of the times his wife had been in acute danger had him bellowing, "Find her and bring her back!"

"Aye, Yer Grace." Flaherty waved to the two men who had already managed to find four of the horses.

"Garahan, you and Tremayne head into town. We need your contact to observe your arriving a bit early and acting as if nothing is wrong."

"It's my fault she went to all of this trouble to go after her husband," Tremayne said.

"How so?" the duke asked.

"After I rescued her from the shack, she demanded I turn around and chase after Buxton and his men to free O'Malley."

"The two of you against Buxton and nearly half a dozen of his men?"

"If I had turned back—"

"The both of you would be bound and gagged alongside O'Malley…or worse—dead!"

Tremayne fell silent as the commotion of a few more horses returning caught everyone's attention.

Flaherty audibly sighed. Every man felt the same…acute relief. They'd be stranded without their horses. Turning back to the discussion at hand, he said, "The lass wasn't thinking clearly— she was reacting to the shock of it."

"I gave my word that I would go after Finn," Tremayne added.

"And we did," Flaherty reminded him. "We discovered where they took him and that there were too many guards posted around the outside of the cave, and inside, for the two of us to handle—especially with Mollie bound and determined to save Finn. We had no choice but to return and bide our time to plan his escape."

"The wait plagued her," Garahan said. "We all knew it. I pray ye reach her before she's recaptured." He nodded to Tremayne. "We'd best head to the village."

A group of men lined up, ready to relieve those on patrol along the coastline. Flaherty walked over to discuss the change in their routine. They would be staying on patrol for eight hours instead of four. Instructions received, the men rode out single file.

The duke nodded to Flaherty. "A word, Flaherty."

"Aye, Yer Grace." The two men walked over to the stairs leading up to the ramparts. Ascending them, they watched the two riders head toward the village, and the group of men riding in the opposite direction.

The duke watched the riders disappear and confided, "I cannot help but remember the actions of the women in my family when the men they love were threatened."

"Her Grace and Lady Phoebe held strong the night of the ball when they'd been told you were dead," Flaherty said.

"The same night that madman held my sister at knifepoint." The duke shook his head. "And the time Lady Aurelia and Lady Calliope deliberately disobeyed direct orders *not* to go to Chalk Farm to prevent the duels their husbands were involved in."

"Ye could add yer nanny—Patrick's wife—and our cousins Michael and Sean O'Malley's wives as well."

"Good God, is it my fate to be surrounded by stubborn women who refuse to listen when their own safety is being threatened?"

"It would seem that ye are, Yer Grace. By the same token, 'tis me fate—and that of me cousins and brothers—to protect the lot of ye."

"I'm grateful, Flaherty."

"I'll say a prayer that we arrive in time," Flaherty said. "Finn will have our heads if he gets out of this alive and finds out Mollie set fire to the kitchen and set our horses loose so she could rescue him."

"Indeed," the duke replied, descending the stairs. "God help us."

Flaherty was right behind him. "A fitting prayer, Yer Grace."

The duke and Flaherty left instructions with those left to guard Penwith Tower, while their horses were saddled. With a nod, the duke let Flaherty lead the way to the cliffs.

"The lass had a head start," Flaherty said as they approached the bend in the path and the ledge they were looking for. He jolted to a stop when he saw the rope wrapped around the nearly rotted tree stump. "Bloody hell!"

The duke beat him to the rope by a second. The two worked to untangle the rope as the wood gave way and split in two. Between them, they held fast.

The stifled scream from below the surface had them reacting with lightning speed. While the duke braced his weight to hold the rope—and the woman dangling from the other end—Flaherty wrapped it around the large boulder they'd used before. With the rope secured, the two men leaned over the opening and saw a glimpse of auburn as the lass dangling from the rope spun around and around.

"Hang on, Mollie," Flaherty called in a low voice. He couldn't take the chance his voice would carry through the cave to where the guards were no doubt stationed.

"How far down is it to the bottom?" the duke asked.

"I never asked Bayfield, though I know he had enough rope to reach the bottom."

The duke frowned. "Did he mention jumping the last few feet?"

"Nay."

"We should hoist her up," the duke said.

Flaherty met the duke's steady gaze and shook his head. "She'll fight like a wildcat if we do."

"Do you want to risk her life if she's captured?" the duke asked.

"Do ye want to risk the skin on yer face if we haul her up?"

"As a matter of fact," the duke answered, "I do."

"Well then, let's put our backs into it," Flaherty said. "When she's close enough, ye can be the one to explain why she's going up instead of down."

A few moments later, they heard mumbled curses and saw the top of her head at the bottom of the opening a few feet down.

Her gaze met Flaherty's, and the tilt of her chin and blaze of hate in her eyes had him nodding to the duke. "I'll be letting ye be the one to reach for her hand, Yer Grace."

The duke lay on his belly and reached down into the opening. When their gazes met, the abject misery on Mollie's face gutted him. "It was my decision not to lower you, Mollie. Do not take it out on Flaherty."

She bit her lip and nodded.

The duke paused, one hand grasping Mollie's, the other beneath her arm. "Your *word*, Mrs. O'Malley."

The first tear spilled over, though she made not a sound. Her nod was enough answer for the duke. He pulled her out of the opening.

Her tears flowed as she fumbled with the knot she'd fashioned.

"Allow me," the duke said.

She drew in a deep breath and slowly exhaled. "Thank you, Your Grace. I promise I won't fight Flaherty or anyone else." Head down, shoulders slumped, she seemed to be waiting for whatever harsh lecture the duke would mete out.

He wanted to yell at her, shake her until she admitted she had been wrong to have taken such rash steps to rescue her husband, but Persephone's voice, and reminder, echoed through his head: *A woman will go to any lengths to save the man she loves.*

Her words calmed him to where he could say, "Wait here with Flaherty."

"What are you going to do?" Mollie asked.

The duke did not bother to answer. He locked gazes with Flaherty, who understood and checked the loops around the boulder before tossing the gloves he'd tucked in his pocket to the duke. "Ye'll need these."

"I don't think—"

Mollie lifted her hands, palms facing the duke. "Neither did I—please wear the gloves, Your Grace."

"Dear God!" the duke said, seeing her injuries.

"They'll heal, Your Grace. Please wear the gloves...and be careful."

He did as she asked, then retrieved the pistol from his frockcoat pocket and slipped it in the waistband of his trousers. He tied a knot in the rope, looped it over one shoulder, and braced himself in the opening. "Ready when you are, Flaherty."

"Give one tug when you want me to stop. Two tugs if there's trouble."

The duke shook his head. "What could you possibly do from up here if something's wrong?"

The Irishman slowly smiled. "Follow ye down, while Mollie here stands watch."

"Then O'Malley will have *both* our hides if anything happens to her."

"Faith, he already will when he finds out the lengths she went to attempt the rescue him without our help."

The duke rolled his eyes. "Pray, then, that nothing untoward occurs while I reconnoiter and release Finn." He turned his gaze to meet Mollie's. "Do not worry, Mollie—we'll find a way to extricate O'Malley from his prison."

✦

FLAHERTY KEPT PROPER tension on the rope as he lowered the duke through the opening. He jolted for a moment when the weight on the other end of the rope disappeared. "He's reached the bottom."

Ignoring her injured hands, Mollie braced her weight against her palms and leaned over the hole.

"Have a care," Flaherty warned.

The sound of a pistol firing—and the report of another—had Flaherty adding an extra knot to the rope to prevent it from moving. He rushed over to the opening and dropped to his knees but could not see anything. Another shot echoed through the darkness.

"Ye gave His Grace yer word, Mollie. Ye'd best keep it. I have to go after him!"

Flaherty checked the pistol he'd tucked in his waistband, then pulled the dagger from his boot and placed it between his teeth. With a look that brooked no arguments, he grabbed hold of the rope and quickly dropped from sight.

Mollie could not wring her battered hands to ease the agitation welling up inside of her. So she did the next best thing—she prayed.

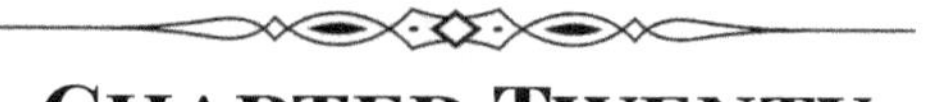

CHAPTER TWENTY

FINN O'MALLEY ROUSED when something poked him in the back. Blinking, he fought to stay conscious. Had he blacked out again? Was it from lack of sleep, or being knocked unconscious? Maybe he was slowly bleeding to death from a wound he could not feel.

He huffed out the breath he didn't remember drawing in, and felt pain welling through his ribcage. *Bloody hell*—he'd broken another rib. Taking stock of the injuries he remembered receiving, he noted the most serious would be the entry and exit wounds from the lead ball he'd taken in the arm—and the knife wound in his back. Thank God Flaherty had insisted on cauterizing the wounds—it was faster than sewing him back together.

Mollie-lass—wherever ye are, I'll find ye. Once I have ye in me arms, I'll never let ye go!

The jab to the back of his arm had pain slicing from one side of the pistol ball wound to the other. Someone was definitely behind him. He reasoned that it wouldn't be one of Buxton's men—they'd be coming at him from the mouth of the cave, not the dark recesses behind him.

"Whoever ye are, state yer business."

The answering chuckle was barely audible, but he heard it.

"If ye're one of me cousins, I'll deal with ye later."

"It's Wyndmere."

Shock had O'Malley momentarily speechless. When his tongue unknotted itself, he rasped, "Yer Grace!"

"Aye. Hold still while I slice through your bonds."

"If ye could nick one of me hands, I'd be grateful. I've lost all feeling from me shoulders to me wrists and hope it's a temporary affliction."

The duke made short work of cutting through his bonds, causing Finn's arms to feel like weights were attached to his wrists weighing them down.

"Did they bind your ankles too?"

"Aye. I'm not sure if can hold the knife in me hands just yet."

The duke moved into Finn's line of vision. With a flick of his wrist, he sliced through the ropes around his ankles, setting him free. "Don't try to stand up yet. I'm going to see if I can get closer and see how many men are standing guard."

"'Tis too dangerous, Yer Grace. I'll go."

The duke sent him a telling look that suggested Finn had lost his mind. "Work the feeling back into your hands and feet while I'm gone."

Pins and needles jabbed into Finn's hands as he placed them on the ground beside his legs and pressed his weight against them. All at once, the feeling returned with a vengeance. He could feel the sharp edges of rocks mingled with the sand on the floor of the cave. Ignoring the discomfort, he rubbed his hands together for good measure.

He worked the feeling back into his legs and ankles, welcoming the pain that came with the reawakening of his limbs.

"Five," the duke said, rejoining Finn.

The crunch of a heavy footfall behind them had Finn freezing.

"Relax," a familiar voice said. "'Tis yer favorite cousin."

The duke released a sigh of relief. "Finn's got the feeling back in his arms and legs, Flaherty."

"His Grace noted there are five men standing guard," Finn said. "If ye give me the blade ye keep in yer boot, Flaherty, we can easily take them between the three of us."

Flaherty handed his dagger to his cousin and met the duke's searching gaze. "Don't be worrying about our man Finn here—he's the devil's own talent with a blade."

"It's not that," the duke said. "I'm worried about Mollie."

"What's happened to me wife?" Finn asked.

"She was fine when we left her a little while ago."

Finn fought to control his temper and keep his voice pitched low. "And where in the bloody hell would that be?"

"Above yer hard head!" Flaherty answered. "She set the kitchen on fire and let the horses loose so we wouldn't notice she left the safety of Penwith Tower."

Finn glared at his cousin. "Did ye tie her up to keep her from coming down through the blasted hole above us?"

"Would have if I'd thought of it," Flaherty admitted. "Before we arrived, the lass climbed halfway down a rope that she'd lashed around a rotted stump."

"Dear God! Is she all right?"

"She's been afraid for yer life, fretting and begging us to go after ye before we had all of the information we needed about Buxton and the men guarding ye."

"I hope she borrowed a pair of yer gloves."

When Flaherty did not answer right away, Finn had his answer. "She'll need her hands tended to. I'll see that she doesn't lift a finger till she's healed."

"An excellent notion, Finn, as you will be waiting for your own injuries to heal," the duke told him.

Finn snorted. "I'll not be arguing with the men freeing me—at least until we're well away from this place and I have me wife in me arms. Then we'll discuss who will be guarding me wife when we go up against Buxton's lackeys."

"How many of those standing guard would you recognize if you saw them again?" the duke asked.

"Every blasted one of them."

"Did you learn any of their names? It will help when they are remanded to the authorities and transported to London."

"Dickens, Hawley, Sanderson, Montgomery, and Clemmets."

As one, the group, weapons in hand, silently moved forward.

Finn glanced at his cousin, and Flaherty nodded. The duke raised an eyebrow in silent question, then nodded. Finn tilted his head back and bellowed his O'Malley ancestors' battle cry. It rang through the cave and bounced off the walls, startling the group of men, giving the duke and his men the advantage.

Two of the men threw down their pistols, while another froze in his tracks. Flaherty disarmed one, and the duke disarmed the other.

"Nice work, men," the duke announced. After slipping the pistol he'd taken from his prisoner into the waistband of his trousers, he lashed the man's hands behind his back.

Flaherty was doing the same to his prisoner when the man who'd frozen at the battle cry tried to slip away. "Finn, behind ye."

Finn didn't bother to turn around as he kicked his foot straight out behind him, connecting with the man's kneecap. "I'll tie him up in a moment. Keep an eye on him, Flaherty."

"Done."

The duke retrieved one of the discarded pistols and handed it to Finn, who tucked it in his waistband, then reached for the other pistol. "I'm thinking we'd best gag them. What do ye think, Yer Grace?"

The duke reached into his waistcoat pocket and retrieved his handkerchief.

O'Malley shook his head. "Too good for the likes of them. The sleeve of me coat's just the thing—'tis slashed and bloody. Hold on while I remove it. We can cut the sleeve into strips to gag them with."

"We may as well use yer other sleeve, too," Flaherty said.

"For?" Finn asked.

"Blindfolds."

"A sound notion," the duke said.

The men made short work of the process, then stood back to survey their handiwork.

Finn urged, "We'd best leave. I need to see me wife."

"She'll be waiting for you, Finn. Don't let your heart get in the way of your head until we're topside," the duke warned him.

"Follow me," Flaherty said, leading the way toward the mouth of the cave. With the five guards bound, gagged, and blindfolded inside the cave, there was no one standing guard outside.

The sun was low on the horizon when they reached the summit of the path. Finn looked over the area, worried when he didn't see his wife. "Where is she?"

"Finn?"

He squinted, and relief swamped him. His wife uncurled herself from where she sat on top of the largest boulder—the highest point on the ledge. She jumped to her feet and ran straight into his arms.

"Mollie-lass!" His voice broke over her name as he pulled her into his arms, desperate to hold her to his heart. "God, I thought the next time I'd see ye would be on the other side of the Pearly Gates." He heard her snort of laughter and laughed along with her, admitting, "Aye, 'twill be a stretch to mend me ways if I plan to make it to Heaven. Sure and ye won't be joining me in the fiery flames of Hell."

"It is my job as your wife to look after your soul."

Finn's deep chuckle surrounded them. "Well now, and here I thought 'twas yer job to take care of me *mmpffhh*—" His voice was muffled against Mollie's lips.

Flaherty's sharp bark of laughter rang out. The duke grinned when he clapped a hand to his man's shoulder. "It would seem all is well with these two. We'd best head back and be ready for the news Garahan and Tremayne bring us."

Ignoring his bruised and battered body, Finn swept his wife into his arms. "We'll be right behind ye."

Flaherty walked over and poked his finger in his cousin's

shoulder. "Ye'll lead the way back. We'll be riding behind the two of ye."

"I don't need ye to guard me back," Finn grumbled.

Flaherty glared at him. "I know ye like I know me own heart, and I'm telling ye, there's no time to do what ye have in mind."

Finn's frown was fierce. "How do ye know what I have in mind?" Mollie tucked her head beneath her husband's chin, but not before Finn heard her soft laughter. "Stay out of this, wife—I'll be dealing with ye later."

"I hope so."

The duke's lips twitched, but he pretended not to hear Mollie's reply and asked, "Has Buxton's guard in the cave changed today?"

"Nay, why do ye—Ah, I see. Their relief should be arriving soon. We'd best be off then, love."

Flaherty and the duke mounted their horses, while Finn carefully set his wife on their horse's back. After vaulting onto the animal, he slipped her onto his lap. "Close yer eyes and rest yer head, lass."

"I can't hold on to your coat?" She stared at the torn and bloodstained sleeves of his cambric shirt, where his frockcoat sleeves should be. "Where are your sleeves?"

"I'll explain later…after ye tell me how ye managed to escape from me cousins and injure yer poor, sweet hands."

She sighed and agreed, adding, "I had to—"

"Listen to what those protecting ye bid ye to do. Ye're to follow whatever they say—no matter if ye agree or not. 'Tis the only way I'll be able to concentrate on me job, knowing ye're safe from harm, love."

Mollie whispered, "I did not think of it that way."

"From this moment forward, ye will."

"Aye, Finn. You have my word."

"We'll tend to yer hands—and the rest of ye—when we arrive at Penwith Tower." Wrapping his uninjured arm around her, he promised, "I won't let you fall."

"I already have," she whispered.

Concern marred his brow. "When? Did ye hurt yerself?"

She motioned for him to lean closer. When he did, she pressed her lips to his a second time. "Bumps and bruises are part of the journey of falling in love with you, Finn O'Malley."

"I love ye, lass."

"I love you too, Finn."

He growled low in his throat. "Now, for the love of God, close yer eyes!"

Mollie did as he bade and let the heat of her husband's embrace, accompanied by the cadence of the horse's gait, lull her to sleep.

CHAPTER TWENTY-ONE

GARAHAN AND TREMAYNE sat across from the Frenchman at a table in the back of the Randy Cock.

"Why do you think *mon capitaine* would wish to join forces with Englishmen?"

Garahan snickered. "I'm Irish." Pointing to the man sitting beside him, he said, "He's English."

"And proud of it, mate," Tremayne added. "We aren't after joining forces with Ruan."

Garahan leveled his gaze at the man sitting across from them. The Frenchman was equal in size to Tremayne, and his cousin Finn—he'd be an adversary to be wary of. "We're after setting a trap for Buxton. He'll answer to his superiors in His Majesty's Excise Office for looking the other way and lining his pockets while the free trade continues along our coastline."

"Ah, but it has been lucrative for *mon capitaine*—and those who are loyal to him. What would we have to gain?"

"Ruan and yourself surely realize—as do we—that smuggling will continue to some extent as long as taxes are levied on imported goods," Tremayne said.

The Frenchman remained silent.

"If ye help us expose Buxton, ye will see more of the profits," Flaherty added.

"And you will not interfere?"

Garahan laughed. "I could lie and tell ye we won't."

The smuggler smiled. "*Oui*, you could. We both know that you will continue to rout us from the caves beneath the duke's tower."

"'Tis our job," Garahan said.

"And mine is to see that *mon capitaine's* cargo reaches your shoreline and is distributed to those who have paid for our services."

"Unless and until we can convince the locals who are struggling to survive along this harsh coast otherwise," Tremayne said, "we will do our best to see that you do not use His Grace's caves for your ill-gotten booty."

"Bought and paid for," the Frenchman corrected him.

Tremayne frowned, and Garahan jabbed him with his elbow. "'Tisn't the issue here. Using His Grace's caves is."

The Frenchman leaned across the table. "You would look the other way if we stored our cargo elsewhere?"

"Aye," Garahan said. This time Tremayne kicked him under the table. Garahan glared at the lieutenant. "As neither His Majesty's Excise Office, nor Customs Office, have hired us to patrol the coastline, to keep smugglers and wreckers from plying their trade, our duty is solely to His Grace, the Duke of Wyndmere. *He* is adamant ye do not use his caves."

"I can assure *mon capitaine* that you do not plan to extort a percentage from him for looking the other way?"

Tremayne snorted. "Aye, but know this—we will *not* be looking the other way. Our efforts will be concentrated on protecting the Duke of Wyndmere, his family, and his properties. There are other authorities who will see to it that your efforts will be curtailed."

"In return, we ask ye to help us rid the village of St. Ives of its crooked excise official and his men," Garahan said.

The smuggler lifted his tankard and drained it. Setting it on the table, he said, "*Bien*, I shall deliver your message and will return with an answer in two hours."

Tremayne and Garahan nodded, then stood to shield the other man as he slipped through the back door into the night. If anyone saw them speaking to the seaman, they would think nothing of it. Patrons of the Randy Cock knew to keep their mouths shut.

The two men shared a look before making their way to the front of the tavern. With a nod to the man behind the bar, they left.

Once they were well away from the village, Tremayne asked, "Do you think Ruan will agree?"

"Yer guess is as good as mine. He may see our offer as a challenge. Ye know as well as I do there are other caves he could use. His Grace's are the most convenient."

"Aye," Tremayne agreed. "If we do not interfere with the smugglers and wreckers, the duke's presence here may no longer be met with resistance. Even though my gut tells me to turn over every free trader we encounter to the authorities, that is not what we are here to do."

"'Tisn't that I want to look the other way—there are times when it is inevitable that we will happen upon smugglers when they are on the duke's property—but Ruan has been warned. Finn and Flaherty have been sending reports to the duke all along as to the state of things in St. Ives. His Grace is well aware of the situation."

"You cousins have other duties that are more pressing than capturing smugglers," Tremayne said.

"Aye, protecting the duke and his family has been more of a challenge than the lot of us ever thought it would be."

Tremayne nodded. "Captain Coventry has mentioned once or twice the gravity of some of the situations you and the rest of the duke's guard have faced while performing your duties."

"And what we're facing at the moment, which is why Coventry loaned ye to His Grace. We're grateful, Tremayne."

"My pleasure, Garahan."

Garahan signaled to the men on the ramparts, then rode

beneath the guards into pandemonium.

Immediately on guard, he and Tremayne dismounted, handed the reins off to one of the stable lads, and strode toward the circle of men arguing.

"ME WIFE GOES where I go."

Flaherty got in Finn's face and growled, "Unless ye expect her to be following ye to the gates of Hell, she stays with me."

Finn immediately replied, "I'd be grateful."

Mollie crossed her arms in front of her and frowned at her husband. "I'm going with you, Finn."

"Lass, I cannot believe ye'd argue when ye know 'tis out of the question. Ye're carrying our babe. Ye're not a cat—though I'm thinking ye've already used up three of yer nine lives."

Flaherty's lips twitched, and Finn shot him a warning look. Flaherty cleared his throat and held his hands up in front of him. "His Grace will return shortly. Hennessey and Bayfield rode with him to the manor house to speak with the caretakers."

"Problem?" Garahan asked.

Finn shrugged. "Other than the building that used to house our kitchen burning to the ground?" He turned to glare at his wife. "'Tis a mystery what happened. Not one man questioned has a bloody clue how the fire started."

"Just because you've given an order, Finn," Mollie informed her husband, "does not mean I will obey it."

"If I have to tie ye to the bedposts, I will." Mollie's eyes widened and her face flushed. She opened her mouth to speak, but Finn beat her to it. "'Tisn't pleasure I have in mind, lass."

Mollie marched over to Finn and poked him in the chest. "How could you embarrass me like that?"

"'Tis a side benefit, if it'll gain yer agreement to obey me."

"Obey you?" She squared her shoulders and tilted her chin up to meet his gaze. "I am never speaking to you again!" She whirled around and stomped away.

Finn glared at her back and started counting. When he reached ten, he stalked after her. "Ye're me wife, and ye'll obey me!"

"When pigs fly!"

Finn's stride was longer. He easily caught up to her and scooped her off her feet.

And that was when the first wager was placed. Flaherty took Finn's side, while Garahan bet Mollie would be the winner in the contest of wills.

When they turned to Tremayne, he raised his hands in the air. "I never get involved in family matters."

Mollie struggled in Finn's arms for a few minutes, then stilled. Garahan stated the obvious: "She's no match for Finn's strength."

"Aye, but he'll temper it. He loves the lass," Flaherty added.

The men agreed and waited until the couple disappeared through the massive wooden door to the great hall.

"Patrick and Finn have chosen well. Their wives will lead them on a merry chase," Flaherty said.

"And keep them on their toes," Garahan murmured, "as will Sean and Michael's wives." He turned to stare at Flaherty and slowly smiled. "I hear there's a lass down at the Mermaid's Glass that has caught yer eye. Thinking of marrying her?"

Flaherty's face paled. Instead of answering, he spun on his heel and stalked toward the stables.

"He's the next one of us to fall," Garahan predicted.

CHAPTER TWENTY-TWO

F INN KICKED THE door closed with the heel of his boot and
kept walking.

"Where are we going?" he asked.

"Somewhere there's a stout bolt on the door."

Mollie's soft laughter soothed the worst of the worry he
carried. "I thought ye weren't speaking to me."

She was smiling when she lifted her chin high. "I'm not."

"Well then, since ye aren't speaking to me, mayhap we can
find another way to communicate." He strode across the wide
expanse of the great hall, his footsteps ringing against the wood
floor.

Mollie wanted to hang on to her anger at being told to obey
in front of Finn's men, but her husband's warmth penetrated her
woolen shawl, gown, and chemise. His powerful musculature
wrapped her in a cocoon of protection she'd never felt before.
Finn was many things, but a brute was not one of them. She
knew she'd angered him with the steps she'd had to take to free
him. And she owed him an apology.

He stopped in front of the stone wall on the opposite end of
the room, and she was about to ask why when he pressed his
hand against the rocks and lifted a latch.

"I thought this was part of the wall," she said.

"Ye're meant to, lass. 'Twould fool anyone unfamiliar with

Penwith Tower, and will be where we'll be spending the next hour—uninterrupted."

Her heart began to pound a wild rhythm. "Will we?"

"However long it takes to convince ye the reasons ye must obey me."

She stiffened in his arms. "I do not like the word *obey*."

He inclined his head and once again used the heel of his boot to shut the door.

Mollie turned her head one way and then the other, taking in the cozy room. There was a bed pushed up against the far wall— big enough for two. A small table and two chairs sat opposite the bed. If not for the thin shafts of moonlight coming through the tiny window at the top of the wall, the room would be in complete darkness.

He placed his knee on the bed and gently laid her in the middle of it, then stepped back. "Now then, lass, ye'll need to pay attention. I'll only say this once."

His stern tone was all the indication she needed to know that he was going to use that word again.

Needing him to understand she had no intention of being a silent and biddable wife, she jumped to her feet. With a glare to match his own, she put her hands on her hips and leaned forward.

The next thing she knew, she was flat on her back with Finn pinning her to the mattress. Her arms were above her head, though he held her wrists in the gentlest of grips. He accidentally brushed the palm of one hand. Pain had her sucking in a breath.

His emerald eyes mirrored the pain she felt. "Ah, lass, why did ye not wait for Flaherty or Garahan to accompany ye?"

The expression on his face—a mix of sadness and worry—had her throat tightening the longer he stared at her. She could not have answered if she wanted to.

"Mollie-lass, I never want to see ye in such pain again." He bent and pressed a featherlight kiss to the side of the hand he'd brushed against. "Yer poor wee hands."

"They will heal. Had I not orchestrated your release, how

long would it have been before your cousins and Coventry's men rescued you?"

His brow furrowed. "I'm not liking the thought of anyone having to come to me rescue."

"The mighty Finn doesn't need anyone's help, does he?" she asked.

"Nay." As soon as he said the words, his expression changed. "He only needs one thing, lass."

Righteous indignation filled her as she prepared herself to hear that he needed her to obey him. Not going to happen in this lifetime—or the next!

He leaned on his elbows and lowered his mouth to hers. Softly, sweetly, he kissed her. "I need to know ye're safe, happy, and waiting for me return." To her utter shock, his eyes filled. He regained control of his emotions, but not before a tear slipped past his guard as he confessed, "On my honor, lass, I love ye more than me own life. It would kill me if anything happened to ye."

She did not realize *she* was crying until she felt the tip of his finger brush beneath her lashes to wipe away her tears. "I thought I would die when I watched Buxton's men drag your unconscious body from the shack and haul you into the back of that wagon." More tears gathered, but she willed them away.

He rolled over so their positions were reversed; he was on the bottom, and she was now looking down into the depths of his brilliant green eyes. Finn wasn't trying to hide his feelings from her. She had to tell him the truth.

"I tried to forget you, but still I was devastated when I found out you asked the duke to transfer you here—so far away from me. I thought you hated me...but then you came back when the twins' lives were being threatened by kidnappers."

"I will always come back to ye, lass."

"I could not let you walk away from me again without showing you how I felt about you."

His lips twitched. The grin she'd dreamed about when they were apart slowly transformed his agony to happiness. "Ye were a wild thing the night I let ye seduce me."

She narrowed her eyes. "*Let* me?"

"Oh aye, lass. I may have pretended not to notice ye intended to have yer way with me. It was a ruse. Yer every emotion was on yer beautiful face—even a blind man would be able to guess what ye had in mind."

"You *let* me seduce you," she repeated.

"Ye seem to be having a bit of trouble with that. Shall I explain it again?"

"No!" Good Lord, he'd known how she felt about him all along, and knew she planned to seduce him? A dark thought slithered through her belly. She tried to shove it away, but couldn't. She had to know the truth!

"Were you ever planning to save my reputation...or did you marry me because of our babe?" she asked. He hesitated for a moment, but it was long enough for her to explode with anger. "I thought you loved me?"

Clearly perplexed by her lightning-fast mood shift, but prepared for her temper, he rolled again until he was once more on top. "I do love ye. Haven't ye been listening?"

"I have," she said, trying to scoot out from under him. "You let me seduce you, and you never intended to marry me."

"I never intended to marry *anyone!*"

His words arrowed through her. The pain drained her, leaving her feeling hollowed out. Broken. Unable to look at him, she turned her head away and closed her eyes.

"Look at me, lass."

She ignored him.

His anger was quick to ignite. She felt his body stiffen before he commanded, "I said, look at me!"

She couldn't care less...and she wouldn't look at him. Finn O'Malley—the man she loved, had given herself to—had never intended to marry her. Good God! How could she spend the rest of her life loving her husband, knowing he could barely tolerate being in the same room with her?

"Set me aside—please, Finn!"

HIS BIG BODY jolted in response to her words. Set his wife aside? Ignore the babe in her belly and the ache in his heart just thinking of his life without Mollie in it? Never!

With jerky movements, he got off the bed and walked to the other side of the room. The knock on the door echoed in the quiet.

"That'll be our meal. I made arrangements for it to be served, thinking ye'd be hungry."

"How did you manage that when the kitchens…" Her voice trailed off. "Never mind."

"I noticed the burned-out structure when we rode in, so I asked one of the stable lads to fetch us something to eat. Ye have to know that a man cannot toil on an empty stomach, lass." He opened the door, thanked the lad, and latched the door once again. Standing with his back pressed against it, he said, "Now then, what will it take to convince ye I wanted this marriage as much as ye did."

Her reply cut him to the bone. "How can I ever trust you again? You lied to me."

"I never lied to ye. I simply left out a few pertinent details of our situation."

The knock sounded again. "I'm giving ye five minutes to make yerselves presentable, then I'm coming in to see to yer wounds."

"James?" Mollie asked.

Pitching his voice low, Finn answered, "Aye. Garahan's been a royal pain in me arse."

"We'll be needing ten minutes!"

His wife's eyes matched the upward tilt of her lips. She was smiling. He knew then that all hope wasn't lost. He could convince her to forget all about setting her aside.

"For the love of God," Garahan called. "Ye're a right beast to think of yer needs while ye wife's hands need attention."

"Nine minutes!" Finn said, drawing his wife into his embrace. There was so much he wanted to tell her—though knowing Garahan, he wouldn't take the hint. He'd start pounding on the door.

"Ye won't be getting food or drink until the both of ye have had yer injuries tended to," another voice insisted from the other side of the door.

"Flaherty?"

"Who the hell do ye think would be standing beside our cousin, while yer poor wife is at yer mercy?"

Finn wanted to shout, but one look at the sadness creeping into his wife's eyes stopped him cold. "Ye're right, lads." He pressed a kiss to the top of her head, settled her onto one of the chairs, and opened the door.

Garahan stumbled into the room. "Ye should be shot for doing what we knew ye were about to do."

Finn's mouth opened, but no sound came out. He clamped it shut and shoved Garahan into Flaherty, who was standing in the doorway. "Ye'll mind yer words—and yer tone—in me wife's presence."

"If ye're willing to listen to reason and let Flaherty see to her injuries," Garahan said, "I need to have a word with ye—in private."

Finn looked over his shoulder at his wife and the dejected expression on her face. "'Tisn't that we're keeping secrets from ye, lass," he said. "None of us are at liberty to speak of our duties to the duke. 'Tis part of the vow we took."

"Aye," Garahan said. "Patrick, Sean, and Michael are held to the same vows. Not a one of them can confide their duties to their wives."

Flaherty nodded as he set a tray on the table where Mollie sat. As he sprinkled a handful of herbs into the bowl of steaming water, he met her gaze. "Surely ye heard Patrick's wife complain a time or two about him being close-mouthed?"

"I've heard tales from our cousins—stationed in London and at Chattsworth Manor—that Sean and Michael's wives have similar complaints," Garahan said.

Finn watched the careful way Flaherty held Mollie's hand. When his cousin looked at him, Finn saw the anguish in his eyes. "'Tis the truth, lass. After what we've both been through since we were ambushed, ye cannot think I would lie to ye."

Mollie's eyes met his. "You wouldn't lie, but you'd hide the truth from me…if you thought it would protect me."

"Ye'll just have to trust me, then. Won't ye?"

Mollie sighed. "What choice do I have?"

Finn's gut clenched. She didn't trust him.

The hand on his shoulder squeezed—his cousin's silent entreaty that it was urgent they speak now.

"Trust that I am protecting ye," he said as he nodded to Garahan. He had one foot across the threshold when he paused to tell her, "I love ye, lass."

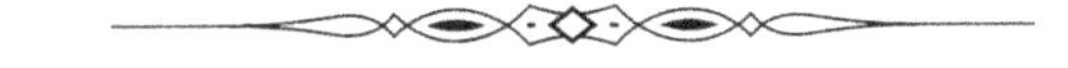

CHAPTER TWENTY-THREE

MOLLIE WATCHED HER husband's retreating form and knew she should trust him. Hadn't she asked the same of him the night she'd given herself to him? Although he hadn't audibly staked his claim with an offer of undying love—or the promise of marriage—truthfully, she had not asked for either.

She had followed her heart—a heart so full of love for the devastatingly handsome Irishman that she'd had no choice but to seduce him when he kept her at arm's length. Their few stolen kisses had fanned the flames of desire that ignited whenever they were in the same room.

Her virtue was hers to give to whomever she chose. She'd planned to save it for the man she married—until the day Finn O'Malley waltzed into her life. Her heart was his from the moment his emerald-green gaze collided with hers. But the worry that he'd married her out of a misplaced sense of honor niggled at the back of her mind. She'd set out to tempt him. His earlier words came back to her...he let *her* seduce *him*—he'd known her intentions all along.

Did that change their situation, or shift the blame? Blame—no, there had never been any blame. Desire? Yes. Passion? Absolutely. Love? Mayhap—at least on her side.

The need to put the question to him was a living, breathing thing. When he returned, his injuries would be seen to, his empty belly filled…and then she would ask him: was it his honor and the babe in her belly that forced his hand?

The sliver of doubt crept in while Flaherty tended to her hands. By the time he'd carefully smoothed the healing salve on the wounds and wrapped them, doubt faded. Certainty took hold: Finn O'Malley would have continued to seek her bed whenever he returned to Wyndmere Hall. But if not for the babe she carried…he never would have married her.

✦

FINN LISTENED WHILE Garahan divulged the details of the meeting at the Randy Cock between Ruan's man, Garahan, and Tremayne.

"And ye're certain ye can trust the Frenchman?"

Garahan snorted. "As far as I can toss him." Eyeing Finn, he said, "I'm thinking he'd be a match for yerself or Tremayne. The three of ye are broader through the chest and shoulders than the rest of us."

An idea took hold. Finn would use the smugglers as the excise official had—only to his own advantage. "Use me as bait."

Garahan held Finn's gaze for a moment before asking, "Are ye daft?"

"I want Buxton captured and made to pay for his crimes." Finn looked away and then back. "If I have to use meself as bait, then so be it. Me life for his—'twould be worth the trade."

"After all the lass went through to save yer skin, you'd toss it all away?"

Finn shrugged. "We can rebuild the kitchen. The lads rounded up the horses. What else would I be tossing away?"

Garahan glared at him. "Ye're an *eedjit!*"

"'Tisn't the first time ye've said that to me."

"Won't be last if ye toss away yer chance at happiness."

Finn flexed his hands, imagining using them on his cousin. A quick jab to the throat, followed by another to his gut.

But his need to pound Garahan would have to wait. Drawing on his resolve, he said, "I'm not tossing anything away."

The door opened behind them, and Flaherty walked over to where they stood on the other side of the great hall. "I think yer wife is in pain."

"Think?" Finn asked.

"Aye—the lass wouldn't answer me when I asked."

Finn wondered if it was her nature to hide her thoughts and feelings from those who cared for her. Bloody hell, he more than cared for her—he loved her! "I'll speak to her."

Flaherty shook his head. "I'd give her a little time before ye go in there half-cocked, demanding to know if her hands pain her."

The lid on Finn's temper threatened to blow off. He crushed it back into place. "I'll be deciding what is best for me wife. I've just told Garahan me plan. Offer me as bait to the Frenchman— he'll have heard all about Buxton's bid to capture meself and me wife. Lucky for us, Buxton's a buggering *eedjit* and could never outthink the lot of us." His heart nudged his head, and he added, "Or me brilliant wife. Hatching her plan to distract ye while she rode to me rescue."

"I thought ye didn't need anyone to rescue ye," Garahan scoffed.

Flaherty looked at Finn, shook his head, and said, "The lass thinks ye'd be better off without her."

Finn grabbed the front of Flaherty's coat and shook him. "Why in the bloody hell would she?"

Garahan tapped Finn on the shoulder. "Let go."

Finn released his grip on Flaherty. "What did she say?"

"'Tis what she didn't say," Flaherty replied.

"Oh, so now ye profess to know what is on a woman's mind?" Finn asked.

"Nay. But I'll wager from the heartbreak I saw in the depths of eyes the color of a spring sky, 'twas what the lass was thinking before she bade me to see to yer injuries."

Finn turned and started to walk away. Garahan's words halted his steps: "If yer wounds fester, ye'll be no good to the duke or the rest of us."

James was right, though God help him, Finn would never tell the man. "I need a word with me wife—just a word, lads. I'll be right back."

"Ten to one he'll muck up the apology," Garahan said to Flaherty.

Flaherty shook his head. "Ten to one he'll drive the wedge further between them."

Garahan held out his hand. "Done!"

Flaherty shook it. "Done!"

Finn's bellow had them staring at the closed door.

A few moments later, Finn burst back through it, letting it bang against the wall. "Why in the bloody hell did I marry a woman as stubborn as me ma?"

Garahan and Flaherty exchanged a glance. Garahan shrugged, and Flaherty replied, "Faith, every blessed one of us is hoping to find women to marry that are as strong and resourceful as our mas."

Finn didn't argue…though he did look back to see the slip of a woman standing in the doorway, glaring at him, openly challenging him. The woman who held his heart and had him by the *bollocks*. "She said I'm an *eedjit*."

Garahan slapped him on the back. "Smart woman, yer wife."

"I have more supplies in the tack room in the stables," Flaherty told him. "Let's get this over with. Then I'm thinking ye need another word or two to soothe yer wife's anger."

Finn's shoulders slumped. "'Twill take more than that."

CHAPTER TWENTY-FOUR

THE DUKE OF Wyndmere was accustomed to the weight of responsibility. The moment he accepted the mantle of duke, those he was responsible for had increased tenfold. And the vast number increased exponentially with each member of his personal guard that married.

Dear God—four of the sixteen men were now married. One was the proud father of a daughter, another was stepfather to a son of four and ten, and two others' wives were expecting.

"Boggles the mind," he said aloud.

"I beg your pardon, Your Grace?"

The duke had been lost in thought, and in the quiet of the coach had forgotten he was not alone. "No need, Mrs. Castleton. Forgive the outburst. I did not mean to startle you."

The housekeeper for his manor house in St. Ives smiled. "My husband and I could only imagine the number of issues you have been dealing with since you arrived the other day."

"There are far more at present than I'd anticipated. A few have cropped up overnight." Looking out the window, he admired the beauty of his surroundings. "Who would think that beneath this lovely landscape, dozens of problems exist?"

Mrs. Castleton frowned. "Far more than that, I'll wager, Your Grace. It is not my place to tell you what to do, but my fifty-plus years of living here should count for experience enough to advise you to be on your guard constantly."

"Thank you. I appreciate and intend to follow your advice. There are four outriders—two of which happen to be retired from His Majesty's forces and are currently working for my London man-of-affairs."

The older woman's relief was evident, as the tension seemed to leave her by degrees. "Mr. Castleton and I were worried. You haven't visited more than a handful of times in the last year or so, and the things that go on below the surface...are frightening."

The duke picked up on her reference to the caves below his cliffs—and Penwith Tower. "Has something happened at the manor house that I need to be made aware of?"

"No, Your Grace. I was thinking of happenings in and around the village."

The duke felt one of the knots in his gut loosening. "I cannot thank you enough for agreeing to take Mollie O'Malley under your wing. I do not believe she should be staying alone in their cottage until this situation has been resolved. With all that has happened to her and her husband since their arrival—I cannot imagine that she won't be asking to borrow a fast horse and leave Cornwall altogether!"

His housekeeper slowly smiled. "From what I've heard from my husband, she's stout of heart and not easily overset."

He agreed. "It does concern me that she does not seem to be afraid. That is what worries me—and her husband Finn. He fears for her health and that of their babe."

"Leave everything to me, Your Grace. I shall keep her busy with tasks inside the manor house, all the while keeping an eye on her."

"I'm pleased to be leaving her in your care. However, she may not be amenable to leaving her husband's side—no matter if it is for her own safety."

The team slowed as they approached Penwith Tower, and Mrs. Castleton said, "If it were me, I'd fight tooth and nail to stay by my husband's side, but I am certain she will be more than grateful to be away from imminent danger."

The duke did not want to admit his fears aloud. Mollie O'Malley was liable to make a fuss and cause more than a stir once she got wind that her husband had conspired to have her removed from Penwith Tower. Finn needed to know she was safe in order to carry out his duties. "Let us hope so."

He watched the men assemble as the carriage rumbled to a halt inside Penwith Tower's curtain wall. The door was flung open before he could reach for it.

"Ah, Garahan," the duke said. "Any news to report?"

If the duke had not been watching Garahan closely, he would have missed the slight wince as James assured the duke all was well.

"And how is Mrs. O'Malley this afternoon?"

Garahan glanced over his shoulder at Flaherty, who was walking toward the carriage. "Resting."

The duke sensed she was not, but decided to wait and question his men later. He stepped down from the carriage and held his hand out to his housekeeper. "Mrs. Castleton and her husband are caretakers at the manor house. She is here to escort Mollie back to the house, where she'll be staying until the situation has resolved itself."

Introductions were made, and the duke led the way to the great hall. Garahan opened the door with a flourish, and they were greeted by the sight of Finn embracing his wife. He lifted his head and met the duke's gaze. With a nod of acknowledgement, he bent and whispered to his wife, "His Grace is here."

Mollie eased out of her husband's arms and turned to greet the duke. "Thank you for your concern, Your Grace, but I—"

The duke raised his hand, and she fell silent. "Arrangements for your safety have been made. You would not want to compromise the safety of my men, would you?"

"No! You know that has never been my intention," she assured him.

"Ah, then the fire that leveled the kitchen was an accident?"

Her face flamed, and he had his answer. It had not been.

"All of the horses have been rounded up," Garahan added.

"And construction of a new—larger—kitchen has begun," Flaherty said.

The duke swept his gaze over the men gathered. They were letting him know, subtly, that they would protect Finn's wife with their lives—and had already done that and more for his duchess, their twins, and a number of his family members, in their tenure as members of his personal guard.

He turned and faced Mollie. "I do hope you will refrain from setting fire to another of my buildings. My men have enough to do protecting my property and those that work for me."

She looked away, then back before replying, "You have my word, Your Grace."

He inclined his head. "Accepted." The duke looked around at the men who formed a circle of protection around him. "Men, I have charged you with putting an end to the corruption slithering in and around the caves beneath these cliffs while overseeing the reconstruction of Penwith Tower and its curtain wall."

Those gathered listened intently as the duke continued, "I am pleased with what you have accomplished so far. Our job is not over as long as the free traders—and those in league with them—stretch their slimy tentacles into St. Ives. The village and its people have gone too long without the protection of my title. I aim to see that they have it for as long as I live and breathe." His gaze met O'Malley's, Garahan's, and Flaherty's. "Are you with me?"

The chorus of "ayes" swelled around him. The duke slowly smiled. "I'm grateful to each and every one of you."

AT THE DUKE'S nod, Finn walked over to his wife and wrapped her in his arms once more. "I hope ye'll rest when ye can, as our babe requires it. I know ye'll worry, while I'll be wishing ye won't."

She smiled, but he could tell it was forced. He silently applauded her effort not to make a scene as they parted.

"His Grace has given his word that I can return to ye at the manor house each night. Ye have me word that I will, lass."

She was trembling when he tilted her chin with the tip of his finger. He pressed his lips to hers, gently, reverently.

"Don't fret while ye're waiting for me to return. 'Tisn't—"

"Good for the babe," she finished for him. "I know. I'm certain Mrs. Castleton has enough work to keep the both of us busy until tonight."

He bent low to lean his forehead against hers. "Be safe, *mo chroi*—my heart." Unable to walk away without one last kiss, Finn crushed her to him and kissed the breath out of her. He tugged on her arm to get her moving toward the carriage. When she stood, dazed, staring at his mouth, it lifted into a crooked smile. "Ah, lass, ye tempt me, but I've duties to the duke."

She shook her head at him and let him lead her to the carriage and help her inside. He handed Mrs. Castleton in beside his wife and closed the door. "Trust me to keep me word. I'll be there by the time ye've put the supper on, Mollie-lass."

He stepped back from the carriage, but stopped when she called his name.

"Aye?"

"I love you."

"Ah, lass. I love ye more."

He watched the carriage, and its outriders, pull away and drive beneath the arch of the curtain wall. As it turned east toward land's end—the tip of Cornwall—he felt a heavy hand on his shoulder.

"She'll be fine," Garahan said. "A strong lass, is our Mollie."

Finn glared at his cousin. "*My* Mollie."

Garahan chuckled. "Face it boy-o—the day she married ye, she became part of the family."

Finn sighed. "'Tis a bit of a worry at times—our family, such as it is—but I wouldn't trade it for anything!"

The duke spoke with a few of the men as they dispersed before walking toward Finn and Garahan. Finn met the intensity of the duke's gaze and asked, "Are ye ready to hear our daring plan, Yer Grace?"

"Are you going to risk your neck twice in one day?"

"Twice?" Finn asked.

The duke chuckled. "If you do not arrive at the manor house by supper tonight, there will be hell to pay."

Garahan snorted with laughter, and Finn shrugged. "Well now, it seems ye have the right of it, Yer Grace. Garahan and I best head out, or we'll be late for our appointment."

"Who will be guarding your backs?" the duke asked.

The two men looked at one another and shrugged. "Ruan's man is canny," Garahan said. "Too much is at stake to chance having a handful of men guarding our backs."

"Are you mad?"

"Me ma has asked me that on more than one occasion," Finn admitted.

"As has mine," Garahan added.

"I know you shall take every precaution," the duke told his men. "Twenty minutes from now, I shall send two men into the village. If they happen to end up raising a pint at the Randy Cock, I'm sure no one will notice."

"Better make that thirty minutes from now," Garahan advised.

THE DUKE AGREED and watched Finn and Garahan mount their horses and take the road to the village.

"I'll need you here, Flaherty, heading up the guard," he said. "Tremayne, you've already been to that tavern. Pick one of the men to ride with you—see if you can cause a diversion after you get there. I don't want anyone paying too close attention to Garahan and Finn's meeting."

"Yes, Your Grace." Tremayne strode toward the stables, signaling to Bayfield as he went. The two men rode out a few minutes later.

"Do you think Ruan will agree?" the duke asked Flaherty.

"He's one for taking chances…as long as he thinks the odds are on his side," Flaherty said.

"Are they?"

"Aye."

The duke was about to press him as to why, when one of the lads from the village approached with a question about one of the horses, and the moment was gone. The duke and Flaherty parted, agreeing to meet on the ramparts to wait for the return of Garahan and Finn.

Little did the duke know—if all went according to plan—Finn would *not* return.

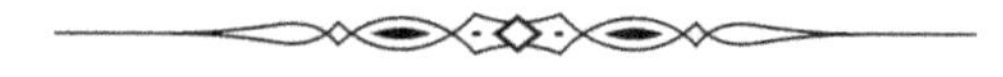

CHAPTER TWENTY-FIVE

FINN AND GARAHAN rode into the village, each man watching for anything suspicious. They were in the minority in St. Ives—working for the duke—unlike the more than half of the village who worked for Ruan or Buxton. When they arrived at the tavern, Finn noticed movement in the alley next door to the Randy Cock.

"I'll make certain no one is loitering in the alley that shouldn't be there," Finn said as he dismounted.

Garahan dismounted and held out his hand to Finn. "I'll tie off yer horse to the hitching post with mine."

Finn didn't bother to answer as the hair on the back of his neck stood on end. Three men jumped him as he stepped into the alley. Two men held him while the third hammered him in the kidneys, driving him to his knees. He wasn't incapacitated—as he knew his attackers would think—but it hurt like hell.

He needed to warn Garahan. Curling into a tight ball, he ducked his head so no one would see him smirk right before he gave a short, sharp whistle.

He'd pay for alerting Garahan, but it would be worth it. Garahan would be free to go for help. Finn was the man Ruan and Buxton wanted—not Garahan. He was ready to put up a credible fight resisting capture, when that had been his plan all along.

GARAHAN HEARD THE whistled warning, and stopped in his tracks. He, his brothers, and his cousins only used that shrill whistle as a last-ditch warning to stay away.

His heart wanted to go after Finn, but his gut and his head told him to heed the warning. He ducked into the shadows and waited until he heard his cousin taunting whoever jumped him. Judging from the sounds of the scuffle, it had to be at least two or three men. A few minutes later he heard the jingle of a horse's harness and saw a wagon pull out of the alley. One man drove—two had a death grip on Finn. One of those two was the man they were to meet inside the Randy Cock…Ruan's man.

Garahan's mind switched into mercenary mode, noting the direction of the wagon. As soon as he was certain they were well on their way and would not notice him, he vaulted onto his animal's back and rode full out back to Penwith Tower.

"Hang on, boy-o!" he murmured to himself. "I'll bring the cavalry and rescue yer sorry arse! Ye'd best not be wrong about Ruan and his man!"

THE WAGON PULLED to a stop on the cliffs above the caves. Finn knew the spot all too well. Needing to reassure himself that Ruan's man was not thinking of getting rid of him instead of sticking to their bold plan, he asked, "Are ye out of yer mind?" Finn glared at Ruan's man. "I did not double-cross ye. I came to meet with ye, and turn meself over to ye, so Ruan could use me as insurance against Buxton."

"That's a lie," one of Buxton's men said, while the other grunted in agreement.

The Frenchman did not show any outward emotion. *Good,* Finn thought. He'd keep his word to Finn and not give away the plan they had concocted between them to prove Buxton had been cheating Ruan for months.

"Ye know for a fact that Buxton pocketed more of the coin he was to turn over to yer captain than he claimed he collected."

Ruan's man did not respond. His silence was convincing, too convincing—had Finn bargained with the devil only to come out on the losing end, forfeiting his life?

The cauterized skin on Finn's arm pulled taut as he was yanked to his feet. "Toss him out of the wagon," Ruan's man said. "He'll soon learn not to double-cross Ruan!"

Finn thought the Frenchman was enjoying their plan a bit too much. He landed face-first in a clump of brambles and cursed as pain shot through his face. "Bleeding bastards! Ye could have broken me fecking nose!"

Someone's foot stomped on the small of his back. He closed his mouth. He'd wait until Ruan's man had executed his part of the plan and freed Finn so they could capture Buxton's men and take them to Ruan.

As they approached the path that would lead to the cliffs, he heard the distinctive jingle of Kelly's team—their man had attached a trio of bells to his team's harness as a way to identify him in the dark of night. Relief speared through Finn. Everything was going according to plan.

"I'll take it from here."

Every hair on the back of Finn's neck stood on end—Buxton?

"I have orders from *mon capitaine* to deliver the Irishman to him," Ruan's man argued.

The click of a pistol being cocked was Buxton's answer. Finn worked the knot in the rope that lashed his hands together. He tugged and pulled…but the knot held fast.

"I said we wait until I speak to *mon capitaine!*"

A shot was fired, and the distinctive sound of a body hitting the ground nearby jarred Finn into action. He turned over to see what was happening, and found himself staring into the barrel of a pistol.

"Now then, O'Malley," Buxton said. "It's time to pay for the inconvenience of having to hire new guards."

Finn could bluff with the best of them, and he did so now. Pretending not to notice the gun aimed at his forehead, he chuckled. "'Tis a shame the last bunch were inept. Outwitting them was too easy."

Buxton lowered the gun and locked gazes with Finn. "And that's why I killed them."

Finn called up his ironclad control—he would not give Buxton the satisfaction of knowing he felt an ounce of remorse for the death of the men who'd been guarding him in the cave. "Well then, Buxton, what have ye planned for me?"

Buxton slowly smiled. "I believe we've already had this conversation. Have you forgotten already? I plan to gut you and then hang you from the gibbet outside the excise building in the village for all to see."

Finn's stomach flipped over. Mayhap 'twas his destiny to die at the hands of this man.

A petite vision with auburn hair and sky-blue eyes flooded his head. The memory of their last kiss filled his heart, giving him the strength to face down his enemy. "Sure and that would be a grand day out for the people of St. Ives, wouldn't it now?"

The sarcastic tone of his voice had the desired effect—his opponent ground his teeth.

Satisfied he'd hit a nerve, Finn said, "Now then, what'll it take to have ye forget yer plans and throw in with meself and the lads?"

Buxton waited a beat before saying, "You work for the duke."

"Well now, I'm a man who likes to keep me options open. His Grace doesn't realize there are a few of us who have been making plans while in his employ. There's a shipment due to arrive on the evening tide—we have men in place to lure it ashore."

His adversary put his gun back in his waistband and raked a hand through his hair. "I don't believe you, but on the off chance you are not lying, I intend to collect my percentage of the haul."

Finn kept his expression neutral—inside, he was grinning. Buxton's greed was the right card to play, while at the same time he was concerned that Ruan's man had yet to move.

"I'm betting my man Simpson and his men will be the ones to lure the ship into the rocks. They will see to it that every man on board dies before they carry the cargo ashore."

Finn dug deep to keep up the façade—and the superior smile off his face. "Yer man Simpson traded his loyalty to ye for a bag of coin."

"I'll kill him."

"Ye'll have to find him first."

Buxton grabbed Finn by his lapels. "Where is he?"

"How in the bloody hell would I know? I've been at the duke's beck and call since handing over the bag of coin. Though I did note Simpson turned his horse inland once he collected his fee."

Buxton and his men walked away, and Finn dared a glance at Kelly, then tilted his head in the direction where Ruan's man had been shot. Kelly gave a slight nod—he'd been close enough to hear the shot and would know to collect Ruan's man and patch him up so they could return him to the ship as Finn had agreed.

He hoped to God the man wasn't dead.

Part of their second plan had been achieved. He'd convinced Ruan's man of Buxton's treachery—though he hadn't planned on Ruan's man getting shot. Kelly had arrived as planned and would have a group of local lads stationed between the cliffs and the caves below.

Kelly waited until the men were out of sight before jumping off the wagon. He slit Finn's ropes and said, "Watch your back. You don't know if you can trust Simpson."

"I'll convince him to trust me." Watching Kelly climb up onto the wagon, Finn knew one thing was certain—Buxton and his men were in for a surprise.

He had to go to the village alone, or else he wouldn't have a chance to discover if the lad he had paid to plant a bag of coin in the excise building had done so.

If he hadn't, then the third and most crucial part of his wild plan would be in jeopardy—the part where he didn't die!

GARAHAN URGED HIS horse into a gallop and leaned forward, urging every ounce of speed from his mount. His horse's hooves sounded like thunder as they approached Penwith Tower. He shouted, "Buxton's got Finn!" Yanking on the reins, Garahan spun his horse around and headed toward the cliffs.

He didn't have time to talk. He had to get back to Finn! He knew they were headed to the cliffs. Following the path, he reached the intersection where the one from the village connected with the one from Penwith Tower. He dismounted and examined the ruts where the wagon wheels had left a depression in the sandy soil.

He noted that the tracks did indeed continue on to the path to the cliffs. He tied his horse to a bush and proceeded to follow the tracks, stopping short when he reached a spot where there was blood on the ground, but no body.

He hoped to hell it wasn't Finn's blood, though it would not bode well for Garahan and Finn if it was Ruan's man either. "I'll be damned either way. What have ye gotten me into this time, Finn?"

His gaze swept the area. There was no sign of Finn, the wagon, or Kelly—who was to meet them on the cliffs with his wagon. Both were missing. Had Kelly gone after Finn? Garahan searched the ground for more tracks, and found them. He had a problem— two sets of wagon tracks, and they were headed in opposite directions. Which way would lead him to Finn?

Flaherty's whistle had relief spearing through him. His cousin leapt off his horse and joined Garahan by the tracks. "Ye were here first," Flaherty said, eyeing the tracks. "Choose first, and I'll take the other direction. Hennessey is combing the area by the entrance through the roof of the cave."

Garahan chose the ones leading to the caves and started in that direction, then paused to tell his cousin, "I think Buxton shot Ruan's man, but if we figured this wrong, it could have been Ruan's man who shot Finn—there's blood back there a ways, but no body."

Flaherty nodded, absorbing the information. He would follow the tracks along the edge of the cliff toward the village.

They mounted and took off in opposite directions.

Garahan kept second-guessing himself as he rode. Should he have revealed himself earlier at the Randy Cock? Would Finn be standing by his side if he had? His gut tied in knots, as he followed the tracks. Shouted curses and an argument had him pulling up and dismounting to follow on foot. Using the rocks to shield him from view, he made his way closer to the cave.

Bloody hell, 'twas the same one Finn had been held prisoner in a few days earlier.

"How do I know you are not lying to me?"

Garahan recognized that voice—'twas Buxton!

"I could ask the same of you, *mon ami*."

Ruan! Garahan wanted to rush the men arguing at the mouth of the cave, but Finn's life hung in the balance. He had no idea how many were inside the cave—could be as many as a dozen, or as few as two. He'd have to wait…or go back for help.

He said a quick prayer, and a large hand covered his mouth.

"Mmmfph!"

"It's me." Tremayne's harsh whisper was the answer to his prayer.

Garahan nodded, and the lieutenant let go. "Finn could be in that cave."

"How do ye know?" Tremayne asked.

"I don't," Garahan admitted. "There was blood, but no body. I'm not leaving until we determine Finn's not in that cave." He studied Tremayne for a moment before asking, "Why are ye here?"

"His Grace sent us off after you—we were to cause a distraction at the Randy Cock, if needed. But on our way to the village, we heard a wagon on the path to the cliffs and followed it."

"We?" Garahan asked.

"Aye," Tremayne said "Bayfield rode out with me. We were waiting to make our move, when we saw you." He turned as the argument increased in volume, and asked, "Who is Buxton arguing with?"

Garahan answered, "Ruan."

"The Frenchman who owns the free trade along this coast?"

"Aye."

"How many are inside?" Tremayne asked.

"I've only been here long enough to hear those two arguing about what to do with Finn," Garahan replied, trying to keep the worry from his voice. He could not accept that it would be his cousin's destiny to find love only to lose it, and die at the hands of a traitor to the Crown.

Tremayne glanced over his shoulder. "They could be arguing about Finn without the man being here."

Garahan nodded.

Tremayne knew from the look on Garahan's face that the man would not budge until they'd searched the cave. "You can fit through the roof of the cave. We need to know how many men we are up against. If it's an entire crew…"

"Could be as many as a dozen men," Garahan finished. "What are ye planning while I'm counting *eedjits*?"

Tremayne reached into his frockcoat pocket and pulled out two hand grenades ready to be lit. "A diversion."

"I thought ye were a Dragoon, not a Grenadier."

Tremayne smiled. "I have many talents."

The argument escalated, easily covering any sound Garahan made scrambling up the path to the top of the cliff or Tremayne's movements below him.

COUNTING ON GARAHAN to do his part, Tremayne studied the scene before him and spotted a longboat a short distance away from the mouth of the cave. He eyed the distance, made a quick calculation, and pulled a match out of his pocket. He lit the fuse, aimed the grenade, and threw it, hitting his target.

The satisfying sound of the explosion, wood splintering, and men shouting had him wondering: how many men were in the cave? "Bloody hell! Garahan better not try to free Finn on his own."

A sound had him spinning on the balls of his feet—ready to leap in any direction to subdue his attacker—but he jolted to a stop when he recognized the man—Bayfield.

"Did the others arrive?" Tremayne asked.

"Aye. Hennessey's headed toward the ledge," Bayfield told him. "Is Garahan going to wait for help before going into the cave?"

"Nay."

Bayfield smiled at the smoking pile that used to be a boat. "Nice aim, lieutenant."

"I have one more—but I'm saving it."

"For another diversion?"

"Aye."

The sound of a gunshot coming from within the cave had both men reaching for their weapons. Tremayne pulled his pistol from his waistband, while Bayfield slipped the dirk from his boot.

"On three," Tremayne rasped.

CHAPTER TWENTY-SIX

"MOLLIE?"

She glanced over her shoulder and immediately braced herself for bad news. "Your Grace. Is anything wrong?"

The duke crossed the room and offered his hand. She hesitated a moment to calm her racing thoughts, then placed her hand in his.

"Aside from my wife," the duke said, "you are one of the strongest women I know."

His words shredded her calm. Tears filled her eyes and spilled over. She whispered the words he did not say: "Finn's dead."

His grip increased. "Nay," he insisted. "Captured. Garahan and three others are missing."

She drew in a deep breath and slowly exhaled. "Who is missing?"

"Tremayne, Bayfield, and Hennessey."

"Then there is hope, if Garahan and Captain Coventry's men are together."

"Indeed." He released her hand and motioned to the settee by the fire. "Would you care to sit?"

She studied the duke's face. Though handsome, he didn't have that extra dash of rakish good looks like Finn. She prayed she would see her husband's twinkling green eyes and crooked smile once more.

The duke's neutral expression slipped for a heartbeat, and she surmised he had not told her everything. Instead of pestering him with questions, she walked over to the settee and sat down.

The duke placed his hands behind his back and paced in front of her. "Shall I summon Mrs. Castleton to sit with you?"

She assumed the worst and blurted out, "Finn's dying."

The duke's mouth hung open for a moment before he closed it. He shook his head. "I had not realized how alike you and Persephone are. My wife is quick to fill in the blanks when I am trying to sort out the words that would lessen the blow of bad news."

"I think there is a compliment in there somewhere."

The duke looked at the ceiling and appeared to be muttering something.

He's counting…just like Finn! She'd best apologize.

"I am sorry for interrupting, Your Grace. Please continue."

His eyes showed a hint of unease, and then it was gone. "I have men searching the cliffs and one of the taverns in the village—where Finn and Garahan were last seen."

There had to be something she could do. She refused to sit in the duke's drawing room, hands clasped, while her husband could very well be about to forfeit his life to protect the duke. "Is there anything else that can be done?"

He frowned before answering, "I have assigned extra men to guard you. Do not let your emotions override your good sense— my men and I will not fail. We'll find Finn and the others."

Her stomach heaved at the possibility that her husband would not return. With a will of iron, she fought and controlled the spasms.

"Your word, Mrs. O'Malley."

She lifted her chin and met the duke's gaze. "I promise to remain here."

"Once an O'Malley gives his word, he keeps it!"

A lone tear escaped, but she ignored it to say, "Once an O'Malley gives *her* word, she would die to keep it!"

His wry smile had her wondering what he would find amusing about the situation.

"Hence the extra guard posted to see that you do not leave."

Frustration twined with anger. "I gave my word!"

"Ah, but unfortunately, I was not able to see your hands as you gave your word. According to my willful wife, if her fingers are crossed, it trumps her vow."

Mollie felt her lips lifting of their own accord. She rose to her feet and splayed her hands, so the duke could see her fingers were not crossed. "I will remain here until either you or my husband return." She crossed her arms beneath her breasts and frowned at the duke. "I trust that will suffice."

"Indeed." The duke spun around and stalked from the room.

Mollie didn't bother to worry about offending the duke. Her husband's life was in the man's hands. Once Finn was free, she'd worry about apologizing.

Having given her word, the only course left open to her was to pray. She bowed her head. "Dear Lord, please keep Finn safe and return him to our babe and me."

Mollie did what any wife in her position would do—she paced the perimeter of the drawing room, pausing at each window to peer outside. She noted two guards at the front of the house. For a brief moment, she wondered if there were two more guarding the rear entrance.

As if he were standing behind her, and she was leaning against the solid wall of his broad chest, she heard Finn whisper in her ear, *"O'Malleys keep their word, lass."*

Her impatient nature was bound to get the better of her if she had to sit here and wait.

Mrs. Castleton knocked on the open door, capturing Mollie's attention. "His Grace is concerned that you'll worry. He asked me to bring tea—and something sweet to tempt your appetite—and keep you company." She motioned to a footman who followed her, carrying the tea tray.

"That was thoughtful of him. I would enjoy your company,

as I'm about to drive myself mad wondering 'what if.'"

"His Grace understands," Mrs. Castleton said, pouring tea. "Cream? Sugar?"

"No thank you." Mollie waited until Mrs. Castleton had served the teacake and scones before sipping from her cup.

"His Grace remembers. I was in your situation fifteen or so years ago."

Mollie set her cup on her saucer and placed it on the table in front of them. "What happened?"

The housekeeper launched into a detailed tale of her husband being pressed into service in the Royal Navy and his years serving—including nearly losing his life when his leg was crushed beneath the cannon he'd been firing. He survived, but his leg did not.

Mollie had noticed the man's limp. He must have a wooden leg. "How did you cope with the worry and the long absences?"

Mrs. Castleton's eyes met hers over the rim of her teacup. "Faith, hope, and many hours of prayer." Setting her teacup and saucer on the table, she asked, "Would you like me to pray with you?"

Mollie felt a bit of her concern ease, and with it, her confidence that Finn would return filled her. "I would like that very much."

They joined hands and bowed their heads to pray.

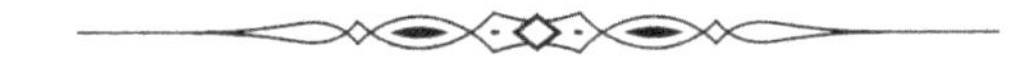

CHAPTER TWENTY-SEVEN

FINN HAD NOT counted on Buxton insisting they find Simpson together, but knew his plan had succeeded when—praise God—the bag of coin he'd had the lad plant was discovered among Simpson's belongings.

Infuriated, Buxton didn't ask questions—he took aim and fired.

Anticipating the reaction, Finn bumped into Buxton's shoulder, causing him to wing Simpson…instead of shooting him through the heart. Furious that Buxton placed little or no value on life, he shouted, "Ye'd kill a man for doing the same as yerself? Lining his pockets with coin?"

Buxton didn't bother to answer—he was too busy reloading. He raised his pistol, but before he could take aim, Finn snatched the weapon out of his hands.

"How do ye expect the lads and I to work with someone completely without honor? How do we know ye'll keep yer word to us?" Finn demanded.

The other man shrugged. "You do not. My men respect me and obey my every order."

Obey—the word hit Finn between the eyes, reminding him of telling Mollie to obey *him*. God help him…if he got out of this situation alive, he'd promise to never utter the word again!

"Well now, truth be told, yer men fear ye—they don't respect ye. The lads and I have recruited more than one of yer men in the past year, or haven't ye noticed?"

Finn was stretching the truth; they'd only managed to pry information from one man—the man standing to his right bleeding from the pistol ball wound in his arm. Thinking to distract Buxton from trying to beat Simpson over the head with the only other weapon nearby—a chair—he said, "Not yer man Simpson, here. 'Twas another."

Buxton whirled around and demanded, "Tell me his name!"

Finn chuckled. "Ye do rile easily, Buxton. For a man who works for His Majesty's Excise Office, I would think ye'd need to have a more moderate temperament."

Finn watched the other man's movements, pleased when he curled his hands into tight fists. He wouldn't mind taunting Buxton to put up his fists. Finn would welcome a satisfying bout of bare-knuckle fighting right about now.

Finn ignored the need to pound someone, reminding himself of their goal—to unsettle and confuse the excise official to the point where he turned on his own men. Remembering the name he'd learned from one of their sources, he said, "Mayhap ye should speak to Richards. Ask him about our meeting a few nights ago at the Randy Cock."

Buxton's face paled, then flushed with rage. Yelling Richards' name, he stormed out of the room.

Finn held his hands up in front of him to show he had no weapon. Simpson eyed him but did not speak. "I'm reaching into me pocket. I've a length of linen in it. I'll bind yer wound."

"Why would you after you lied to Buxton, and he shot me!"

"Ah, but he missed his target. Sure and ye won't expire from a flesh wound, if ye remember to have someone tend to it properly." He wrapped the cloth around Simpson's arm and tied off the knot. "Are ye willing to face the retribution ye'll be held to when facing charges of aiding smugglers and wreckers—and pocketing a percentage of Buxton's fees?"

Simpson remained silent, until Finn added, "I'm certain His

Majesty will be happy to allow ye to keep the ill-gotten coin ye've been collecting"—he paused to nod at the open doorway—"working for that crooked excise official."

Simpson stared at the makeshift bandage around his arm, then looked at Finn. "He threatened to kill my wife and son—what would you have had me do?"

"Tell someone—anyone—"

Simpson exploded with anger. "When the entire village is either collecting coin for Buxton, or from the Frenchman?"

Finn frowned. "I see yer point. Well then, I'm asking ye now. Are ye willing to tell the truth when the time comes?"

"Aye."

"Are ye willing to give back the coin?"

"I haven't spent a single pence!"

Satisfied he had judged the man's character correctly, Finn asked, "Who else has Buxton threatened?"

Simpson shook his head. "Every man working for him."

Finn digested the news, then asked, "How many can ye trust yer wife and son's lives with, if they give their word to speak the truth against Buxton when the time comes?"

"Half of the men."

"I'll be needing their names."

"Done," Simpson said.

"Now then, I'll let ye in on the plan the lads and I came up with—if ye swear ye'll be keeping yer word."

"I swear on my life. I will tell the truth if it'll put that bloody bastard away."

Finn snorted. "I'm thinking His Majesty may have something else in mind to deal with the man—he may even be after sending a message to others working in the Excise Office, and the Customs Office with his justice."

"Buxton is not looking the other way and accepting coin to do so because his wife and family are being threatened," Simpson said. "He has a black heart and a greedy soul."

"Does his family live in St. Ives?"

"Aye. His wife and daughter. Both are lovely, sweet-tempered, and trusting. I doubt they know what Buxton has been up to these last two years."

"I'll need ye to trust me. I'm going to tell Buxton that I'm taking ye to the lads. We're planning to hold ye hostage until the next load of contraband arrives."

"I'll need your word not to harm my wife and son."

"We'll be taking care of that as soon as we are away from here. Hold out yer hands. I'll lash them in front of ye—it's easier to ride a horse that way."

Understanding showed in Simpson's expression as he complied. "Buxton needs to think I'm your prisoner."

"Aye. Let's be on our way. We need to ensure your family is protected. If need be, they can stay in the great hall at Penwith Tower."

Simpson murmured his thanks as they moved from shadow to shadow until they reached a side door and disappeared into the twilight. Finn waited until they were a good distance away from the excise building before untying Simpson's hands.

"We'll stop at your home first," Finn said, "then at the homes of the others whose families have been threatened." When Simpson quickly agreed, Finn added, "Yer wife and son might feel more secure if the other wives and children accompany us to Penwith Tower."

For a moment he wished Mollie was waiting for him. Shaking that thought from his head, he felt only relief that she was safe at the duke's manor house—under guard. He hoped she would not be angry with him when she discovered he would not be returning to the manor house tonight, nor would he return to Penwith Tower. If all went according to plan, he would be either bound and gagged or in shackles—held at gunpoint at the excise building.

He had to get word to the others of his change in plans. Flaherty and the duke should be at Penwith Tower. He had no idea where Garahan and Tremayne were, and sent up a quick prayer neither had run afoul of any more of Buxton's gang of cutthroats.

They mounted up and rode through the village, turning down the side street Simpson indicated. "The third house on the left is our cottage."

Finn slowed to a stop outside the small home. He removed Simpson's bonds. They dismounted as the door swung open wide. The willow-slim woman standing in the doorway held a little boy on her hip. She stared at the man beside Finn and slowly smiled. "You're early."

In three strides, Simpson had the woman and child in his arms. Finn placed a hand on the man's shoulder, and said, "Best get inside…away from prying eyes."

With his arm around his wife, Simpson urged her through the door and quickly followed. Finn paused to scan the perimeter. All seemed quiet. He entered the house and closed the door behind him.

"I need you to promise me you will not worry," Simpson told his wife.

She glanced at Finn, then turned to frown at her husband and the bloody bandage wrapped around his upper arm. "I cannot help but worry when you are gone at all hours of the night and have stopped confiding in me these last few months. You are home earlier than normal—and have been injured and are still bleeding. Why wouldn't I worry?"

Finn snorted to cover his laughter, then apologized. "I beg yer pardon, Mrs. Simpson. I mean no disrespect."

When her husband remained silent, she sighed and looked at Finn. "You're Mr. O'Malley, aren't you?"

"Just O'Malley—Mr. O'Malley's me da."

"The duke's man," she added.

He nodded. "One of them."

Her son's eyes closed. She shifted him from her hip, cradling him against her breast. The little one sighed then snuggled close. "As my husband seems incapable of speaking at the moment, mayhap you can tell me what is going on and why I should not worry."

Finn nudged Simpson, who glared at him, but refused to speak. Finn explained, "There is unrest in St. Ives, and we don't want ye and yer fine boy in the middle of it."

She seemed to be waiting for him to continue. Her next words confirmed his suspicion. "Smugglers, wreckers, or both?"

"'Tisn't me place to say. Ye can put yer questions to yer husband later. We need to get you to safety. I'll give ye five minutes to pack a small bag. I'll bank the fire for ye."

Simpson waited until his wife was out of hearing range. "I'm not telling her anything. The less she knows, the better off she'll be if there is an inquest. I'll not have her caught in the web of Buxton's lies and deceit."

Finn spread the coals far enough apart that they would not continue to burn. "Do ye need anything?"

"My wife and son are all I need."

Finn turned toward the staircase and nudged Simpson. "Carry the bag for the lass. I'll help her onto yer horse."

Simpson ignored him and swept his wife off her feet and onto his horse—her son still nestled in the crook of one arm and her small bag clutched in her other hand. "Whatever happens, promise me you'll listen to O'Malley. He's promised to protect you and our son with his life."

Tears glistened in Mrs. Simpson's eyes. "You'll tell me later?"

"Aye," Simpson agreed.

A SHORT WHILE later, Mrs. Simpson and her son had been settled in the great hall at Penwith Tower along with three of the other men's wives and four children. Including Simpson's two-year-old son, there were two boys, aged four and six, and a babe...a girl just two months old. The men were to arrive at Penwith Tower one at a time, so as not to draw attention.

Given the fact that Garahan, Tremayne, Hennessey, and Bayfield had yet to check in, Finn and Flaherty agreed it would be best if the families were transported to the duke's manor house.

There were already four guards stationed there protecting Mollie and the duke's elderly staff. Finn knew they would need every available man on hand if their plan to trap Buxton was to succeed.

The first part had gone according to plan, Finn thought as he led the wagon hauling the women and children and neared the manor house. He'd convinced Buxton that he too was working against the Crown and lining his own pockets, all the while using his position as head of the Duke of Wyndmere's Cornwall guard as a cover.

Finn had uncovered that the excise official had bribed more than half of Buxton's men, threatening harm to their families if they did not collect Buxton's percentage from those accepting smuggled goods. The fact that not all of the men were willing to throw in with O'Malley and the duke's men was worrisome, but they were running out of time. Finn would see if he could help pick up the pieces when all was said and done. The women and children of those choosing loyalty to Buxton would have the opportunity to tell what they knew—or did not know. Finn would see to it that no other families had to suffer from being wrongly accused, as Da and Uncle Sean had been.

He reined in his horse and dismounted when a blur of movement caught his attention. He spread his legs and lifted to the balls of his feet, ready to fend off the attacker—when he recognized the auburn-haired whirlwind barreling toward him.

He caught Mollie as she flung herself at him. Shifting her in his arms, he felt his worry slip away. Her heart beat in tandem with his as the soft sound of her sigh wrapped itself around him. "Ye were not supposed to leave the manor house, lass."

She lifted her head and met his gaze. "I haven't left the property," she reminded him.

"'Tisn't the same thing, and ye know it."

She pressed her lips to the edge of his jaw and tightened her grip around his shoulders. "I was worried."

"Are ye going to put yerself through worry every time I leave yer side to do the duke's bidding?"

"Aye," she said. "It is my job."

"Yer job is to rest and take care of our son while I'm away." He meant to keep frowning at her, but the disgruntled look on her face had him smiling. "And when I'm home," he said, pitching his voice to a low rasp, "ye're to take care of me every need."

"If that is all you expect me to do, Finn, you may as well have left me at Wyndmere Hall and my duties to Her Grace."

He narrowed his eyes at her and was about to remind her what her duties were to him—as his wife—when the duke joined the group. Finn needed to explain why he'd brought the women and children to the manor house.

But before he could offer an explanation, the duke swept his gaze over the group and settled it on Finn. "I take it you offered protection to these families."

"Aye, Yer Grace." Finn set his wife on her feet and put his arm around her. With a nod to the man at his side, he said, "Simpson and three more of Buxton's men have had their families threatened if they did not do the man's bidding."

The duke's eyes blazed. "I see. I take it you have a plan in mind to see that he is brought to justice."

"Aye, Yer Grace. But first let us see to the women and children." He turned to Mollie. "Would ye mind lending a hand? I'm thinking the little ones may be needing a cup of milk and something sweet to fill their bellies before they lie down for a nap."

She agreed, and he kissed the top of her head.

Simpson helped his wife dismount. "I'll leave you to make the introductions, O'Malley."

Finn's gaze never left Mollie's as he said, "I'll be letting me wife take care of that while we speak to His Grace." He started to turn away, then swore, grabbed hold of his wife, and kissed the breath out of her. "That'll have to hold ye until we return."

Mollie placed her hand on his forearm, entreating him, "You had better return, Finn O'Malley."

"Ye have me word. There's only one way I won't be coming back."

She put her hand over his mouth. "Don't tempt fate, Finn." She stood on her toes and pressed her lips to his. "Remember that I love you."

Undone, the warrior held his wife to his heart while he breathed in and breathed out—three times. Steadier for having seen her, fortified by her love—and the taste of her sweet lips—he was ready to face down the enemy.

"Faith, I love ye more."

CHAPTER TWENTY-EIGHT

L UCK WAS ON their side as Tremayne and Bayfield stormed into the chaos at the mouth of the cave. The smoke was thick enough to hide them as they snuck past Buxton and two of the men arguing with him.

Once they were inside the cave, Coventry's men paused to assess the situation and were surprised to find no one standing guard. "Follow me," Tremayne said.

Bayfield nodded, and the two men made their way deeper into the cave. There were barrels stacked along one wall, and crates against the opposite wall. Finn assured them the French smuggler would no longer use the duke's caves. Either Ruan could not be trusted to keep his word, or Buxton had ignored the similar warning and was the one using the duke's caves to hide his smuggled goods.

"Doesn't feel right. Where's Finn?" Bayfield asked.

The sound of flesh pounding on flesh caught their attention. Tremayne lifted his head toward the sound. "Sounds like more than two men fighting. Think Hennessey made it inside?"

Bayfield shrugged and followed him toward whoever was fighting. Pausing to listen, the two men chose the opening to the left. The sounds grew louder. A punch, followed by a grunt, and Garahan's question: "What have ye done with me cousin?"

A muffled groan was followed by a voice exclaiming, "Ruan's

man pulled him out of the wagon. I thought Buxton would shoot him, too."

Tremayne and Bayfield stopped to exchange a look of concern. "Who do you think Buxton shot?" Tremayne asked.

Bayfield shrugged.

Then they heard Buxton's man answer, "Ruan's man."

Tremayne digested the new information and said, "Finn isn't here, and we didn't see him come out of the cave. He must have returned to the village—we would have seen him if he returned to Penwith Tower."

"Aye. There is only one other way out, and neither Finn, nor you, could fit through the opening in the roof of the cave," Bayfield said.

"We have to find Finn. I'll take my chances leaving the way we came in," Tremayne said. "You and the others use the rope."

Bayfield widened his stance and said, "No. There are only three men out front—and from the sound of it, one just up ahead. We leave together."

Tremayne wanted to argue with him, but there wasn't time. "Let's haul Buxton's man out of here and take him with us."

They nearly bumped into Garahan and the man he was leading out of the cave. He locked gazes with Tremayne. "You've obviously been successful." He glanced at the other man. "Bayfield, where's Hennessey?"

"Hennessey's busy," Bayfield answered.

"I could use a hand," a voice called from behind Garahan. Hennessey appeared with a man slung over his shoulder. "Had a bit of trouble with this one. He tried to jump me as I let go of the rope."

Tremayne smiled. "Glad to see you haven't lost your touch. Need me to carry him for you?"

"Nay," Hennessey answered. "I have him." He glanced around and asked, "Where's Finn?"

Garahan prodded his prisoner in the middle of his back, and the man quickly answered, "He was standing beside the wagon—

with his hands bound behind his back—last I saw him."

"He was yer prisoner?" Garahan asked. "And ye don't know where he is?"

"When Buxton left, we went with him," the man answered.

"Finn could have gone back to the village," Tremayne suggested.

"We'll find him," Garahan said.

"Let's take these two back to the tower," Hennessey said.

"After we take care of the three men outside," Garahan added.

It got lighter the closer they were to the opening. Weapons raised, ready to attack—or defend—Tremayne and Bayfield led the way. No one challenged them. The men were gone.

"Where are they?" Tremayne demanded.

"I don't know," Buxton's man insisted.

Tremayne didn't bother to ask again. He told the men, "We'll split up."

"Aye," Garahan agreed. "Hennessey, ye'll come with me. We'll take the prisoners to Penwith Tower."

Tremayne looked to Bayfield. "You and I will take the path to the village and see if we can locate Finn."

"If you don't find any sign of him, report back to Penwith Tower," Garahan said.

"Aye," Tremayne agreed as the men went their separate ways.

GARAHAN NODDED TO the men on the ramparts as he and Hennessey walked beneath the archway, their prisoners draped over their horses' backs.

Flaherty flew down the steps. "Where in the bloody hell have ye been? We've sent men out looking for ye."

Garahan shook his head. "Bayfield's with Tremayne, headed

to the village searching for Finn—'tis a long story. I'll tell ye after we find Finn."

"What have ye brought us?" Flaherty asked, eyeing the men now struggling against their bonds.

"Two of Buxton's men who disagreed with Hennessey and meself when we were searching for Finn."

Flaherty scrubbed a hand over his face and shook his head. "Finn was here earlier, but he left again. We'll have to let His Grace know ye've returned in one piece."

"How long ago did Finn leave?" Garahan asked.

"Not that long. Finn and one of Buxton's men arrived with a wagonload of women and children. The duke decided 'twas best if they took the women on to the manor house. Mollie's already there."

Hennessey dragged his prisoner off the back of his horse. The man lunged away from him, but Hennessey grabbed hold of the man before he could make a break for it. "I thought we were to capture Buxton's men—not their women?"

Flaherty sighed. "That bleeding bugger threatened his own men. Said he'd hurt their wives and children if they did not follow orders. Not a one of the children is a day older than five or six." He raked a hand through his hair and rasped, "There's a babe—a little girl—just two months old."

"And the women?" Tremayne asked. "How are they holding up?"

"Disbelieving that Finn and Buxton's man Simpson weren't bringing them here to lock them up," Flaherty answered. "We're hoping Mollie'll be able to assure them that 'tisn't the case."

"If anyone will be able to soothe them," Tremayne said, "Mollie can."

"Buxton's orders were to extort money from those in the village who purchased smuggled goods from Ruan." Garahan pulled his prisoner off the back of his horse, grabbed him by the front of his coat, and warned, "Don't even think of trying to escape."

The man looked at the other prisoner held in Hennessey's grip and let his shoulders slump forward.

"Wise choice," Garahan said.

Two men walked over, and Flaherty ordered them, "Let's lock these men up." After they left to do his bidding, Flaherty looked to the men standing in front of him. "Tremayne, ye and Bayfield need to ride to the manor house and let the duke know what's happened."

Garahan waited for Coventry's men to leave. When they did, he glared at his cousin. Finally, Flaherty looked away and swore. "Finn's headed back to the village to see if Kelly was able to tend to Ruan's man—Buxton shot him. Finn mumbled something about making sure Ruan's man makes it back to the ship. Finn gave his word to the Frenchman."

"He's nothing but a bloodthirsty pirate!" Garahan said. "Did ye remind our hardheaded O'Malley kin of that?"

Flaherty clenched his hands into fists at his side, then relaxed them. "I did, but his argument made sense."

Garahan shoved his cousin.

Flaherty clipped Garahan on the side of the head. "Ye haven't been here for the last year or so. Finn and I have been. We've men spying for us as well as working to rebuild the wall and protect those doing so."

"What of it?" Garahan asked.

"Never once have we heard that Ruan had to threaten any of his men to do his bidding."

"The lot of them are smugglers," Tremayne said. "Ruan obviously promised them a percentage of the coin earned."

"He is a smuggler, and a pirate," Flaherty agreed. "But his word is his bond."

"Is it now?" Garahan asked.

"Aye. He tolerates Buxton," Flaherty added. "But his patience with the man's wearing thin—since he learned of Buxton's tactics for keeping his men in line."

Garahan blew out the breath he'd held. "So, we wait in the

hopes that Ruan is an honorable pirate, and Finn'll return? What do we tell Mollie when he doesn't?"

"I repeat, ye haven't been here and don't know the situation like Finn and me."

Garahan shook his head. "If ye're wrong…Finn's a dead man."

When Flaherty did not dispute his words, Garahan asked, "Are ye planning to wait here, or row out to Ruan's ship?"

"Finn said to give him an hour's time, and to make certain his wife stays at the manor house with the other women—well guarded."

"And?" Garahan asked.

Flaherty met his cousin's gaze. "Then we wait at the excise building for Buxton to return."

"What kind of a plan is that?" Garahan demanded. "We need to go after Finn!"

Flaherty's eyes blazed blue fire. "'Tis Finn's plan and his honor at stake. Ye'll follow his plan."

"It wasn't part of the plan that Buxton would shoot Ruan's man. It bloody hell wasn't part of the plan for Finn to take the wounded man to Ruan's ship," Garahan said. "Finn would have told me."

"Finn knew ye wouldn't agree, as ye hadn't been here more than a fortnight and did not know what we know." When Garahan stared toward the archway and the cliffs beyond, Flaherty said, "Trust us—trust Finn."

Garahan squared his shoulders and glanced over his shoulder. "How many men are going to the village with us?"

"None."

"Bloody fecking hell!"

Flaherty snorted. "That's what I said to Finn."

"And ye want me to trust him?"

"A handful of men are already stationed in and around the excise building, waiting to spring the trap on Buxton and his men."

"How many men does Buxton have left?" Garahan asked.

"We had a couple transported to London before ye arrived," Flaherty answered. "Five that were guarding Finn in the cave when the duke helped him escape, but they haven't been seen since…"

"The two we captured," Garahan said. "Two that were arguing with Buxton."

Flaherty stared off into the distance, and his cousin prompted, "Well?"

"Possibly five. Definitely three."

Garahan's eyes locked on Flaherty's. "And would four of those men include Simpson and the three others whose families were threatened?"

Flaherty slowly smiled. "That they would. Are ye done blathering? We've a job to do before Finn's lovely bride takes it upon herself to go after him."

Garahan grinned. "She's got a fire in her belly and is not afraid of anything."

Flaherty sighed. "A fine Irish lass, but ye're wrong."

"Am I now?"

"Aye," Flaherty said. "She's afraid Finn will die protecting the duke."

Garahan agreed. "Every one of the women who married the O'Malleys knew of their vow…our vow to protect the duke and his family with our lives."

"And every last one of those women would fight to save their husbands."

Garahan's worried gaze met Flaherty's. "How long do we have before she follows after Finn?"

"I'm thinking she's already halfway to the village by now."

"God help us if she ends up in the middle of this!" Garahan said.

"Faith, don't forget, the Lord helps those who help themselves."

"Ye knew she'd leave," Garahan said. "What's yer contingency plan?"

"She trusts Tremayne," Flaherty said. "He'll catch up to her and protect her with his life."

"A good man to have at your back in a fight. What if she's hurt?" Garahan asked. "What of the babe she carries?"

"'Tis out of our hands, and ye know it," Flaherty said.

Garahan shook his head. "Finn'll tear our hearts out."

Flaherty grinned. "He can try."

CHAPTER TWENTY-NINE

MOLLIE HELD THE tiny babe in her arms and felt a warmth sweep up from her toes to wrap around her heart. She glanced at the babe's mother and noticed the poor woman's hands were still trembling. The need to soothe was second nature to Mollie. She'd done that, and more, from the time she and Francis learned the duchess was expecting—through the nightmare of the kidnapping attempts to the day she had to say goodbye to Her Grace and her darling twins after she and Finn were married. She missed her family at Wyndmere Hall terribly.

"Let me take that for you, Mrs. Humbolt." Mrs. Castleton retrieved the cup and saucer and placed it on the table. The duke's housekeeper did not mention the spilled tea—or the woman's obvious distress—reminding Mollie of Merry, the duke's housekeeper in the Lake District.

"Please, Mum, may I have more tea?"

Mollie glanced at the oldest of the children, Mrs. Marks' son. The hopeful expression on the six-year-old's face was endearing. She hoped his mother agreed.

Having a bit of a tea party was more to keep the mothers occupied than the little ones. Anything to keep the women's minds off the danger their husbands were in...the danger Finn was in!

Mrs. Beverly's son was not to be left out—though only four

years old, he was more of a charmer than the Marks' boy and tended to boss the older boy around.

Though Mollie was concerned for Mrs. Humbolt, there was a deep-seated worry for Mrs. Simpson. Buxton relied on Mr. Simpson to keep order in the village of St. Ives. The excise official had secured the man's loyalty with the worst of the threats against the families gathered in the drawing room. Nightmares equal to what the duke and duchess had endured.

Mrs. Castleton settled the boys down with their half-cups of tea (mostly milk) and busied herself refilling plates with slices of the fist-sized meat pies she'd been preparing for the duke's men who were assigned to guard Mollie, and the staff, at the duke's manor house.

As no one had been staying there for the last few years, there was no cook in residence. Mollie had donned an apron to help Mrs. Castleton prepare the meat pies—the men working for the duke had voracious appetites. While they rolled out pie dough and chopped and cooked the filling, she'd regaled the duke's housekeeper with tales of the first time the cook at Wyndmere Hall had prepared the handheld meat pies for the duke's guard as a filling meal to grab in between patrol rotations.

Mrs. Castleton had just taken the first batch of pies from the oven when the women and children arrived. The kindly housekeeper had taken one look at the shaken families as they entered the manor house and began mixing up another batch of pie dough and a big bowl of filling. The men would have to wait for the second batch to eat.

As she was elbow deep in pie crust, the memory of the first night the duke's cook had prepared those meat pies filled Mollie. It was the night a madman and his men attempted to lay siege against the duke and his family gathered at Wyndmere Hall. She'd seen the courage and resourcefulness of the women in the duke's family that night. They'd cooked, cleaned, and bandaged from midnight—when the attack began—until dawn the next morning and into the afternoon. Exhaustion and pregnancy did not stop the brave women from doing their part.

Those same women had defied their husbands to attend duels their husbands had been involved in, and traveled alone—save for their lady's maids—in a bid to reach their husbands in time to stand by their side when everyone else had deserted them.

She vowed that she too would be brave, steadfast, and defiant. Finn's harsh words to her earlier, when she offered to accompany him to the village, had cut her to the quick. But she forgave him, sensing his worry was at the heart of his fury.

She stared at the babe sleeping peacefully in her arms now and wondered if the babe she carried was a daughter or a son. Since leaving the Lake District, she and Finn had only been able to share a few stolen moments together. She'd been nauseated during the journey to Cornwall. Then they were ambushed.

He'd put his life in danger too many times to count since they'd arrived in Cornwall. Was this the Lord's way of letting them know they were not meant to be together? Had their vows—though in truth, she'd never expected Finn to offer for her hand—resulted in the string of calamitous events keeping them apart? She did not believe in coincidences. If it was not a sign from Heaven, what else could it be?

Worry scraped the lining of her stomach until it felt raw. Her head warned her to stay put—wasn't that what Finn had told her to do? Ah, but her heart had urged her to follow after him. Though it was not ladylike, she had pressed her ear to the door to the duke's study and listened to the plans discussed. Finn was going to meet with the French smuggler. She feared Ruan more than the English excise official. She would not let him face it alone!

Ignoring logic, reason, and her husband's stern warning to not get involved, she slowly rose to her feet to follow her heart. "If you will excuse me, ladies, I need to lie down."

Mrs. Castleton was quick to react. "Of course, Mrs. O'Malley. We cannot have you tiring yourself out—it isn't good for your babe."

The women gathered in the drawing room agreed as the housekeeper rose and accompanied Mollie to the door to the drawing room. "Would you like me to walk you to your room?"

"No thank you, Mrs. Castleton. Please stay and keep everyone company. I only need a half an hour or so to rest my eyes."

"Take as much time as you need," the housekeeper said.

"Thank you." Mollie walked slowly until she knew she was out of sight of the drawing room's open doors, then slipped around the corner to the door leading to the servants' side of the manor house.

No one was about. The newly hired footmen were stationed outside of the drawing room, while the duke's guard stood watch around the perimeter of the house. She let herself into the kitchen. She wished she'd had the forethought to acquire a weapon, though she had no idea how to load or fire a pistol. She took one of the knives stored on the sideboard. Not the largest, although she knew it was deadly sharp—she needed one that would fit into her apron pocket.

Heart pounding, belly churning, she let herself out of the servants' entrance and darted from the corner of the house to the hedge for cover. Waiting to catch her breath, Mollie gathered her strength—and her resolve—and let herself into the stables.

Setting the horses loose had worked once, and may work again. Her nerves taut, her mind taxed with worry for Finn, she could not think of another distraction. The village was too far from the manor house. She needed to stand beside her husband when that foul excise official was captured. The men of the duke's guard would see to it that the official was made to pay for the crimes he'd committed—as well as the dastardly ones she'd just learned of from the ladies in the drawing room. The bastard had threatened the lives of those innocent children, and their mothers, to ensure his men would continue to collect his blood money.

Mollie didn't waste any more time. She cautiously slipped past the first of two guards—both had their backs to her—and entered the stables. After working her way from the back of the building to the front, she unlatched the doors to the horses' stalls until she reached the last stall.

"You're going to take me to the village," she told the roan gelding. "Hold on—I need a bucket to stand on." She found one, turned it over, then opened the door to the stables. She met the horse's gaze and knew he was ready to go. Holding his bridle, she walked him over to the bucket, stepped on it, and grabbed hold of his mane. It took two tries, but she managed to pull herself up onto the gelding's back.

Leaning close to the horse's ear, she rasped, "Take me to Finn!"

In the chaos of half a dozen horses running loose, she and the gelding shot past the guards and galloped down the path that would take them to St. Ives.

TREMAYNE RODE UP to the manor house straight into bedlam. Riding up to the first guard, he demanded, "Where is Mrs. O'Malley?"

"In the drawing room with the other women," the guard answered.

"How long have the horses been loose?"

The man stopped, obviously to think before he answered. "Not long."

"Bloody hell. Where is His Grace?"

"Tremayne!" The duke strode toward him. "Mollie's done it again. Garahan and Flaherty warned me that she might, but I didn't believe them. I overheard Finn demanding her promise that she would not leave the safety of the manor house— everyone within a half-mile heard the man's bellow. She gave me her word!"

"Garahan and Flaherty know their cousin well." Tremayne

met the duke's concerned gaze, adding, "Truth be told, I had thought Finn would have ordered his wife to obey him."

"Good God, she's more like my darling duchess than I'd imagined! We've got to find her before she gets to the village!"

Tremayne spun his horse around and set off at a gallop. His heart thundered in time with the horse's hoofbeats, while his mind replayed each and every scene involving Mollie. The brave, stubborn wife of Finn O'Malley had been bruised and battered since arriving on the outskirts of St. Ives.

No one deserved happiness more than Finn and his bride. He admired them both—for different reasons—and felt their actions were justified. If Mollie were *his* wife, he would have ordered her to stay behind, too.

She'd craftily arranged a distraction, and he'd been charged with the task of bringing her back. He hoped chasing her all the way to the village was not necessary, but Garahan and Flaherty were right—she'd gone after her husband. God only knew what the woman thought to do when she arrived in the village. There was a chance Finn was still on Ruan's ship…if he made it to Ruan's ship. Bloody hell, he could be held prisoner—after explaining how the smuggler's man had been injured—or not anywhere near the ship!

Would Ruan shoot first and listen second?

As his horse's hooves thundered along the road to town, Tremayne's mind raced, coming up with every possible outcome he could envision. None of them good. Buxton was not a man to be trusted. He prayed Mollie wasn't headed into a trap.

"Bloody hell!" He rounded the last of the curves in the road and could see the village in the distance. Where was she? "How could the woman outrun me on a horse?" *Idiot! She doesn't weigh half what I do.*

Leaning over the saddle, he covered the distance at a gallop, slowing down when he reached the first building. The excise building—his best guess as to where Mollie was headed—was in the middle of town.

A scream of pain pierced through his heart.

"Mollie!" Finn's guttural roar of anguish tore through Tremayne. He threw back his head and answered with a battle cry that bounced off the buildings as he rode.

The scene in front of him was surreal and could not be happening. Mollie O'Malley was standing on the raised scaffold in front of the excise building—facing Finn, who stood legs braced apart, a rope around his neck.

"Let her go, ye bloody bastard," Finn roared, "or I'll rip yer fecking heart out!"

Mollie stopped struggling and lifted her chin high. "Whatever you want, Buxton, I'll do it. Please, promise to let Finn go."

Tremayne wondered why no one heard his war cry—or noticed him. Taking in the crowd gathered, he had his answer. Men that worked with O'Malley and the duke's guard, including Garahan, were interspersed throughout those gathered. Why hadn't they attacked Buxton and freed Finn? What were they waiting for?

"Anything?" Buxton's slimy voice caught Tremayne's attention. It reminded him of offal floating in the Thames.

"Anything," Mollie answered.

"Release her," Buxton ordered the man holding Mollie's upper arms behind her back. When she was released, Buxton beckoned for her to come to him.

Tremayne watched her lift her chin high, square her shoulders, and walk toward the man.

"Keep yer hands off me wife," Finn warned.

Out of the corner of his eye, Tremayne watched men slip from the crowd, one at a time. *Finally.* Whatever plan was in place, he did not want to interfere. He had his orders to protect Mollie.

Buxton licked his lips when she drew closer. "She's a lovely bit of fluff." He glanced at Finn and slowly smiled. "Bet she's a wildcat in bed."

"Touch one hair on her head, and I'll slice ye, gullet to *bol-*

locks!"

Buxton didn't bother to answer the threat—he was too busy pulling Mollie into his arms. She scratched Buxton's face and clawed at his eyes. When he did not release her, she kneed him in the groin.

Buxton let go of Mollie as his eyes rolled back in his head.

Tremayne saw his chance and yelled, "Mollie! Move to the right!"

She threw herself to the side as Tremayne tackled Buxton and men swarmed onto the scaffold.

MOLLIE SCRAMBLED TO her feet and rushed to Finn's side. Hands trembling, she reached for the rope around his neck. Her fingers struggled to loosen it.

Buxton screamed, "Pull the lever!"

Finn heard the official's order. His gaze met hers and time stood still. "Dying to save ye, Mollie-lass, is the greatest of honors."

Mollie felt the scaffold shift beneath them, and watched with horror as the expression on her husband's changed from love to one of acceptance, as he was jerked out of her hold.

She screamed his name. The breath whooshed out of her lungs as she was tossed out of the way and landed hard on her side. She struggled to draw in a breath but couldn't.

The last thing she heard, as darkness claimed her, was Finn's hoarse rasp. "Take care of our babe, lass."

CHAPTER THIRTY

TREMAYNE HAD BUXTON by the throat, but tossed him off the scaffold when he saw the trapdoor open beneath Finn's feet.

Tremayne roared in anger, pulled the pistol from his waistband, and shot the rope. It didn't break. Would Finn's neck break before he had a chance to reload? He couldn't risk it.

He jumped off the platform and dove toward the Irishman hanging from the gibbet. He wrapped his arms around Finn's knees and lifted him high—until Finn's feet were above the trapdoor opening and the rope went slack. "I've got you, Finn!" He looked over his shoulder and bellowed, "Somebody cut the bloody rope!"

Garahan leapt onto the scaffold, wrapped his arms around Finn's waist, and helped bear his cousin's weight, easing more of the rope's tension. "Ye're not dying today, boy-o! Ye saved me sorry hide from a similar fate once. 'Tis time I paid ye back."

Finn struggled against the ropes binding his arms behind him.

"Don't move," Garahan warned. "Ye cannot risk the rope tightening around yer neck!"

Finn immediately stopped, and the strain on his face relaxed as his color faded from beet red to nearly normal. Between Tremayne and Garahan, they were holding off the inevitable.

Tremayne bellowed, "Where in the bloody hell is Hennessey!"

The echo of a sword unsheathed, and the swish of the lethally sharp blade above their heads, answered their question…and ended the threat to Finn's life. He was free!

Neither man had been prepared for the full weight of the huge Irishman—they'd only been concerned with holding him up so the rope wouldn't snap his neck.

Hennessey stared at the tangle of men at his feet and shook his head. Sheathing his sword, he offered his hand to Finn and helped him to his feet, then loosened the noose and lifted it over Finn's head. "I got here as soon as I could."

"Ye were almost too late," Garahan said as he stood.

Tremayne pulled himself up through the trapdoor, and Garahan bent to lend a hand. Finn abruptly turned around, and his elbow smacked into Tremayne's nose. The resounding crack had Garahan snorting with laughter. Tremayne grabbed hold of Garahan's ankles and yanked. Garahan landed on his back, but came up cursing.

Before the fight started, Finn rubbed his throat and asked, "Where's Mollie?"

"The duke carried her over to his carriage," Hennessey answered.

FINN WILLED HIS brain to think, and his body to move. For a brief moment, he felt as if they were no longer working in tandem. A little longer and his weight, added to the rope around his neck, would have snapped it.

He drew in one breath and then another, filling his body with much-needed air. He leapt off the scaffold and rushed to the carriage where the duke still held an unconscious Mollie in his arms. "What happened? One minute she was staring into me eyes…and the next…I couldn't see her."

"Sit down before you fall down, Finn," the duke ordered him.

Finn climbed onto the seat and held out his arms for his wife. The duke passed Mollie to Finn and said, "I lost sight of her for a moment. Buxton was making a run for it, and I had to stop him."

"I hope ye killed him." Finn stroked the tip of his finger along the curve of Mollie's cheek. It had a bruise on it. Had she landed on her face? Why wouldn't she open her eyes?

"Not for the first time in my life, I was tempted to," the duke admitted.

"He was going to stretch me neck and take me wife for his own amusement!" Finn thundered. "If ever a man needed killing—"

"It isn't up to us to act as judge and jury. We'll leave that to the king, and his court, to decide."

"Prinny will probably interfere and let the man go," Finn mumbled. He brushed a lock of auburn hair off Mollie's forehead. "Do ye think she hit her head? Is that why she's unconscious?"

A tear slipped from beneath her lashes—and then another.

"Mollie-lass, open yer eyes."

Her lashes fluttered against her parchment-pale skin as she slowly opened her eyes. "Am I dead?"

Finn chuckled. "Nay, lass."

"But I saw your face, and the trapdoor open—I watched you die!"

"Faith, 'twas yer mind playing a trick on ye."

Mollie blinked then locked gazes with Finn. "The rope tightened around your neck…did you bargain with the devil?"

"Nay, lass," he said, laughing.

"The expression on your face—surprise and acceptance."

"Sure and it was a shock to feel the bite of the rope digging into me neck."

"How can you laugh at a time like this?" Mollie asked.

"He's alive," the duke answered. "I'd say that was cause for celebration, wouldn't you?"

Mollie turned to look at the duke. "When did you arrive, Your Grace?"

"Right before one of Buxton's men opened the trapdoor. It took me longer than I'd anticipated…I had to catch two of the horses you set free, hitch them to the wagon, and drive it here."

"Tell me ye didn't set His Grace's horses loose a second time, lass," Finn said.

She sighed and tucked her head beneath his chin. "It's all a bit fuzzy," she said, obviously lying. "I don't recall."

"Did ye hit yer head?"

"We'd best take her back to the manor house," the duke said. "Any dizziness or shortness of breath, Finn?"

"Nay. I have me cousin and Tremayne to thank for that. If they hadn't kept me weight off the rope—" Mollie's sob of anguish had him pulling her closer. "Cry if ye need to, lass. Best not to keep it inside of ye."

Finn held his wife to his heart as she wept. Her tears, and her breathing, finally slowed. She slept as the duke drove them through town. Neither man spoke as they traveled along the road past Penwith Tower. Content just to be alive, Finn was reassured with every beat of his heart and the flutter of Mollie's. They made their way along the winding road through the duke's property until they reached the turnoff that would lead to the manor house.

The sound of a lone horse coming up behind them at a fast clip had Finn looking over his shoulder as the duke pulled back on the reins in front of his home.

"Tremayne!"

The duke stepped down from the carriage and held out his arms. "Let me hold Mollie while you get down."

Finn jumped down, swayed a little, but quickly righted himself. "I'll never be able to thank ye for all ye've done for meself and me family, Yer Grace."

"I believe I've said the same to you more than once, Finn."

He grinned as he held his sleeping wife in his arms. "That ye have, Yer Grace."

"Is Mollie all right?" Tremayne asked as he dismounted and

walked toward them.

One of the men guarding the house stepped forward to take the horse to the stables. Another climbed onto the carriage and followed the horse and rider.

"She will be, Tremayne," the duke answered for Finn. "After Mrs. Castleton checks her for injuries, she'll be needing rest, and a hot meal."

Tremayne nodded to Finn. "I hope you realize what a treasure of a woman you have there."

Finn frowned. "I do—why?"

"She was willing to bargain with her life—and Lord knows what else—with that devil to set you free."

"He never intended to set me free," Finn said.

"Mollie didn't know that," Tremayne said.

Mr. Castleton held the door open for them, and the duke motioned for Finn to precede him. "That's because of the rare qualities Mollie and my wife share."

"What's that, Your Grace?" Tremayne asked.

"Their faith, an unstinting supply of hope, a deep capacity to love without restriction."

Finn started toward the drawing room, but the duke stopped him. "Take her upstairs—she may rest more comfortably without the questions the other woman are likely to bombard her with when she wakes up."

"Would ye send one of the footmen up?"

The duke frowned. "What do you need?"

"'Tisn't me place to ask it of ye, Yer Grace."

"For the number of times you've stood between death and my family, I believe it is. Now what do you need?"

"Some tea and something light to eat, if it 'tisn't too much trouble."

"No trouble at all. I'll speak to Mrs. Castleton directly. I'll also ask one of the footmen to carry in water to heat for a bath. Persephone often reminds me that a long soak in a hot tub soothes frazzled nerves."

"Thank ye, Yer Grace. I'm certain she'll enjoy that."

"Mrs. Castleton can check for injuries—"

"Begging yer pardon, Yer Grace," Finn interrupted. "I'll take care of that meself, if ye don't mind. Mollie might take it into her head to hide her injuries from others—including me—but I have me ways to encourage her to listen to me." He grinned. "The lass doesn't like me to worry."

The duke inclined his head. "Tremayne is right, you know."

"About what?" Finn asked.

"You have found a treasure of a woman, Finn. The feisty ones always are."

Finn sighed. "She's a handful."

"I believe you and the rest of my guard already realize that my darling duchess is, too."

Finn's lips twitched. "It has come up a time or two in conversation as we're planning our patrols." He quickly added, "But never said in a disparaging way, Yer Grace. We think the world of Her Grace and yerself."

"Persephone and I feel the same about you and the men of my guard." The duke was smiling when he asked, "Do you think you can let go of your wife long enough to put her on the bed?"

"I'm thinking I need to hold her for a bit longer. Mayhap I'll be strong enough to let her go when the tea tray arrives."

The duke placed his hand on Finn's broad shoulder. "At least sit in the chair by the bed while you wait."

"I think I will. Thank ye, Yer Grace."

"Thank *you*, Finn."

Finn waited until the duke closed the door behind him before lowering his brow to rest against his wife's. The first tear that fell symbolized his heart breaking at the thought of dying and leaving Mollie and their unborn babe alone.

The second was for the pain she'd suffered from the day she entrusted him with the gift of her virtue.

The third was for stubbornly believing he could only honor one vow at a time.

The next symbolized the gratitude he felt toward Garahan and Tremayne for holding him up until the rope around his neck was severed.

The tears that followed were the relief that nearly cut him off at the knees when he realized the good Lord had given him a second chance. He planned to live his life to the fullest with Mollie and their son or daughter, whichever they would be blessed to welcome into the world.

Spent from the emotions racking his soul, he pressed his lips to the top of her head, closed his eyes, and drifted off to sleep.

MRS. CASTLETON KNOCKED on the bedchamber door and listened, but there was no sound. She turned the knob, opened the door a crack, and peeked around the edge of it. The sight had tears springing to her eyes. Finn held his wife in his arms—and they were both fast asleep.

She backed out of the room and whispered to the footman to quietly place the tea tray on the table beneath the window. Satisfied they would have something to eat when they woke, she put her finger to her lips and motioned for the footman to follow her downstairs. She'd keep the pots of water hot until the couple woke and sent down for their bathwater.

She hummed to herself as she and her husband put the finishing touches on the meal they planned to feed the crowd gathered in the drawing room. She'd already prepared a large pot of stew and baked enough loaves of bread waiting for the duke, Finn, and Mollie to return. The stew would more than feed the small army of men tasked with guarding the duke and those who served him.

She smiled as she instructed the footmen to start serving the meal and waited for the summons to come from Finn O'Malley, *the duke's dragoon.*

CHAPTER THIRTY-ONE

MOLLIE SLOWLY WOKE, grateful to feel the warmth of her husband's strong arms wrapped around her. The soothing sound of Finn drawing in a breath and slowly exhaling was a gift. She'd lost all hope when her husband suddenly dropped, and the rope pulled tight.

"Thank you, Heavenly Father, for sparing Finn's life."

His chest expanded and his breathing changed as he rumbled, "Thank ye, Lord, for me stubborn, feisty, beautiful wife."

She leaned against him and lifted her gaze to meet his. The need to touch him filled her. She traced the tips of her fingers along the line of his jaw, stopping at the bruise purpling on his chin. "Who hit you?"

"Does it matter, lass? I'm alive, and ye're in me arms. A man cannot ask for more." He bent his head and gently kissed her mouth. "Ye taste of hope, lass." He pressed another to her forehead. "And rain-soaked roses." She sighed and closed her eyes as he kissed the tip of her nose. "Ye taste of love, Mollie-lass." His voice broke as he added, "I never thought to see ye again in this lifetime."

Her eyes opened, and she saw the truth of his words in the depth of his emerald eyes. "My heart broke, Finn, when I saw you facing that madman, ready to sacrifice your life for the duke and his family."

"'Twasn't just for the duke, lass—'twas for our babe and yerself, too. I knew Buxton planned to kill me. I made a bargain with Ruan to help me spring a trap on the Englishman."

Her heart ached with the knowledge that he had. "At the cost of your life, and you didn't tell me?"

"Between Ruan's men, the duke's, and Coventry's, I knew they wouldn't let that happen."

"Why did they wait so long? It was torture watching them place the rope around your neck, knowing I only had one thing to bargain with to set you free—me."

"I'm sorry for yer worry, lass. But I couldn't tell ye of our plans. Couldn't take the chance someone would overhear me telling ye."

"You could have trusted me."

"Faith, but I did! I made me peace with me Maker and trusted ye would believe I'd die to protect ye."

Reason returned, and she added, "You trusted that Buxton and his men believed it too."

"That I did. Is there anything else weighing on yer mind, lass?"

She thought of everything that had occurred since the night nearly two years ago, when she'd bathed his face while he lay unconscious from a wound to his head, during the attack on Wyndmere Hall. "I have prayed for your safety every day, Finn. I do not think I could survive if I'd lost you."

He cupped her face in his hand and stared into her eyes. "You are the bravest woman I know, Mollie-lass. Yer heart and yer head may be constantly at war with one another—as ye plan ways to defy me commands—but I wouldn't have ye any other way."

He lowered his mouth to meet hers and kissed her, softly, tenderly at first. As desire flared to life, passion took hold, and he plundered her mouth, kissing the breath out of her.

Finn placed his hand to her belly. "Ye wouldn't leave our babe to face the world alone. Ye would survive for his or her sake."

"But I—"

"Would not have anyone else raise our babe. Ye'd whisper tales of me courage in the face of death, me strength, and me love for ye and our babe."

"Finn…"

"Ah, lass. The day ye gave me yer greatest gift—yer virtue— was the day I gave ye me heart, and me undying love."

"I love you, Finn."

"Ah, lass, and well I know it."

She was laughing as Finn lowered his mouth to hers and captured her lips in a kiss filled with promise.

"Now then, I promised His Grace and Mrs. Castleton that I'd check ye for injuries. When ye jumped out of the way, ye landed hard on yer side. Did ye hit yer head as well?"

Given the aches and pains slowly making themselves known, she didn't think so. "It doesn't pain me."

"Ye were unconscious," he reminded her.

"I knocked the wind out of myself when I landed on the wooden platform."

"Well then, lass, let's have a look." He shifted her off his lap and stood next to her, studying her face as if he'd never seen her before. He blinked, and his expression changed to one she could not read. He must use it to keep his thoughts from showing while working for the duke.

"This gown will have to go." He gently turned her around and undid the top button. But a knock on the door had him mumbling as he refastened it. "Come in."

"You are both awake," Mrs. Castleton said. "Wonderful. It's always best to settle into the hot tub as soon as it's filled." She motioned for one of the footmen waiting behind her to start emptying the first bucket, while instructing the other to remove the tea tray with the cold pot of tea.

Finn guided Mollie to one of the chairs. Once she was seated, he stood near the door, feet spread, poised and ready to spring into action, if need be, to protect her.

Her sigh was audible as she studied the handsome-as-sin Irishman she'd married. She would rather have not been interrupted, knowing Finn's intention was to strip her bare and make a thorough study of her body from head to toe—looking for injuries. God, she needed the reassurance of his callused hands touching her, soothing her—inflaming her.

The housekeeper was only following the duke's instructions. His Grace had been instrumental the first time they rescued Mollie's husband. He'd been there today, too, when she thought all hope had been lost.

She met her husband's gaze and sent up a prayer of thanks that the men who'd banded together to save Finn had looked past their own interests and worked to free the man they all admired…her husband, Finn O'Malley.

The flash of desire in his eyes had a shiver racing up her spine. For the rest of their lives, for however long that may be, she knew one look from Finn would set her body on fire. She locked gazes with him and poured out what she was feeling in her heart for the man she loved.

His eyes darkened and his nostrils flared. He felt the same. Needing to control her emotions, she forced herself to return to the scene outside of the excise building. Ice gathered in her belly as she remembered the scaffold, the rope…Buxton.

She drew in a deep breath and exhaled to concentrate on the outcome and not the fear. Because of Tremayne and Garahan, Finn was alive and standing in front of her…frustration coming off him in waves.

The need to soothe him, to feel the weight of him, as they joined their bodies and spoke with their hearts, washed over her. She stood and walked to his side then leaned close to whisper, "I'll go mad if they don't leave soon."

He pulled her into his embrace and pressed his lips to her forehead. "Aye, *mo chroi*. Shall I hurry them along?"

"Please. I need—"

She could feel Finn's need pulsing against her side, and knew he was hanging on to his control with the last of his strength.

"Shall I help you with your bath, Mrs. O'Malley?"

Before she could refuse the housekeeper's help, Finn said, "I have not had a chance to check for injuries yet. Mollie needed her sleep. I didn't wake her."

Mrs. Castleton nodded toward the bellpull in the corner. "Just ring if you need anything."

"We will," Finn said. "Thank ye."

He locked the door behind the duke's overly helpful staff and rasped, "I have ye now, lass."

"Oh?" She feigned disinterest, while her heart pounded in anticipation.

Finn strode over to where she stood and let his gaze drift from her head to her toes. "I'll have to go slowly. I wouldn't want to miss any injury—no matter how small. I won't be satisfied until I'm certain yerself, and our babe, are unharmed."

Her heart full, she let him sweep her into his arms and carry her into the dressing room. The scent of roses drifted toward them from the steaming water. He lowered her to her feet and, once again, reached for the buttons at the back of her gown.

This time, no one disturbed them as he slipped the gown off. When she shivered, he pressed a kiss to the top of her head before pulling the pins that held the weight of her auburn hair in place. Waves of silk settled over her shoulders, settling against the small of her back.

"God, ye're a beauty, wife of mine."

She reached for the buttons on his waistcoat and undid them. As he pushed it off his shoulders, she did the same with his cambric shirt, until his powerful chest—and bandages—were laid bare before her.

Her eyes widened as she stared at the damage the hemp rope had left behind—a deep purple ring and raw, abraded skin where it bit into Finn's neck. Sweat broke out behind her knees as oily nausea settled in her belly.

Finn swept her off her feet and over to the chamber pot. He

held her hair out of her face as she retched until she was empty.

"*Mo ghra*," he rasped, holding her to his heart. "I would spare this part of carrying our babe if I could."

"*Grha?*"

"Me love," he said. "Now then, do ye need the chamber pot again, or are ye ready for yer bath?"

"Bath, please."

He set her on her feet, and she reached up to cup his strong jaw in her hand. The memory of the first time she saw Finn O'Malley filled her. The impressive breadth of his chest and shoulders, garbed in unrelieved black from head to toe, denoting his high rank within the Duke of Wyndmere's household. A symbol of his homeland, the word *Eire* and the Celtic harp, was embroidered over his heart—the insignia of the duke's guard.

She lifted to the tips of her toes and pressed her lips near the edge of the bruise that had spread since she first noticed it. "You know I would love nothing more than to make love with you."

He frowned and nodded. "Ye're exhausted and yer belly is empty. Let's get ye into the tub while it's still warm."

He helped her remove her chemise and clenched his jaw when she stood before him. She had bruises coming up beneath one arm and on her hip. "Is this where from when ye landed on yer side?"

She nodded, and his frown intensified. "We should be grateful that is all that occurred...it could have been far worse." She shook her head to dispel the dark thoughts she had yet to erase. "Let me help you undress."

She undid the placket on his trousers and noticed him struggling to breathe when they stood facing one another.

"Finn, are you all right? Is it your throat?" She stared at the reminder of his brush with death and prayed she would be able to help him forget the ordeal in time. "Does your back pain you?" Taking in the long, slashing scars crisscrossing his chest and the more recent one from a lead ball, she asked, "Is it where you were shot?"

"Nay, lass—'tis me flagging control. I seem to have none

where ye are concerned after preparing meself to meet me Maker."

Understanding and compassion filled her. "Why don't you have something to eat? Mrs. Castleton's tray had meat pies and sandwiches as well as cream tarts and scones. I can manage to bathe myself."

He inclined his head and strode into the bedchamber and the waiting tray of food.

"Do you know, you are as handsome walking away from me as you are walking toward me?"

His snort of laughter soothed the edges of her worry. It would take time, but they would both recover from the anguish of watching him plunge through that bloody trapdoor!

"Well now, I can say the same. Watching yer hips sway is poetry in motion, lass."

She stepped on the low stool beside the copper tub and tested the temperature with her toes. "It's still warm." She slipped into the fragrant water, leaned her back against the tub, closed her eyes, and sighed.

"Hungry, lass?"

The memory of the last time they'd made love filled her. She was reaching for him as she opened her eyes. Though desire swirled in the depths of his gaze, it was tempered with the steely control she had come to expect from him.

He stood before her—battered and bruised with bandages that needed to be changed—as if nothing had happened. "We'll be making love soon, lass. First, I have to feed ye and our babe." He nodded to the plate in his hands. "Cream tart or meat pie?"

Her stomach rumbled and he chuckled. "Meat pie first, then the tart." He fed her and then himself. Brushing the crumbs from his hands, he eyed the size of the tub and the water level within it. "I'm thinking there's enough room for two, if I bail out a bucket or two."

Mollie was laughing when she said, "Hand me that bucket!"

The laughter went a long way to ease the heaviness in her heart as they ended up filling three buckets before he was satisfied the water wouldn't spill over onto the floor. Finn stepped into the tub, sat down, wrapped his arms around her, and settled her in his lap.

"Wait! You cannot get your bandages wet!"

"Lass, I've survived being shot, stabbed, beaten, and nearly hanged. I'll chance it." He settled into the warm water and sighed. "Ah, 'tis as close to Heaven as I'm wanting to get for the next twenty years, lass."

"Sharing a bath?"

"Aye. Ye're a part of me now, lass—and there's an emptiness when we're apart."

She sighed as he dipped the linen cloth into the water and stroked it up her arm across her chest and between her breasts. "The water feels warmer now."

He paused before dipping the cloth in the water again. "It should."

"Should it?"

"Aye—I burn for ye, lass."

They took turns washing one another, interspersing nips, licks, and kisses with each swipe of the rose-scented cloth.

"Now then, lass, are ye ready for me?"

In answer, she turned in his arms, straddled his lap, and took him into her. No other words were necessary as they replaced worry with desire, fear with passion, and despair with love.

She met his thrusts, rocking her hips to take him deeper. Sighs became moans; whispered words of love became urgent rasps.

Finn thrust one last time and groaned deep in his throat.

Mollie's head fell back. As she felt her climax rip through her, Finn pulled her to him and swallowed her cries as he plundered her mouth with lips and tongue, until she collapsed against him.

She shivered, and Finn gathered her close. "As I'm thinking they don't have rose-scented water and copper tubs in Heaven, we'd best make good use of this one."

She wrapped herself around him and let him take her to the stars.

CHAPTER THIRTY-TWO

MOLLIE MET HER husband's gaze. He stood tall, proud, though his hands were bound behind his back and a thick rope lay around his neck. "Dying to save ye, Mollie-lass, is the greatest of honors."

She screamed Finn's name and was enveloped in warmth. The solid wall of her husband's chest pressed against her breasts and belly had pinpricks of desire erupting as the heat emanating from his powerful frame flowed through her, all the way to her bones.

The memory clung to her, as her nightmare evaporated. He rubbed a hand along the length of her spine, soothing her until she relaxed in his arms. "I dreamed that you died." She met his gaze and could not control the tears welling in her eyes. "How will I survive, if you are ever in such peril again?"

FINN SHIFTED UNTIL Mollie lay on her back staring up at him. Did she realize she was crying? Tears fell in a steady stream from the corners of her eyes. He brushed them away with the tips of his fingers.

Knowing she hated to cry, he didn't mention it. Instead, he

dipped his head to sip from her lips. Softly, gently, like the brush of a butterfly's wings—stirring the air as it landed on a flower to drink its nectar.

"Ye've grit enough for two, lass. Determination, conviction, and faith. Ye may not want to survive—if, and when, the good Lord calls me home—but ye will." He leaned on one elbow and placed his hand over her heart. "Our son will grow up knowing how much we both love him—whether—tis one of us, or, Lord willing, the both of us who will raise him."

He slid his hand beneath her and held her to his heart. "Can ye feel that, lass? Me heart beats for ye—and ye alone. Ye're the other half of me…the better half. Make me proud, no matter if I'm standing beside, or hours away seeing to the duke's protection."

Her smile bloomed slowly, like a flower in the sun after a recent rain—a rose, reminding him of the scent of her skin, the taste of her throat. He'd never thought to marry, nor could begin to fathom the depth of the love he had for Mollie. For a heartbeat, fear tried to grab hold of him.

He looked into eyes the color of a summer sky. As he accepted the fullness of the love she offered, his fear evaporated. Mollie's love was now key to his survival—and a part of him. Her love enhanced his strength, his faith, his integrity.

"Our *daughter*," she corrected him, wrapping her arms around his neck and pulling him closer, "will grow up knowing the love of both her parents, because you are right. I do have grit enough for two. I mean to see that you stay in one piece if I have to follow you to the gates of Hell to drag you back."

"Don't ye mean Heaven, lass?"

They were laughing when their lips met. He kissed her deeply.

A lingering kiss that held the promise of a lifetime of love.

EPILOGUE

Seven months later…

FINN'S HEART SWELLED with pride. "Sure and ye're a warrior queen, Mollie Catherine Malloy."

She snorted. "That's O'Malley—or have you forgotten our vow taking and everything that happened between then and now?"

"I'll not soon forget the injuries ye suffered from the moment we pledged our lives to one another, lass."

She lifted her hand to the side of his face. He placed his on top of hers, leaned toward her, and gently pressed his lips to hers. Concern marred his brow as he stared down at the bundle in his wife's arms—barely an hour old. "Are ye certain ye wish to name our daughter Boadicea?"

Mollie's lips twitched, and he knew she was making the most of his promise to her during the last hours of her laboring to bring forth their babe.

"'Tisn't right to tease a man who's gone through all seven levels of hell waiting for our daughter to be born."

She pulled her hand free and smacked him on the back of the head. "You are an arse if you think that comes close to what giving birth is like."

Before she could blast him again, he pulled her close and

kissed her with all of the passion and worry that tangled inside of him still as he relived the hours of her labor—helpless to ease her pain as she battled to birth their babe.

"Mollie-lass. If I could have taken the pain for ye, I would have. Ye have to know that it sliced across me heart, sitting here with you unable to help ye."

Mollie brushed the tip of her finger along the curve of their newborn daughter's cheek before lifting her eyes to meet his. "I could not have handled the pains if you were not here beside me, holding my hand and rubbing the knots from my back. I needed your strength," she rasped. "And you willingly gave it to me."

His eyes filled. "I never want to see you go through that pain again."

She sighed. "It'll be awfully cold in our bed without you in it."

Finn gaped at her, then shook his head. "Ye are a wicked woman, Mollie Catherine O'Malley."

She smiled at him. "But you love me anyway."

"Only the good Lord knows why."

"If you give me a little time to regain my strength, Finn, I will be happy to remind you."

He was laughing when he pressed his lips to hers.

About the Author

Historical & Contemporary Romance "Warm...Charming...Fun..."

C.H. was born in Aiken, South Carolina, but her parents moved back to northern New Jersey where she grew up.

She believes in fate, destiny, and love at first sight. C.H. fell in love at first sight when she was seventeen. She was married for 41 wonderful years until her husband lost his battle with cancer. Soul mates, their hearts will be joined forever.

They have three grown children—one son-in-law, two grand-sons, two rescue dogs, and two rescue grand-cats.

Her characters rarely follow the synopsis she outlines for them...but C.H. has learned to listen to her characters! Her heroes always have a few of her husband's best qualities: his honesty, his integrity, his compassion for those in need, and his killer broad shoulders. C.H. writes about the things she loves most: Family, her Irish and English Ancestry, Baking and Gardening.

C.H.'s Social Media Links:
Website: www.chadmirand.com
Amazon: amazon.com/stores/C.-H.-
Admirand/author/B001JPBUMC
BookBub: bookbub.com/authors/c-h-admirand
Facebook Author Page: facebook.com/CHAdmirandAuthor
Facebook Private Reader's Page ~ C.H. Reader's Nook:
facebook.com/groups/714796299746980
GoodReads:
goodreads.com/author/show/212657.C_H_Admirand
Instagram: c.h.admirand
Twitter: @AdmirandH
Youtube:
youtube.com/channel/UCRSXBeqEY52VV3mHdtg5fXw